beg the night

MYSTICS OF ASHORA

BOOK 1

EMILY BLACKWOOD

PLEASE NOTE

Beg The Night contains some themes of sexual abuse.
Though everything on-page is consensual between the
main characters, there is one scene of sexual activity
occurring under the influence and there are multiple
mentions of sexual coercion. Past child abuse, government
kidnapping, graphic violence, and death of family
members also appear in this book.

"I am terrified by this dark thing that sleeps in me."
- Sylvia Plath

athena

Everyone was finally dead.

Everyone but me, anyway. Ironic, since I was the one who deserved it the most. The sun roasted my skin as I gripped the tarp that held my younger sister's body. She wasn't nearly as heavy as my father was, thank god. Last week, it had taken all my strength to move him the ten feet through the yard to the grave I'd spent hours digging.

Burying bodies was a new thing for me. My muscles still screamed at every movement.

Jasmine's body felt too small to be burying. It *was* too small to be burying. At seventeen, she had just barely started her life. Now I was burying her in the yard with the rest of my family.

Mother, Father, Kylar, Jasmine.

Jasmine's death hurt the most.

Her body rolled into the grave, landing with a sickening thud, and I quickly got to work covering her with the brittle dirt. My palms were blistered from the wooden handle of the shovel, but I barely felt them ripping open as I continued to fill in the hole.

Even the torture of the first death didn't match this. I cried for days after Mother drowned in the stream up north, so did the rest of the family. It was a freak accident, apparently, because she had been swimming in that stream her entire life.

An *accident.*

The word replayed in my mind until it gnawed at my every thought. I couldn't get away from that word. Couldn't move past it.

Accident.

Kylar died next. Snake bite to the leg. The infection that set in took him just days after Mother drowned. We hadn't even begun to feel the grief that awaited us. Father and I buried them without saying a word. What was there to say? By then, our family had already been destroyed.

Then Father. Heart attack, it seemed.

That's when Katherine left us. My older sister swore that this house was cursed, that we would all die if we stayed.

She had been acting strange since Mother died. I blamed it on the grief. She wasn't thinking clearly when she chose to leave. None of us *ever* left town. It wasn't safe out there. Not with the war raging on, with the Ministry hunting mystics. I hoped Katherine made it out safely, even if I hated that she'd left us.

It was just Jasmine and me for weeks. And after those

first few miserable days, the silence of the house grew almost comforting.

Do you think Katherine misses us? she asked me just last week. Her blonde hair was pulled into a loose braid, and the time she'd spent in the sun had given her cheeks a pinkish glow that made her look even younger than she was.

How could she not? I forced a smile. Jasmine's relationship with Katherine was vastly different from mine. She had been protected from some of the cold, hateful things I had seen over the years.

It was hard to hold it against my older sister. It's what she did to survive. Katherine's bitterness hadn't been there all our lives. It grew like an old oak tree, branching and taking over until it was the only thing visible for miles.

The memory stung the back of my throat as I hauled more dirt over Jasmine's cold body.

The worst part? I'd actually begun to believe Jasmine might survive.

But then the flu wrecked her body. She slept through most of it, not even aware of the torture that slowly shut down her organs.

It wasn't a bad way to go.

My entire family—aside from Katherine—lie dead and decaying in this dirt. And as much as I hated to believe it, Katherine was likely dead, too. A woman alone never survived long. Not with the Ministry on the hunt. That's what Father had taught us. We were earthly—not mystic —but it didn't matter to them. No one was safe anymore. They would take people from their families in the middle of the night just to run tests to determine whether they were mystics.

And nobody ever returned.

That's why my family lived way out here in the middle of nowhere, far from anyone who might notice us. Far from anyone working for the Ministry.

Not like it did much good. Everyone ended up in the ground eventually. The last few weeks had been testament enough to that.

Once Jasmine's grave was filled, I wiped my dirty palms on my trousers and sat back in the grass. Birds chirped above me, swarming the skies. I would have traded any amount of money for the kind of freedom they possessed.

Sick bastards.

The birds didn't know the world was ending. They didn't know we were killing each other one by one, fighting for something that didn't exist.

A cool breeze brushed my dirt-brown hair over my shoulder. I wouldn't normally risk sitting outside like this, but my ability to give a shit was dwindling with every passing second.

Jasmine.

She was the last good thing left in my life. The final hope I had that we might actually survive this war. *Hold yourself together*, she would say. *We need you to stay strong, so when this is all over you can put our family back together.*

A sharp laugh racked through me, painfully piercing the silence. What family? What life?

Gunshots rang out in the distance. I'd stopped

flinching at the sound months ago. What was the use? My family and I had been hiding from the Ministry since the war had started two years ago.

But I'd only fought as hard as I did in order to keep my family safe. Now, I had no family. If I was right about Katherine, then there wasn't a soul alive I cared for. No reason to keep going.

I dropped my head back as I took in the bright blue sky above me. *Forgive me, Jasmine. I'm not nearly as tough as I pretended to be.*

The truth was, my sister's death took all the strength and determination I possessed, and I feared I would never get it back. I no longer cared enough to fight.

To run.

To hide.

If the Ministry wanted me, they could damn well come find me. I was too tired to keep fighting. I was too—too—

A single tear fell from my eye, rolling down my dirt-covered skin and lingering on my chin before dripping to my tattered shirt.

Though I wasn't a mystic, it didn't matter. I was a woman. And in the depths of this war, the Ministry was gathering all the women they could find.

In some ways, I envied Jasmine. She would not have to endure what came next.

The voices and gunshots grew louder, but I didn't even have the strength to stand. They wouldn't shoot me. My long, wavy locks and womanly figure would be a dead giveaway. They'd want to take me alive. Not that I'd stay that way for long.

More silent tears fell.

The birds scattered, launching themselves from the trees noisily, evading the horror that approached.

I didn't turn around, didn't even bother to move from the spot near my family's graves as the footsteps approached.

A deep voice shouted unintelligibly. More male voices followed, disturbing and harsh. The ground vibrated with footsteps.

A sharp needle pierced the side of my neck, and in seconds, it felt as though I was flying.

It was nice.

And then it was all over.

athena

We were moving.

My consciousness faded in and out, accompanied by a sharp pain in my temple.

I didn't flinch. Didn't move. Not when the familiar buzz in my palms warned me that I wasn't alone.

The Ministry.

I shouldn't have been afraid. Hell, I wasn't expecting to be. I had no family left to fight for. No friends left to care about me. There wasn't a soul left on this entire planet that knew of my existence. Still, my adrenaline spiked, causing a tingling sensation in my chest.

These were the people my family had feared all those years. These were the people we were taught to avoid.

To run from.

Now that they'd found me, I would finally discover what the dark whispers of the Ministry were truly about. *It was about damn time, honestly.*

For now, though, the longer I feigned sleep, the better.

The vehicle rocked as the terrain shifted. We transitioned from a smooth road to a surface so bumpy, it had to have been the forest ground. The vehicle was large, but based on the ragged breathing, there were at least three people surrounding me.

"We're almost there," a deep voice said. "Wake the girl. Director will want to see her talking."

I kept my breath steady, not moving a muscle. But it didn't matter. Two seconds later, someone was shaking my shoulders with big, rough hands. "Hey!" the owner of the meaty hands shouted. "Wake up, bitch. Nap's over."

Jig's up. Coming face to face with my captors was inevitable, so without any more hesitation, I blinked my eyes open, adjusting to the darkness inside the vehicle. The men surrounding me wore black tactical gear. Each had more than one gun strapped to their belts, along with god knows how many other weapons.

As if they'd need any of it to deal with me. Each one of those men were double my size, and their muscles bulged beneath the tight gear.

The hand on my shoulder tightened until I suppressed a squeal. He yanked me into a sitting position, dragging me along the bench until the side of my body pressed against his.

"You cannot escape," he said in a muffled voice beneath the bandana covering his nose and mouth. "You cannot run. You cannot fight. There is no use wasting your energy. You'll do everything we say, and when you meet Director, you'll keep your pretty mouth shut. Understand?"

My stomach roiled. Ew. *Double ew.*

When I didn't respond, he dug his fingers into my upper arm. "Understand?"

"Perfectly." I mustered a sassy smile, though it slipped when I remembered that I was alone in the back of a creepy-ass van with three strange men.

Apparently, I had more survival instincts than I'd realized.

I bit my cheek and kept my head lowered for the remainder of the ride. The men didn't talk. I wasn't surprised. According to Father, the people who worked for the Ministry had been brainwashed into zombies who would obey every command they were given. Their minds were probably too fried to string more than two words together unless they were ordered by the—

The van jerked to a halt. "We're here."

More voices shouted from outside. Everyone sounded angry. Urgent. The doors at the back flung open, flooding the small, dark space with sunlight. I squinted and turned away, but my captors shoved me toward the door without even an ounce of gentleness.

Rude.

We were in the middle of the woods, though this area was nothing like the forest I'd grown up in. There were no chirping birds. There was no stream trickling in the distance. The trees did not move in the wind, and the wind did not sing through the rustling of leaves.

This place was still. Dead, almost. Everywhere I looked, there were soldiers in black tactical gear. The weapons strapped across their bodies made them look even larger.

Some ran. Some barked orders. I stood frozen until I was shoved from behind.

What the hell were we doing way out here?

"Bring her this way!" someone in the distance yelled. "Director is ready for her inside."

One of my captors led the way while the other two gripped my arms, hauling me forward. We passed piles of weapons, mounds of supplies.

I was dragged to a steel door in the ground where yet another soldier kneeled. As we approached, he pulled it open, exposing a dark staircase beneath.

My captors shoved me forward. "Go," one ordered.

"Down there?" My heart lurched. "Underground?" Being kidnapped and thrown into a van was one thing, but walking into an underground cave that could collapse at any second?

Just shoot me.

"Now."

All right, all right. I took one last gulp of fresh air, then forced myself to take the first step into the underground. A string of dim, orange light lit the way as sunlight disappeared behind me. *Deep breaths, Athena. This is totally normal. The men are following you, and surely they wouldn't come down here if you were going to be buried alive at any moment.*

The pep talk did little to settle my nerves.

At the bottom of the steel staircase, I scanned my surroundings, realizing only then that it was an entire underground compound. The light expanded ahead, exposing a massive hallway with dozens of steel doors on either side. Damn, this must have taken up miles of space beneath the forest floor.

"This way," one of my captors ordered. The guys flanking me gripped my arms again and roughly guided me down the dark, oddly sterile hallway. They didn't speak, and with each step we took, the air grew more and more still. My dirty boots clicked against the floor, matching the deep thud of my heart.

From what I knew, the Ministry had slowly been taking over the continent of Ashora for years. They were a virus, seeping into city after city, wreaking havoc as they went.

But all my life, they'd been nothing more than a mystical force in my mind. The subject of many, many cautionary tales. My parents had done an exceptional job keeping us separated from the world. They told us enough to keep us safe, to keep us fearful of the Ministry.

Rather than fight in the war with the other earthlies, we had stayed hidden. Quiet.

I much preferred living in that delusion.

This was them in the flesh. Pure evil, brute force.

And I hated them with every ounce of my being.

Outside the last door, we stopped. One of my captors knocked once with a solid fist. I would have flinched if I wasn't too damn stunned to react.

The door ahead of us opened. More men filled the small space, *go figure*, but there was someone else inside, too.

A woman.

She sat on the far side of a long table, leaned back in her chair with her arms crossed over her chest. Her flaming red hair was pulled into a tight bun that didn't leave a single piece out of place. Her makeup was perfect, her body lithe and strong. Her black gear matched that of the men, though she wore no weapons or tactical vest. Her smile, though. Her smile was just as dangerous.

And she was zeroed in on me. "Welcome," she said. *Was she talking to me?* "Come in."

The men shoved me forward, but didn't follow. The others moved to the perimeter of the small room as if they wanted to stay as far from me as they could.

"Leave us," the scary woman said without diverting her eyes.

The men immediately rushed out of the room, and when it was just the two of us, I suddenly felt as if I were in more danger than I'd been in the van with those freaks. Especially when that heavy metal door clanged shut.

Yep. I was certainly better off dead.

The woman shifted in her seat, head cocked to one side, and gave me a thorough once-over. I fought the urge to cover my tattered white shirt and loose trousers. Did I look my best? No. But it's not like I expected to be meeting strangers within minutes of burying my dead sister.

If I had, I definitely wouldn't smell this bad. *Could she smell me? That was me, right?*

"Have a seat, please." Her voice was smooth and alluring, almost calming.

I obeyed, moving to the chair across from her and easing into it.

She didn't speak at first. Just sat there, staring at me. I could only imagine what I looked like, with messy hair and dirt caked into my fingernails. But I pulled my shoulders back and met her stare.

The woman's eyes were bright, but her smile faded. "What's your name?"

"Athena." I cleared my throat.

She hummed and dipped her chin. "Hello, Athena. My name is Sandra, but people around here call me Director."

My heart stopped. *This* was the leader of the Ministry? The commander of all these evil, brainless, manly robots? *This* was the person leading the wars and massacring thousands of innocent people?

Clearly sensing my confusion, she clasped her hands on the table in front of her and said, "I'm sure you have questions, and you likely have concerns, but I can assure you, Athena, that you are in good hands here."

I shifted. "What do you want with me?"

Her eyes widened for a second like she was surprised I'd spoken up at all. "You're direct. I like that. No use in wasting precious time." She cleared her throat and straightened in her chair. "As I'm sure you know, an army of mystics can easily wipe out an army of earthly soldiers. Since the war began, the Ministry has been working to harness the power of the mystics. And for some time, we did so relatively easily, using tier one and two mystics who wanted to aid our cause. Tier threes were more rare, but we worked with as many as we could find." Lips pressed together, she watched me for a moment before confessing, "Now, we have nearly none."

Tiers. I had heard my brother speak of them before. Every mystic fell into one of the three categories, depending on the level of power they possessed. Threes were the most dangerous, but also the most desired by the Ministry. No wonder they'd become so rare. Any tier threes remaining out there were probably deep in hiding.

The room fell silent, as if she was waiting for a response from me. As if I had any idea what to say to that. "That certainly sounds like a predicament."

"A predicament, it is. You see, if we do not win this war, life as we know it will cease to exist. You may never see freedom again if the Ministry does not succeed in finding the mystics and harnessing their power. We need tier threes. And we need your help."

I choked on a scoff, a wave of disbelief washing over me. "You think *I* can help you? Why?"

She assessed me with an arched brow. "Do not play games with me, Athena. I am a busy woman. I have it on good authority that you are a mystic. You're going to tell me exactly what type of power you possess, and then you'll help me win this damn war."

I blinked once. Twice. Did she just say what I thought she said? This woman had *clearly* lost her mind. "I am definitely *not* a mystic. Your 'good authority' must be mistaken. I have no power."

Director's fake smile quickly faded.

"I said do not play games with me." She brought a palm down on the table with a sharp slap, her first sign of a loose temper. "It will be beneficial to all of us if you come clean right now."

Hands in my lap, I surveyed the room. If this woman was crazy enough to think I was a mystic, then how the hell was I going to talk sense into her? She didn't even know me! Her men had kidnapped me from my home while I mourned my dead family. What proof did she have?

"I'm sorry to disappoint you, I really am, but I've spent my life as a regular-ass person living with my family. My now *dead* family. I've minded my own business. I've never even *met* a mystic, and I certainly don't possess any magical powers."

Her jaw clenched, and I braced myself for a stronger outburst of her anger. Instead, she leaned back in her chair once more. "You seem like a nice girl, Athena. I don't want to have to use force to get the truth out of you, but you and I aren't the only people at risk here. The entire continent of Ashora is at risk if we do not win this fight." She nodded to the door behind me, and two men walked in. If the room felt small earlier, it felt downright minuscule now.

I fought to keep my breathing steady. Panicking would only make the situation worse.

"Bring her," Director ordered as she stood.

The men each clutched an arm and hauled me to my feet. I tensed, but didn't fight them. I had a feeling I'd need to conserve my energy for what came next.

"Where are we going?"

Director didn't look at me as she walked past, heading back into the steel hallway. "We're going to find the truth."

THREE HOURS LATER, my voice was raw from screaming. The two brutes had dragged me to another door, but behind it, I did not find a clean, sterile room. No, we were in the depths of the underground, inside a dark, dank cage that smelled of death and blood.

My blood, surely.

Maybe my death, too.

Breaths sawing in and out of my lungs, I rested my head on the back of the chair I was now strapped to.

"Tell us what you know and the pain will end," Director ordered.

It took all my strength to hold in the sob clawing its way up my throat. "I swear to you, I am not a mystic. I've *never* wielded power."

"You're lying," she retorted. "It's doing you no good, Athena. Lying to us will not change your fate. You will help us whether you do it willingly or not."

The man who'd been torturing me since they tied me to this chair stepped forward, the knife he'd been using held up in front of him.

He hovered close, leering at me. It was tempting to lie and tell them I was a mystic just to make the damn torture stop. What did these people want from me, anyway? Did they want me to burst out in magic and save the world? What was the point of all this?

"I'll give you one more chance to come clean," she said. "What tier are you? Two? Three?"

This woman was truly obsessed. It was her loss. By no stretch of the imagination could I even be considered a tier *one*. There was no way in hell I could even *fake* having enough power to help her in this war.

Not like I would want to. This war she spoke of? The

Ministry was to blame for it and for the deaths of hundreds of thousands of innocent people. They were power-hungry monsters who couldn't control themselves. Tired of living normal lives among the earthlies, they'd formed territories of mystics. And when they'd stolen from innocent people and the earthlies had fought back...

These people were the reason the world was burning to the ground around us.

"I can't help you." I squeezed my eyes shut, preparing myself for the pain that knife would bring me. My legs were now numb, my body's self-preservation instincts kicking in after the dozens of shallow wounds the nameless man had created. "Please, just stop."

The worst part? I caught that bastard *smiling* as he sliced into my flesh.

If I had any magic at all, I would use it to kill everyone in this creepy, underground establishment.

"That's the thing," Director said softly, stepping in close and angling over me until her perfectly smooth face was inches from mine. "You *will* help me, Athena. You're too stubborn to see that it's for your own good."

My brain was too tired for riddles, too exhausted to comprehend what this psychotic person was talking about.

"Are you familiar with the claiming?"

My vision blurred. "Can't say I've heard of it."

A devious smile appeared on her face. "You're in luck. And we are too. Tier threes are powerful, yes, but during the blood moon, if the claiming ceremony is performed, we can harness the power from two mystics and wield it. This is how we win the war, you see. We wait until the blood moon and then we strike. We will be virtually unstoppable."

My stomach twisted into a painful knot. "You want me to complete the claiming ritual? What even is that? Doesn't sound fun."

She stood and crossed her arms over her chest. "You must mate with a tier three on the night of the blood moon. The transformation that happens to both mystics during the ritual will render you as one of the deadliest weapons in existence."

Mate? I really wished I had enough energy to look shocked. Was she saying what I thought she was saying? She wanted me to have *sex* with a mystic on the night of the blood moon so she could harness the power I didn't even possess? If they were this out of their minds, it was no wonder the Ministry kidnapped women under any suspicion they might be a mystic.

This was a dream. A very bad, sick, twisted nightmare that I would be waking up from any minute now.

"You can't possibly think I'd be willing to *mate* with someone so you can steal our magic. Did you forget the part where I'm not even a mystic?"

Director turned away and spoke in low tones to the man with the blade.

Despite my best efforts, I couldn't make out a word she'd said.

When she turned back, her expression was a shade harder than it had been since I'd met her. "We'll see about that. We've just missed the blood moon, so you've got a month until the next. A month to change your mind,

Athena, and I'm confident you'll come to your senses soon enough."

God, if you're listening, just kill me now. Maybe this lady would come to her senses and understand that she sounded like a total lunatic.

"Take her to the dungeon," she ordered.

I could barely feel my body as I was untied from the chair and forced back onto my feet.

"I'll check in on you in a few days to see whether you've changed your mind. I think you'll find it is in your best interest if you do." She cocked her head to the side, dragging her attention down my body once more. "The other mystics will show special interest in someone like you."

With that, she was gone.

Before I could inhale a steadying breath, I was dragged farther into the underground cavern, closer to the smell of death. The ceiling was so low in some parts, the men escorting me had to duck so they didn't smack their heads on the stone.

Because that would be a real shame.

As we continued, I tried to pay attention to each turn we took, tried to burn every defining landmark into my memory so that I could get out of this prison the first chance I got, but the path was long and confusing, and by the time we made it to a barred, steel door, I'd lost hope that I'd remember. It was darker here, and this door was heavier than the rest. One key slipped into keyhole after keyhole, and the reinforced steel creaked to life as the men spent a handful of minutes undoing the locks.

The door cracked open, and I instantly regretted

fighting so hard to stay alive. A massive, cavernous space just beneath the earth opened up to this strikingly disgusting pit made of rock walls and metal reinforcements. At least thirty men stared back at me from inside the *dungeon*, as Director called it. These were not the Ministry men I'd spent the last several hours with, though. These men looked just as shitty as I felt, some sitting on the dirty floor, others standing along the walls, each one looking at us like it'd give them great pleasure to snap our necks.

"Welcome to hell," one of my captors whispered in my ear as he shoved me inside.

I landed hard on my knees on the stone floor of the nasty cave as the door slammed shut behind me.

Hell, indeed.

athena

Men worried me. Truly. Their sheer strength and ability to overpower a woman was enough to put me on edge. And that was in the presence of just *one*. Here, there had to be dozens.

I scrambled to my feet and scanned my new prison, working to temper a look of disgust.

It was *gross*. We were in an underground cave, like a hole had been dug in the earth and these men had been shoved inside with no extra accommodations. Tiny cracks and natural openings in the rock near the top of the cave walls let in just enough sunlight to illuminate small cots lining either side of this underground dungeon. The walls were damp and rigid, looking as if the entire structure could cave in at any second. Everything was black or brown and covered in dirt. The smell of musk and old air nearly suffocated me, but I forced myself to take a few steps forward.

Some men stood in groups, speaking softly. Some

worked out amongst themselves on the far side of the cavern. Others lounged around on the ground. But after a longer assessment, it was clear my first impression was correct.

I was the only woman here.

As fear ignited inside me, I froze. Maybe if I stood still, none of these monsters—sorry, *men*—would see me.

But unfortunately, within seconds, every conversation in the dungeon dwindled to a halt. Every single pair of eyes fell on me.

This was so much worse than living alone with my family buried in the yard. Was it too late to join them?

"What do we have here?" A blond man approached from my right. He was a foot taller than me, but his black T-shirt hung from his shoulders loosely, exposing his thin frame.

I could take him if I had to.

But I sure as shit couldn't take all of them.

I probably couldn't even fight off the two other men who flanked him with their arms crossed over their chests.

With my mouth sealed shut, I lifted my chin and crossed my own arms.

Rather than back off like I'd hoped, the man only tilted his head in delight. "A shy one." He clicked his tongue. "Good. That'll make our jobs easier."

The men beside him snickered, and a bolt of dread ran up my spine.

Cheeks heating, I willed my body not to tremble. "And what is your job, exactly?" I mustered as much sass as I could as I looked him up and down like the trash he was.

He only seemed to like that more.

"Didn't they tell you?" he sneered, coming one step too close for comfort. "You're here so we can finally complete the damn claiming ritual. We've been waiting for months, and I'll be damned if I let your smart mouth talk your way out of this."

Stomach sinking, I took half a step back. Had *everyone* here lost their damn minds?

"You're all mystics?" I scanned the room, and when every eye was still on me, I swallowed thickly. Some even stopped what they were doing to stand, circling me like I was their new form of entertainment.

The blond man just laughed. "Of course we're mystics. If not for the claiming, why would any man have any interest in someone like you? Now," he said, flashing a wicked smile, "tell us. What tier are you? By the look of you, I'd guess a one. There's no way someone covered in dirt and gore would have real worth in this world."

He scanned my body again, lingering on the blood and wounds that covered my right thigh. I stood tall. I would not flinch in front of these monsters. I would not show weakness.

Arms still crossed, I pulled myself up straighter and squinted at this sad excuse for a human. "I'm not telling you anything," I sneered. "And I suggest you take a step back before you piss me off."

With his hands held up in front of him, he widened his eyes and let his mouth drop open sarcastically.

While his buddies laughed, my heart raced. Shit. I hoped these bozos couldn't tell. This was so, so much worse than lying unconscious in the van with those Ministry freaks.

"Let's get one thing straight here, *sweetheart*." Rather than step back like I suggested, he got so close I could smell the revolting musk wafting from him, his green eyes boring into mine. "You don't get to talk to me like that. As a matter of fact, you don't talk to anyone like that. Not even Henry over there." He pointed to one side, but I refused to look away from him, not when he was so close. "Who I'm convinced was only brought here because Director had no other use for him. Now, keep your pretty little mouth shut and stay out of my way. We all know a woman like you has only one use here."

He reached out like he was going to touch me, but a massive figure stepped into view, and Blondie immediately froze and turned to look up at the male who approached us.

Good god, he was huge. He had pale skin but thick, dark lashes fringing his nearly black eyes. His arms were crossed, causing his biceps to bulge as he looked at Blondie. Then me.

I almost shit my pants right there.

"What are you doing over here, Carter?"

Blondie—*Carter*—tensed and turned away from me like he hadn't just been antagonizing me. "Nothing, Sinner. Just welcoming the new girl to hell."

The massive and terrifyingly attractive man—*Sinner*, I supposed, which wasn't disturbing *at all*—nodded.

His jaw clenched, the muscle there ticking. "Do I need to remind you of our rules here?" Sinner asked.

Carter immediately dropped his eyes to the ground. "No. You don't."

"Good." The bigger man smacked his lips. "Because I was starting to think you'd forgotten the whole reason we're here, and that's to get the fuck out of this place. And in order to get the fuck out of this place, we need female mystics—like her."

Blood rushed to my cheeks from the sudden burst of attention. Why did that sound oddly flattering?

"I know, she just—"

"Leave her the fuck alone," Sinner interrupted. His tone was flat, bored, if anything, and he still hadn't given me a second of his attention, so I figured it had more to do with his obvious hatred of Carter and less to do with the need to protect me. "The next blood moon isn't for four weeks. Can we all fucking behave until then?"

His voice was still even, but the power of it boomed off the cavern wall. Carter and his friends murmured an array of submissive responses, which lit a satisfying fire in my chest.

Men loved to act tough, but in reality, everyone was someone's little bitch.

Everyone but Sinner, apparently.

"And you," he said.

It took me a second to realize he was talking to me. When I did, all I could do was blink up at him.

"Keep to your fucking self. Don't talk to him," he pointed to a retreating Carter, "and definitely don't fucking talk to me. Showers and bathrooms are that way. We're fed once a day if the Ministry cares enough to bother. You're on your own. We've been here for a hell of a long time, so don't assume that your presence is going to change anything for us. Got it?"

I swallowed, trying to stop my eyes from bulging out of my head.

"I'm sorry," he gritted out. "Are you fucking mute?"

Ah, shit. I cleared my throat and willed my vocal cords to work. "Yes, no, sorry. I mean, yes, I understand."

His lip curled up, his expression making it clear he thought I was the biggest idiot here. Honestly, I didn't blame him.

"Can I ask you one question?"

His eyes darkened. "One. And it'll be the only time you get to talk to me, so make it quick."

"What are we doing here? Why does the Ministry keep mystics locked up like this?"

His chest rose and fell. His eyes flickered away for a moment, and when they made their way back, they seemed almost sad. "We're here to mate on the blood moon. That's it. You have one month until then, and if you're lucky, the Ministry will decide you're useless and kill you when it's done. But..."

"But what?"

That massive jaw clenched again. "But you're a woman. Clearly, you're outnumbered here. I don't predict you'll be that lucky."

My stomach plummeted. *Great. This day was really looking up, wasn't it?*

Without another word, he turned and walked back into the crowd of gawking men. They followed his lead, thank god, acting as if they weren't going to watch my every move.

In the dim light, I found a semi-empty corner to the left and made my way to it. The numbness in my legs was wearing off, making each step painful. I prayed to whoever would listen that I wouldn't fall on my ass. Not in front of these people.

The Ministry was my enemy, yes, but here? In an underground cave full of men who'd been brought here with the sole purpose of mating?

It looked as though my list of enemies had just grown exponentially.

Sinner, as scary as he was, was right about one thing. The lucky ones would be killed before they had to endure torture like that.

But there were many of them and only one of me.

The odds were not in my favor.

I finally reached the wall and pressed my back against the stone, sliding down until I met the floor. I sighed in relief, but tried my best to keep my expression neutral. I would not show weakness.

Not like it mattered much. Along with being covered in dirt from my family's graves, blood and sweat coated my skin. I didn't even want to know what all these men saw when they looked at me.

In reality, looking repulsive might help my cause.

Repulsive might keep me untouched.

The male voices returned, the volume pitching to a dull roar. It was preferable to the creepy silence that had taken over when I was pushed into this cavern. Water dripped nearby, and the stone was cold against my body. I ignored the chill sinking into my bones.

I would find a way out of here. Four weeks? That was plenty of time to make my escape.

There wasn't a single other woman here. Could it be because they'd been smart enough to find a way out?

I curled myself into a tight ball and let my eyes flutter shut. Sleep was inevitable. I just hoped that the men were all as afraid of Sinner and his rules as they appeared to be.

If it came down to it, I couldn't fight off more than one or two of these men.

So I silently prayed that they'd forget I was here.

And exhaustion took over.

"SHE CAN BE SUCH A BITCH SOMETIMES!" *I picked up another log from the pile right outside the house. "It's not my fault. You saw how she was acting!"*

When I turned to look, Kylar was smiling and shaking his head, his arms laden with logs as well. "You're too predictable, Thena. She knows how to push your buttons and you let her do it every time."

Annoyance flared hot inside me despite the frigid temperature. "I do not."

"Oh, really? How do you explain your bad mood, then?"

"I am not in a bad mood!" I picked up another log and stomped toward the house. "I'm sick of her getting away with treating me the way she does."

His footsteps trudged the ground behind me. "She gets away with it because she's better at keeping a level head. And because Mother and Father are tired of dealing with you both."

"That's very nice, thank you."

All our lives, Kylar had done his best to be a buffer between my older sister and me, but he didn't understand. Katherine had no issue with him. She was nice to him, even. Why couldn't she treat me with even an ounce of the same respect?

Kylar stepped in front of me before I made it to the front door. "Just..." He huffed a breath. "Try to ignore her. I think it would do you both some good."

I rolled my eyes at his optimism and stormed inside. Once the door was shut behind us, I kicked my boots off and brought the pile of wood to Father, who was stoking the fire.

"Thanks, darlin'," he mumbled. "Your ma's waiting for you two in the dining room. Hustle up!"

I brushed my hands off on my trousers and followed the smell of roasting chicken.

"There you are!" Jasmine cheered from the table. "Come sit by me, Thena! I saved you a seat!"

I couldn't help but smile at my younger sister. She was lit up, beaming from ear to ear. Jasmine sat across from Katherine, whose scowl was so intense I could practically feel it as I sat. How the hell had Jasmine ended up so kind and perfect when Katherine was nothing more than a rotten turnip?

"Did you two wash your hands?" Mother asked as Kylar took the seat next to Katherine.

We glanced at each other before lying in unison, "Yep!"

Father joined us as Mother started passing around the food, and we quickly fell into the comfortable rhythm we always had.

Day after day, we ate dinner as a family. I didn't think I'd ever get tired of it.

I forked a healthy chunk of chicken, and when I'd finished chewing, I cleared my throat. "So, Father, any news on the war with the mystics?"

The air around us stilled, and Father gave me that look again—the look that told me to stop talking. He knew more than he was letting on. He always did. I could see it in his eyes —in the heaviness that lingered there.

"You know better than to ask those questions at dinner, Athena."

"But I—"

Katherine kicked me beneath the table.

I reared back and glowered at her. "What the hell—"

"No cursing at the dinner table!" Mother yelled.

"I'm just trying to ask Father about the war! We sit around pretending that everything's fine, but we all know that's not true!" I looked at my brother, my ally, and said, "You agree with me, right?"

Kylar's face went blank, his focus averted.

"They're going to find us eventually!" I argued.

The whole family was silent. Even Father waited for Kylar's reply. But Kylar stared back at me, curly dark hair a mess and his soft brown eyes as kind as ever. Only now, there was another emotion lingering in his gaze. One that looked an awful lot like pity. "I think I'd prefer not talking about the war during dinner."

"Yes!" Jasmine chimed in from beside me. "I agree with Kylar!"

Across the table, Katherine looked from Father to me like she was trying to determine who would break first. And when her eyes landed on me, they were filled with anger. "You really have to do this every time?" she asked.

"Do what?!"

"We have a nice life here. A peaceful life. I don't see why you can't be grateful for what Mother and Father have built for us and—"

"Who the hell said I'm not grateful? I just wanted to have one damn conversation! My god! You act like the whole world is going to burn down if I even mention the Ministry!"

"That's ENOUGH." Father pounded the table with a fist, causing Mother's dishes to shake.

I shut my mouth immediately.

But my anger could not be as easily contained.

I'd always had a temper, but this? The entire family ganging up on me this way? It was enough to send me spiraling.

Mother couldn't look me in the eye. Jasmine put her hands in her lap and lowered her focus to her dinner plate. Nobody else cared. No, they were perfectly fine living in igno-rance, fully unaware of the mystics and what was happening to the world around us. Hell, the Ministry could come knocking on our door tomorrow and we wouldn't have a single ounce of warning because Father kept us hidden like this—

"Athena." Kylar's soft voice interrupted my thoughts. "You need to calm down. Right now."

The house started to shake, most likely originating from the anger in my own damn body.

Jasmine whimpered next to me, but my head was hot and my ears were ringing, making it impossible to make out her words. Everyone was staring at me like I was going to explode, like I was going to tear the whole place down like some—

"ATHENA!"

A SHARP POKE to my shoulder jarred me from the dream. I'd been lost to my nightmare. It had felt so damn real. As if my family was still whole. Seeing their faces again...to hear their voices, was—

The sharp poke continued, and I snapped my eyes open. It took me all of three seconds to remember where I'd fallen asleep. To recall how dangerous my situation was. I had been sleeping around a group of strange, starved, mystic men. I pushed myself to a seated position on the dungeon floor, hit with a rush of adrenaline.

But the figure hovering over me wasn't a man. The blue eyes peering through the darkness belonged to a young woman who couldn't have been more than nineteen.

"Oh good," she said. "You're alive."

Her long hair was pulled into a loose braid down her back, and even in the darkness of the caves, I could see freckles scattered across her pale skin.

"Holy shit." My mouth was so dry, the words came out in a jumbled mess. "I—I thought I was the only girl down here."

Her responding laugh echoed off the stone walls, startling me.

Breath hitching, I scanned the space, expecting every eye to be on us.

Instead, the men paid us little mind.

"I've been the only girl here for months," she said with a scoff that told me she thought my assumption was ridiculous. "I was starting to think I was the only one left."

I frowned. "The only what left? Girl?"

"The only female mystic, silly." She inched toward me and cocked her head. "I'm Margaret. I think we're going to be great friends."

"Well—" I cleared my throat, in desperate need of water. "It's nice to meet you, I guess, Margaret. But I'm not sure I'm ready to make friends in this rancid place yet." *God, my head hurt.* "How long have I been asleep?"

"Two days," she said, her expression a little more cheerful than one would expect in a place like this. "You must have been exhausted. We haven't had anyone new in quite some time. You're all anyone's been talking about. I would have woken you up to eat, but you looked so peaceful. And you're, like, really pretty."

I blinked at her words. I wasn't exactly proficient at socializing, having spent most of my life relatively isolated, but she seemed a little pushy. "Thanks, but I'm not sure that's a good thing around here."

She shifted so she sat in front of me with her legs crossed beneath her. She wore a simple black shirt and trousers like most of the men down here were dressed in.

She was cleaner and more well-groomed than I'd expect of any person who lived in a literal dungeon, especially a lone young woman in a cavern full of monsters. And she actually seemed to look...happy?

"Oh, it's a good thing," she said. "Here. I saved this for

you." She slid a plate of food to me. "I had to hide it from the others. They're not very good at sharing."

At the sight of the small portion of chicken, my stomach rumbled, reminding me that I hadn't eaten in days. I picked it up with my fingers, not hesitating for a second as I shoved it into my mouth.

As I picked up a second piece and all but inhaled it, I couldn't help but think that maybe this Margaret girl wasn't so bad, after all. She had a nice energy to her. At least I wouldn't starve to death.

Not yet, anyway.

I cleaned the plate in record time, and when I finished, Margaret stared at me with a smile on her face.

"What?" I asked. "I was hungry."

"I knew you would be," she said. "And I cleaned those wounds on your thigh as best I could while you were sleeping. They're not too deep, they should heal soon. The Ministry likes to use small knives." She paused, inching closer. "See? We're friends already. That wasn't so hard, was it?"

Aside from Jasmine and Kylar, I had never had a friend. And really, did siblings even count? Probably not, since they'd been stuck with me since birth.

Not anymore.

I ignored the tightness in my chest and turned my attention back to the mystic. "What did you mean when you said being pretty was a good thing?"

"Oh!" She looked over her shoulder and when she turned back, she hunched lower and angled in like she was about to share a secret. "The pretty ones get paired with the higher tiers. Director will like you. She might even pair you with a three."

I nearly choked. "There are actually tier threes down here? I thought the Ministry was fighting to find even ones and twos."

"They are." She leaned in, her voice barely a whisper. "There's only a single tier three here now. You know." She frowned. "I take that back. Maybe you don't want to be paired with a three. At least not this one. He's scary. Like, *scary* scary. I would stay far away from him if I were you."

"Really?" I lowered my voice to a whisper, too, even though the nearest man was a good twenty feet away. "Who?"

She turned over her shoulder, surveying the room. And then, in a way that didn't surprise me at all coming from her, she actually pointed at him.

I followed her finger.

And my stomach dropped.

The large man leaned on a blanket-covered cot. His bed was in the very back of the dungeon beneath one of the tiny holes in the cavern walls. He had his legs stretched out in front of him in a way that made him look way too large for that cot.

"You're kidding, right?"

Margaret let out a small giggle. "Not at all. The guy is a total loner down here. We all steer clear. I heard he once used his magic to kill someone for looking at him wrong. I believe it, too. He's totally creepy."

I looked away before he caught me staring. The last

thing I needed was unwanted attention from the only tier three in this dungeon.

"If he's that strong, how have they kept him contained here? Why doesn't he use his power to escape? There are so many of you. Couldn't you team up and—"

Margaret's eyes widened and she reared back. "There is no escaping here," she whisper-shouted. "And if you try, they'll punish you." She nodded at my thigh. "That's only the start of it. The mystics working for the Ministry somehow know when we use our power, and they have dozens of soldiers outside that door ready to fight anyone who's dumb enough to try. You're here until you die or until the Ministry proves you're powerful enough to be used on the battlefield."

I shook my head, my breath escaping me in a whoosh. This was so bizarre. "How long has this been going on? How long have you been here?"

She held her hand out in front of her and lifted one finger, then another and another, squinting at them. "Three months. No—four. Yes, four months."

I bit my tongue to keep from cursing aloud. "And have you done the claiming ritual? That sounds absolutely terrible."

Shaking her head, she smiled softly. "They haven't found me useful enough for it yet. I'm a tier one with very little power. That's what Director told me, anyway. I think they've been waiting for someone stronger than me. Someone like you."

"Why the hell do people keep assuming I have power? I'm not a mystic, Margaret." I pressed my fingers to my temples and rubbed in circles, willing the buzzing sensation in my brain to abate. "This is all some sick, twisted joke."

She sighed aloud. "Of course you're a mystic," she said. "You wouldn't be here if you weren't."

"But I've never used magic before. Ever."

She leaned in until she was only a few inches from my face. "Don't worry," she whispered. "Your secret is safe with me."

For the next several hours, Margaret filled me in on everything she knew regarding this dungeon and the Ministry. She was a bit of a nutjob, but I liked her. She lightened the mood in this incredibly depressing dungeon, and that alone was a near-impossible task.

Her sweet demeanor reminded me so much of Jasmine.

From what I could tell, the men ignored her entirely. That was a blessing, I was certain. She held my hand and dragged me around the cavern, pointing out the dirty walls and the much-too-low ceiling as if she were a tour guide showing me around a luxurious lodging space.

At the edge of the cavern, she pointed out a couple natural inlets in the rock walls. They had no doors, yet they offered far more privacy than any space in the main area.

I made a mental note to worm my way into one and claim it for sleep. Maybe Margaret and I could do it together.

She showed me the showers and the bathrooms, too. The plumbing and running water surprised me, but the showers and toilets were essentially thrown into a dug-out extension of the dank dungeon. A few small lights on the walls illuminated just enough to see. When I voiced my concern about her safety in here, Margaret laughed. "They would never hurt me," she said. "And trust me, they won't hurt you, either. They just like to act like they will."

Great. Really great. I was absolutely not going to believe this lunatic if she actually thought we were safe with these men.

After we settled back down in our little vacant corner, she launched into a detailed account of all she knew about the tiers and the claiming ceremony.

According to her, the last time tier threes mated during the claiming, the power they created was exponentially greater than what any mystic could summon on their own. The Ministry could use that power against an entire army. It didn't have to be a man and a woman, but there was a shortage of female mystics, nonetheless.

Margaret didn't know the specifics, but she seemed very confident that it was the truth.

I was in no position to question her.

"I'm not letting them touch me. Not a single one of them," I said. Most of the men had fallen asleep already, so I lowered my voice to a whisper so my words wouldn't echo off the damp walls.

Margaret did the same. "Well, there is one way to get out of it. Both people have to willingly perform the ceremony. It cannot be forced."

I let her words sink in. "If that's the case, then how do they get anyone to agree to doing it? Mating with a random mystic for some strange ritual? That sounds awfully creepy to me."

She lifted one shoulder and let it drop. "People have their reasons. Maybe they can't handle living underground any longer. Not long after I got here, two people who hated each other made an alliance so they could leave. And now, they're gone!"

I shuddered. "Ugh. That's disgusting. I would never have *sex* with one of them to get out of here."

She looped her arms around her legs and rested her chin on her knees. "They're not all that bad."

"Really? None of them have given off the best vibes since I've been here. If I've learned anything in this life, it's to assume men will always hurt women, and their behavior when I got pushed into this cavern only solidified that."

Her lips tugged down. "You're very cynical. It's making me sad."

I picked at my dirty pants aimlessly. "I mean, the tier three's name is *Sinner*. Where do you think he got that name? I can't imagine he earned it by being nice and loving to his friends."

Margaret just shrugged. "I wouldn't want anyone judging me without getting to know me first. I like to give others the same courtesy."

It was a damn miracle Margaret had survived this long down here. She was too nice. Too trusting.

These men had ignored her completely, yet when I'd arrived, I'd garnered the attention of every one of them. Being invisible would have been far more palatable than the verbal abuse Blondie gave me.

He and his friends slept on the far side of the dungeon,

a few feet away from where Sinner sat up in bed, using the moonlight filtering in from the window to read an old, tattered book.

His expression was softer than seemed possible for a man as roughened as he was. He almost looked peaceful.

It was disturbing.

If he was as strong as Margaret claimed, he should have no problems escaping this place. He could easily kill Director and slaughter the soldiers guarding the facility. Then we could all be free.

What was keeping him here? Who was controlling the prisoners?

Had Director really brainwashed them into believing they weren't powerful enough to escape?

Either way, I wouldn't sit around all month and wait for my death or worse. I'd spent my entire life taking care of myself.

And I would die before I let a man violate me in the name of governmental power.

athena

Three more days passed. At first, I spent every waking hour expecting Director or one of her lackeys to storm into this damn room and... I don't know. *Do* something. I couldn't believe the way they were pretending like we didn't exist. They fed us, but barely. And Margaret and I were left to share meals because the men ate about ten times more than we did.

We were lucky they left us anything at all. If Margaret weren't here, I would have starved by now. They seemed to have a basic level of respect for her that they did *not* have for me. I wasn't sure why, but the more I learned about Margaret, the more I discovered that there was something special about her level of crazy.

It was growing on me.

Aside from chatting with my new companion, there was nothing to do but sit around and become very, *very* bored. I had been here for days. The others had been here for months—maybe years. How the hell had they not lost their minds? The only thing they did for fun was partake in the occasional fight, which typically ended in a pathetic brawl that had to be broken up when one of the guys got too aggressive.

I waited for someone to use their powers, but they never did. Not one of the guys tried to bust out or even wielded magic during a fight.

Margaret was right. The Ministry was nowhere to be seen. Yet they still held all the power.

"I'm your friend, and you're my favorite person here, so I don't want to hurt your feelings when I say this, but you stink. You need to shower and change into clean clothes, okay?"

I was shaking my head before she finished the sentence. "There is no way in hell I'm stripping naked only feet away from an entire dungeon full of men."

"They aren't going to hurt you. I shower all the time and they all leave me alone. They won't even enter the bathroom when I'm there."

The couple of times I forced myself to use the bathroom, I made Margaret come with me. Strength in numbers, right? Even though it only limited my privacy further.

Margaret seemed to understand. She was right, though. Every time she entered the bathroom, the men took notice and steered clear.

Again, there was some underlying respect I didn't quite understand.

And I wasn't confident they would extend me that same courtesy if she weren't here.

So I'd deal with the smell of my own body odor. It beat risking a shower.

"I know you're scared," she said softly. She grabbed my hand and held it in both of hers. "I'll wait outside the whole time, okay? You can't expect to go the entire month without taking a shower."

"Like hell I can't."

With a roll of her eyes, she stood. Then she tugged me up beside her. "Come on," she whispered. "Everyone is sleeping, anyway. Now's your chance."

Every cell in my body told me this was a very, very bad idea. It wasn't safe for me when I was fully clothed. Showering only left me more vulnerable.

It was different for Margaret.

But she seemed very confident that I'd be okay. And she was right about one thing. *I did smell.*

"Fine," I whispered. "But you're waiting outside the door. And if anyone comes in, you scream. Got it?"

A smile spread across her face. "Thank god. I wasn't sure I could go one more night sleeping next to you like this."

I shoved her lightly on the shoulder, and with a chuckle, she led the way to the showers. We stepped over sleeping bodies and silently crept our way to the back of the dungeon. The rusty metal toilets and sinks were to the right of the small opening in the corner, and the showers were to the left. We waited by the entrance for a few seconds, ensuring the rooms were empty, before slipping inside.

My heart pounded so hard, I thought my chest would

burst open. But Margaret slipped her small hand into mine and pulled me forward. There were four or five showers, all separated by thick curtains, and my boots squelched on the wet dungeon floor as Margaret led me to the last makeshift stall.

"Let the water warm up for a few seconds before you step under the stream. Trust me, it gets cold." She pointed to the far wall. "I'll get a towel and some clean clothes from the supplies over there, okay? Then I'll wait here."

I nodded, still not totally convinced this was a good idea. I mean, I did possess basic survival instincts.

Or at least I thought I did.

"Don't you dare leave me, Margaret."

She held her little finger up in the space between us. "Pinkie promise." With a wink, she moved to the surprisingly neat pile of supplies in the corner, where she rummaged for extra clothes. I stepped behind the curtain and yanked it shut, ensuring there weren't any gaps in the thick fabric before I finally kicked my boots off.

My feet ached, and as I peeled off the socks that had practically bonded with my flesh, the blisters I'd developed from wearing my boots for days on end screamed at the sudden hit of fresh air. I bit my lip to keep from crying out in relief as my bare feet hit the cold dungeon floor.

I pulled my shirt off next, then folded the filthy fabric neatly and placed it on top of my boots. Same with my pants.

Rather than shuck my bra and underwear, I chose to keep them on. At least for this first shower. If Margaret was right about this being totally safe, I would consider taking them off next time.

See? I wasn't a complete idiot.

I reached for the partially rusted nozzle and turned the shower on. It sputtered for a couple seconds before a solid stream of ice-cold water fell from above.

The hot water in our home had stopped working years ago, so I'd been accustomed to the cold for quite some time. I'd come to appreciate it, actually.

But when the steam began to accumulate in the stall, I nearly cried with relief.

I stepped into the spray and tilted my head back, letting the water wash over my disgusting, matted hair and dirty body. And damn it all, it was nice.

I picked up a bottle from the line of supplies on the floor and poured a generous amount of liquid into my palm. Head tipped back and eyes closed, I lathered my thick hair. I had to shampoo and rinse twice before the caked dirt and blood began to wash away in earnest.

I did the same with my body, and when I scrubbed my face, my hands came away covered in dirt and blood.

Of course the twisted, sick people keeping us prisoner would shove us together in this underground dungeon but give us *soap* for good hygiene. That made total sense.

"Who knew the Ministry would be so evil but actually give us hot water," I joked.

When Margaret didn't reply, my heart lurched. I waited a few seconds, but I heard nothing.

"Margaret?"

A few more seconds went by before I heard her voice.

But she wasn't talking to me. She was speaking in hushed tones to someone else, and from the way the unintelligible words bounced off the walls, it sounded like she was on the other side of the room.

"Margaret?" I repeated. "Who's out there?"

I instinctively crossed my arms over my chest, ready to grab my clothes and dart at the first sign of trouble.

Before I could, the curtain enclosing my shower was ripped open.

I inhaled sharply, ready to scream, but a large male hand wrapped around my throat and slammed me backward, knocking the air from my lungs.

When my senses returned, I found Sinner towering over me, a much-too-menacing look dripping across his features. He was under the hot stream of water now, the droplets ricocheting off his body and onto mine as he pinned me against the cave wall.

"Start talking, New Girl. Who the hell are you?"

"What?" I choked out. "What are you talking about?" *Where the hell was Margaret?*

"What tier are you? What magic do you have?"

"For the last time," I grasped his hand, trying to pry his fingers from my throat, but it was no use, "I don't have any magic. I'm earthly, not mystic. This is all a massive mistake."

He tightened his grip on my throat until I could barely breathe. I squirmed beneath him. I knew what would come next. Someone like me would have no way to fight off a man as large as him.

"You're hiding something," he growled into my ear. "I

could tell from the first second I saw you. You can disappear in the shadows all you want, but if you're a mystic, you better tell us before the blood moon. You put all of us in danger by being here."

A harsh laugh escaped me with what little air I had access to. "You really think I want to mate with one of you crazy freaking mystics? News flash, you *brute*, I actually like my body to remain unviolated!"

Brow furrowed, he released me like I'd burned him. "I don't like you. And I sure as hell don't trust you."

I gulped air, then immediately coughed at the burn in my lungs.

"My sister may think you're special, but to me, you're nothing. If you fuck this up for us, you won't live to find a way out of here."

Confusion rolled through me. What the hell was he talking about? "How could I *possibly* fuck anything up? I was kidnapped and dragged here like a piece of meat!"

His jaw clenched, his dark eyes hardening. "And stop sleeping out in the open where every man here has access to you. You're an even bigger idiot than I thought you were."

With that, he was gone, storming out of the empty showers and leaving me gasping after him.

Margaret appeared a few seconds later, wringing her hands. "I'm so sorry! I tried to stop him, but he promised he wouldn't—"

I held my hand up to silence her. "Margaret, you've been kind to me so far, so I'm going to ask you this question once and I want you to tell me the truth."

With an audible gulp, she nodded. "Okay."

"Is that guy your *brother*?"

She sucked her plump bottom lip between her teeth, tears welling in her blue eyes.

My blood pressure shot up. "Are you kidding me? No wonder all the men ignore you! You're the doe-eyed sister of the *only* tier three here!"

"I didn't want you to be afraid of me!" she pleaded. "Everyone avoids me because of who my brother is. It gets lonely down here! And when I saw you, another *girl*, I knew I'd have to keep it a secret if I wanted company. It's not a big deal, is it? Please tell me it's not a big deal!"

Annoyance flooded my veins. *Un-freaking-believable.* "You lied to me."

"I didn't lie! I simply omitted a small detail about my life."

With a groan, I stepped back into the hot water. My mind still reeled, replaying each detail of what had just happened.

Sinner was Margaret's brother, and he thought I was hiding mystic powers, just like the Ministry.

If the two were siblings, couldn't he simply ask Margaret if I was a mystic? Did he really need to bombard me in the showers and demand the answers like that? My heart was still busy returning to a normal rate. Yeah, my instincts about remaining partially dressed had been spot-on.

"Get out of here," I sighed. "If you let anyone else in here—including your brother—I'm going to be pissed. Understand?"

Margaret's wide eyes lit up. "Got it," she nodded. "Again, I'm so sorry. I really didn't expect him to barge in here."

"It's okay," I sighed, my body deflating. "I have a feeling it won't be happening again." I hoped not, at least.

Now I understood why Margaret was respected around here. Her brother was terrifying.

I finished my shower without more intrusions, and when I stepped out, Margaret had found clothes for me. I rinsed my disgusting boots in the water, but there was no way I was going to put my feet back in those things. I wasn't even sure I could, not after taking them off for the first time in days.

I took off my wet bra and underwear, washed them quickly, and tucked them away with my boots. I wasn't sure my clothing would remain unbothered around here, but if they were still here in the morning, I could put them back on. Margaret had found a shirt that was three sizes too big for me and a pair of men's slacks I had to roll over at the waist to keep in place, but they were better than nothing.

I slipped the fabric over my now semi-human skin.

"Ready?" she asked me.

I nodded, tucking them under my arm. Margaret walked around barefoot, as did half the men in here. I guess I would be doing the same.

She slipped her arm through mine as we walked back out to the main dungeon. What the hell had Sinner meant when he said not to sleep in the middle of the room? It wasn't like there was a wide selection of available cots to choose from.

The men had claimed just about every one, especially those in the corners, where there was a little more privacy, and no one had offered to give theirs up. They may be afraid of Sinner, but they weren't exactly chivalrous.

I turned to head toward our usual spot, but Margaret stopped me, her lip caught between her teeth. "Um, why don't we sleep over there tonight?" she asked, pointing to a cot that hadn't been available before I stepped into the restroom. And of course it was the cot directly next to Sinner's.

"Absolutely not."

"Oh, come on. Why not? It's way better than sleeping out there on the floor!" Though she whispered, her voice carried in the dank cell.

"You know exactly why," I sneered as I scanned our surroundings. "I much prefer our spot on the floor. Come on."

"Something wrong?" a male voice boomed from far too close for my comfort. "Or are you disobeying my direct orders already, New Girl?"

sinner

God, she looked even more shocked now than when I'd snuck up on her in the shower. Her eyes widened, and she instinctively took a step back.

Was she surprised that I was speaking to her? Or that I insisted she and my sister sleep on this cot instead of on the floor like rats?

I couldn't care less about the new addition, but my sister had chosen to befriend her, and I did have some family loyalty, after all.

New Girl stood frozen in place, mouth agape, staring at me.

"What?" I pushed, taking another step forward. My voice was drawing attention now, but I didn't give a fuck. This was *my* dungeon. New Girl would follow my orders. Someone needed to teach her that lesson, it seemed. "Can't speak now? Or is there some other reason that you'd rather not sleep over here?" I pointed to the cot.

Yeah, I'd told her to leave me alone, but I had the right to change my mind, didn't I?

I had to admit, now that she wasn't covered in dirt and blood, she didn't look half bad. If I had to guess by her lean frame and sculpted muscles, she wasn't a stranger to hard work. But I wasn't going to let her physical features distract me.

New Girl here was hiding something. I could fucking smell it.

"Can I talk to you for a second?" Mags hissed.

Squinting, New Girl looked from my sister to me and back again, clearly suspicious.

Mags gripped my arm and pulled me a few feet away. She was small, but damn, the girl was strong. And from the look on her face, she was about to piss me off.

"What do you want, Mags?"

"Why did you have to go and scare her? We were perfectly fine minding our own business!"

"Are you kidding?" I raised a brow. "She shows up here and you wander off to play house with a complete stranger. How's that cold dungeon floor treating you, by the way?"

Her nostrils flared as she took a deep breath. "I've done everything you've asked of me since we got here. I'm lonely and I'm tired, and Athena is actually nice to me, unlike any of you. You didn't have to freak her out, now she's never going to take a shower again!"

I glanced over Mags's shoulder to where New Girl stood, arms crossed, watching us. "She needed to learn how things work around here."

My sister huffed, throwing her arms out. "How things work? You mean how *you* work, going around here and bullying everyone until you get what you want?"

Lips pressed together to tamp down on a smile, I hummed. "Pretty much. Yes."

"She's my friend," Mags huffed. "I haven't had a friend in a long time. Not since—"

She didn't finish the sentence. She didn't have to.

My chest did the strange tightening thing that it did only for her. With a long breath in, then back out to break up the tension, I nodded. "Fine. I'll leave her alone. But the two of you are sleeping on your cot. I'm sick of fighting off the other guys. They're like damn vultures when it comes to the beds, you know."

Her eyes immediately lit up. "Thanks, Elijah."

Annoyance flared in my chest. "Don't call me that."

But she was already walking back toward New Girl and her dripping wet hair. "Yeah, yeah," she called over her shoulder, "you have a big, scary new name now. I know!"

I clenched my fists to keep my shit together rather than following after her.

"Come on," Mags whispered, pulling her new friend toward the bed they'd now share. "This is usually where I sleep, anyway. It'll be much more comfortable this way."

Damn fucking right it would be. And now that they'd be three feet from me, I could actually sleep at night knowing they were safe.

"He might be your brother and a tier three, but none of that gives him any right to boss me around."

My head snapped back in her direction. New Girl did have

some backbone after all, huh? I supposed that was better than most of the newcomers. Typically, the people thrown in here were too afraid to stand up for themselves, too afraid to speak to me, too afraid to even look in my direction.

But New Girl? I caught her staring at me nearly every time I looked at her. Which made it even more clear to me that she was, in fact, hiding something.

And I was going to find out what that was.

I closed the distance between us, only stopping when New Girl's chest brushed mine with every inhale. "Let's get one thing straight here." I balled my hands into fists at my sides. "I *do* get to boss you around. You will do anything and everything I ask you to do, New Girl, but it has nothing to do with my tier. I could be a fucking one, and you would still obey me. Hell, I could be an earthly, and you'd get on your knees before me if I asked you to. Understand?"

My sister grasped her friend's arm and tugged, trying desperately to pull her away from me, but New Girl wasn't the type to back down from a challenge.

Jaw set firmly, she zeroed in on me. She was small. Too small. She'd do the fucking Ministry no good in battle. Not without power, anyway.

Hell, part of me *hoped* she was hiding something. That she was secretly a tier two or three and not some useless earthly the Ministry would use as dog meat the first fucking chance they had.

As irritating as she was, things got boring around here month after month. And I was finally starting to have some fun.

New Girl remained silent, but a fight simmered right behind her eyes. Her fists clenched around her worn, battered boots and dirty clothes.

I locked my own jaw and glared back.

I used to possess that kind of fight. I used to care about winning, about arguing.

But now? Now there was no fight left in me. No resistance. That had all been stripped from me months ago. Hell, it disappeared long before Mags and I were ever brought here.

It was refreshing, honestly, to come face to face with someone who wasn't done fighting.

Even if she was fighting the wrong damn person.

"Sleep tight." I winked. "And if you snore, I'll fucking kill you." With that, I straightened to my full height, then retreated to my bed. I lay back on my cot and picked up my book, pretending to read. I was much too aware of the girls whispering together to actually focus on the words. Much too aware of how many eyes now lingered on them after our little show.

I didn't talk to people in here. I much preferred my solitude. I rarely even talked to Mags these days, though she certainly never stopped making an effort. It was better if people like me didn't make friends. It was better if everyone here hated me.

They would all learn to hate me eventually, so there was no use dragging out the inevitable.

After a few painfully long seconds, the two approached the cot. I had forced the original owner to move, and although he still glared at me every time we made eye contact, he didn't say a goddamn word.

My dungeon. My rules.

And I needed these two where I could see them at all times. Mags practically dragged New Girl behind her, fighting all the way about who would take the side closest to me.

Mags wanted the outside, because the owner of the next cot was Carter, whose prick fucking friends all bunked nearby.

I shifted, flipping another page. I scanned the page from left to right, unseeing, while keeping my ears perked and my focus locked on the movement beside me.

New Girl eventually set her nasty, wet boots down on the edge of the cot. She moved slowly, as if the careful movements would save her from the horrible fucking fate of this place.

I didn't look up from the book as the bed beside me shifted. I waited until their quiet whispers stopped, waited until their breaths had slowed to a dull, even pace.

Only then did I dare a glance in their direction.

Moonlight from the small cracks in the cave ceiling filtered across the bed, allowing enough light for me to make out their forms. They slept back-to-back, as if on guard. And when I dragged my eyes up to New Girl's face, I found her watching me.

I didn't look away. Neither did she. We stayed like that, practically killing each other with the daggers in our eyes, until she slowly moved her hand up.

And flipped me off.

If I had any emotions left in me at all, I might have been amused.

Instead, I simply returned my attention to the book, pretending to read the same page over and over again until I finally drifted off to sleep for the first time in days.

athena

Something was wrong.

The sun was just rising in the distance, its light filtering through the small window above my new cot. I sat up in bed and surveyed the silent, still dungeon.

I wasn't sure what caused my heart to race and my palms to sweat. I couldn't pinpoint what made adrenaline surge through me. But it was *something*.

My body was always one step ahead of my mind, always ready to fight before I knew what the fight was for.

To my right, Sinner was laying in his bed, shirtless, propped up on an elbow and staring at me.

He didn't speak. He only watched me, his dark eyes intense and his brows drawn together like he wanted to ask why the hell I was freaking out.

The answer came seconds later when the massive steel door, the one that only opened on the occasion the Ministry felt generous and came to feed us, creaked, the locks turning.

Sinner went rigid, his focus flying to the door. Margaret stirred in bed next to me, but didn't wake. I couldn't blame her now that she was no longer sleeping on the dungeon floor.

It was probably better if she stayed asleep rather than witness whatever the hell was about to go down. Though, the sounds of the locks were anything but silent, so with each one that clanged, more men around us stirred.

When Director entered, I sucked in a gasp.

"Morning, gentleman," she called out. Her voice echoed off the walls, vibrating through my bones. "Ladies." She scanned the room once before landing on my cot.

Beside me, Sinner grumbled and pushed himself all the way up to stand.

I did the same, suddenly feeling vulnerable seated like this.

Director entered the dungeon for the first time since I had been dragged here. Five armed, masked men followed, each holding a baton as if prepared for us to attack.

As if any of us had the energy to.

The men and their weapons weren't what had the hair rising on the back of my neck. No, what scared me the most was the way Director stared directly at me.

I took two steps forward, my bare feet aching, only then realizing Sinner was doing the same, his expression neutral but his arms crossed. He was clearly eager for them to get to the point so they'd leave again.

Feeling was mutual.

"Athena," Director started, "it looks like you've made

yourself comfortable here. I trust your new roommates are being warm and welcoming?"

A few of the men around me scoffed.

I mustered a smile that probably looked more like a grimace. "They sure are," I spat. "Just like home."

Behind me, a man coughed a laugh. I didn't bother turning to see who.

"I'm here to have a little chat with you," she pushed, her fake smile dropping. "To see if you've changed your mind about what we discussed previously."

Changed my mind? Did she really think I'd grown magical powers overnight? Because I was fairly certain I had *not*.

My stomach dropped. "I couldn't change my mind if I wanted to." The panic of the threat slowly creeped into my chest. "Like I said before, I don't have any powers. I can't help you."

Flanked by her guards, Director stopped a few feet away from me, head cocked. "Such a disappointment," she said. "I really thought you and I could work together. Be friends, even."

Now it was my turn to choke back a laugh. Though I was tired and slightly pissed off, so I hardly succeeded.

"Don't make me hurt you again," she said, clearly annoyed by my response. "You wouldn't want to damage yourself even further, would you? Scar that pretty skin? If you're not careful, you'll ruin any chance you have at finding a willing partner for the ritual."

I tossed my head back and laughed. *Really* laughed. I sounded freaking psychotic, and based on the way a few of the men around me flinched, I probably looked it too. I didn't care. "You really think I care about the claiming ritual? You really think I care what my skin looks like after being kidnapped and thrown into a dungeon? You can do whatever you want to me. I'm not a mystic."

The room fell silent. Nobody moved. Nobody snickered this time. Even Director froze in place, taking the time to process my words.

Eventually, she pulled her shoulders back. "Fine, then," she ordered. "I guess we'll have to do this the hard way."

As one of her freak guard dogs stalked toward me, I forced myself to keep my chin lifted. With a sick grin, he swung a baton, as if he was looking forward to what came next.

Margaret screamed behind me as the black steel hit my knees.

I let out a cry and fell to the dungeon floor. Pain radiated through my body, rendering me immobile. But that didn't stop my attacker from hitting me again, his baton landing in the center of my back this time.

I fought to stay on my knees, but I would not let them break me completely. I would not let them see me crumble.

"Stop!" Margaret screamed. "What are you doing to her?"

"Athena can easily stop this," Director replied far too coolly for the situation. "All she has to do is tell us what tier she is. As soon as we know that, we can match her with a partner for the claiming."

The weapon struck me again, this time below my

shoulder. I grunted in pain, squeezing my eyes shut to keep the tears from falling.

When I opened them again, my vision blurred, everything around me spinning. Hands roughly grasped my arms and hauled me up, then into a chair one of the guards had dragged in.

"Are you ready to fight back? Are you ready to show us what your power is?" Director asked as she loomed over me.

God, I wanted to. Maybe I would have come up with a half-decent lie if I'd had time to prepare before a blade impaled my upper thigh, the cool metal slicing through the clean pants and my flesh.

That hurt. My vision went spotty. Air rushed from my lungs.

Margaret screamed again, something about how ridiculous this all was.

Yes, it was freaking ridiculous. I didn't have any powers. I wasn't a mystic. I was an ordinary, dull earthly. I didn't belong here.

But that didn't stop Director from believing I was hiding powers.

The man with the blade raised his arm again, and I squeezed my eyes shut, bracing myself for another hit.

But none came.

Instead, a gasp echoed around the stone walls.

I blinked my eyes open, dumbfounded by what stood before me. Or *who*.

Sinner was standing in front of me with a thick hand

wrapped around the man's wrist, keeping the weapon frozen in midair.

The whole room had frozen in surprise, actually. I couldn't see Director from here, but I could imagine the shock spreading across her face. She was probably just as confused as I was, though I wasn't sure I was seeing all this correctly since each wave of pain threatened to pull me into unconsciousness.

"I'll do it," Sinner said.

What. The. Hell? Blood poured freely out of my leg, and my head spun.

Director cackled lightly. "You'll do what, exactly, Tier Three?"

Sinner slowly let go of the guard's wrist. "I'll perform the claiming. If she really has power, it will be exposed then. She won't be able to hide it from a three once she's claimed."

I opened my mouth to argue, only to choke on a mouthful of blood. Had I bitten my tongue that severely? And was I really hearing this all correctly?

Or had I lost so much blood that my mind was creating a false reality?

Yeah, that had to be it.

When the guard with the knife moved again, Sinner's chest rumbled with fury. "She's *mine* now. If you touch her again, I'll kill you."

Margaret knelt at my side, murmuring something about me and her brother that I couldn't fully comprehend.

I was too focused on Director, who hadn't immediately

shut this idea down. She couldn't really be considering this, right? There was no way she'd pair me with a tier three for a claiming that I had no right to take part in.

Was the Ministry really that insane? I shook my head. Of course they were. How else had they earned their horrid reputation?

"You'll willingly claim with her?"

Sinner stood, slightly rigid, with his hands clamped behind his back. "Yes."

"And why is that? You haven't been exactly forth-coming in the past."

He took a long breath, his focus sliding over to me.

I froze under his scrutiny. Nothing but distaste and hatred lingered there. Disgust, even. Hell, I didn't blame him. I was feeling all the same things.

"Maybe I'm ready to get out of this shithole."

His words were so sharp, Director actually stepped back. But she quickly recovered, huffing a laugh. "Well, well. Our tier three wants to cooperate now, and we might have what we've been looking for since this war started." She turned to me, one brow arched. "Isn't that right, Athena?"

Blood now ran down my chin and dripped onto my thighs. That didn't stop me from glaring into that bitch's face. "Like I've said a million times before, I can't help you. Find someone else for him to perform your weird claiming ritual with."

Director laughed again, sharper this time, as she saun-tered around me. For an instant, she was completely out of sight, so when she grasped my hair and yanked my head back, I couldn't stop the surprised, pained gasp that escaped me.

"You will perform the claiming. Either that, or you die. Those are your only options. The blood moon is in three weeks. I expect you to get acquainted with your claimed now that you've been spoken for." She shoved my head forward, sending a shooting pain down my neck.

Margaret squealed again somewhere nearby, but I was too disoriented to locate her.

What the actual hell just happened? Sinner hated me. He was *repulsed* by me. Now he wanted to have sex with me during the claiming?

It made no sense.

Through the ringing in my ears, Director's next words were barely audible. "Get the healer in here. I don't want her dying on us when we're this close."

Blood poured from my thigh, making it impossible to think straight. My head rolled forward and stayed there as the boots of Director's companions moved past me. I faded in and out of consciousness. The next thing I registered was another set of shoes approaching. Shoes. Not combat boots. The healer.

It wasn't a doctor. Not a real one, anyway. The person wore a mask, no doubt another mystic the Ministry had forced into servitude.

They didn't want me to die? How kind of them to care so much.

When the healer touched my face, I reared back and threw my hands out to fight them off, but my vision blurred further and the world faded in and out. A moment later, warmth radiated down my thigh, making me even angrier.

"Stop," I mumbled. "Don't bother fixing me up just so they can stab me again tomorrow."

The healer stopped for a moment, and for a sick, twisted second, I thought I recognized the dark, blurry figure in front of me.

But then my vision tunneled again. Yeah, I was definitely losing my mind.

More warmth radiated down my thigh, then eventually faded. A few other figures appeared, all of them blurry, and within minutes, they stepped back and were gone.

The sound of that massive lock clicking shut shook my bones.

For the space of several breaths, nobody spoke. Nobody moved.

Not until Margaret darted forward and dropped to her knees in front of me, applying pressure to the mostly healed wound on my thigh. "Why would you do that!" she yelled to Sinner over her shoulder. "Athena doesn't want to do the claiming!"

"You think I give a fuck about what your friend wants?" His harsh tone made me flinch. "This is our way out, Mags. I'm not staying down here to rot and die."

Margaret sobbed, tears spilling down her cheeks as she frantically looked over my beaten body.

I, thankfully, was past the point of feeling pain—my legs were numb, and so was my back. The bruises I was certain were blooming all over me didn't register. Neither did the absolute dread that should have plagued me.

A familiar voice snickered to my right. Carter. "Nice work, man. I was wondering who would get the chance to have a piece of that. You're open to sharing, right?"

I lifted my head to shoot him a glare, and as I did, I caught a glimpse of Sinner, his jaw clenched, his arms crossed over his chest. His biceps bulged while his fists tightened. "Say that dumb shit one more time and I'll kick your teeth in."

The chattering and laughter in the room ceased immediately. It was impossible to deny that everyone here respected Sinner. No, they feared him. I didn't blame them. He could have looked like a frail, helpless boy with zero strength at all and he would still be intimidating. As a tier three, he likely had the power to kill using only his mind.

It wasn't wise to piss off tier threes. They were the worst sort of enemies. These men seemed smart enough to know that.

As Sinner assessed me, a chill rolled down my spine.

Margaret scrambled to help me stand, ignoring my grunts of pain. She dragged me closer to her brother, though I wanted to be literally anywhere else in this damn dungeon. "Are you going to tell me why you did that?" she said, her tone hushed.

The men around us averted their gazes, clearly pretending like they weren't eavesdropping.

"You said you wouldn't perform the claiming."

His focus drifted over me for one agonizing second before he homed in on his sister. "Plan's changed."

"I won't do it," I mumbled, voice weak. "I won't claim with you."

Margaret stiffened under me, her grip tightening to the point of pain as she fought to keep holding me up.

"The fuck did you say, New Girl?" Sinner stepped closer, now only a few inches from me.

God, everything was fading in and out. "I'd die before I let you touch me."

He laughed slowly, his tone a strange mix of amusement and fury. "You better think long and hard about that before you commit to it because there's only one way you walk out of hell alive, and that's with me. We're getting out of here." He looked back at Margaret. "We all are."

With a low snarl, he spun. He stalked to his cot and picked up his book, and when he sat again, his expression went blank, as if nothing had happened.

Okay, so maybe I did feel something. I felt a never-ending, burning hatred for that man.

He thought he could do whatever he wanted, treat me as if I were an enemy, and then convince me to perform the claiming with him so he could escape?

The joke was on him. I hadn't survived this freaking long just to allow a man to determine my fate. I had three weeks to come up with a new plan. Three weeks to get out of this place.

And I'd do whatever it took. Even if it meant killing him.

sinner

An entire day later, I could still smell the blood from her thigh. Literally *smell* it. The small pool on the dungeon floor had dried, but it didn't matter. The memory of the dark, thick liquid pouring out of her made me fucking sick.

I tossed and turned, trying my best to think of literally anything else, but it was no use. My mind was fixated on her. There was no air flow in this damn dungeon, and the smell of copper was slowly suffocating me.

New Girl slept all day long, which wasn't a surprise after how much blood she'd lost. It was better for her that way, though. The more she slept, the less she would have to live in this torturous reality.

Not that I gave a fuck.

I, however, was wide awake. The sun had set about an hour ago, leaving our dungeon of a home so dark I couldn't see more than a couple feet in front of me. I tossed the thin blanket from my cot and made my way to the showers. I'd do about anything to get away from the rancid smell of her. How Mags slept beside her, I had no idea.

It was sickening.

Most of the guys were already sleeping. There wasn't much to do around here otherwise. This place was hell, yeah, but I supposed having a cot to sleep in each night beat living on edge, constantly in hiding. I'd spent years looking over my shoulder, waiting for the day the Ministry would find me and bring me here. And when they had, it was almost a relief. If it weren't for my sister, I wouldn't give a fuck about what happened to me here.

Because, though I might deserve this fate, Mags did not.

So, for her sake, I'd perform the claiming. Then I'd get her the fuck out of here.

Silently, I padded, barefoot, across the cold stone floor. I needed to clear my head, and laying so close to New Girl was making that impossible. The showers were empty, as I expected, so I quickly made my way to the first stall. With the curtain closed, I stripped off my trousers and started the water.

When the temperature was scalding, I scrubbed the filth of the day from my body. The heat should have been painful, but I'd quit feeling pain a long time ago. Instead, I let it ignite my senses, bringing my dead limbs back to life.

Three weeks. The look on New Girl's face had been absolutely priceless when I said I would perform the claiming with her. She had no right to be flattered. My decision had nothing to do with her. That Director bitch had been wanting me to perform the claiming for some time now. I didn't blame her. They were losing the war and they were desperate. As the only tier three in residence, I was the only thing in this damn dungeon that could help.

Well, me and New Girl.

New Girl swore she didn't have any power, even while being tortured, but just being in her proximity made it obvious that wasn't true. It was like I could sense it, like the air changed slightly any time she was around. If she was willing to go through that much pain to keep it hidden, her power must be strong.

And I had three weeks to find out what it was.

I'd finished and had slipped my trousers back on when someone entered the bathroom.

"Can you believe that shit?" a low voice muttered.

Carter. The asshole who'd messed with New Girl when she arrived. I hated the arrogant prick.

Another man huffed. "Can't you? She doesn't look half bad, and it's been months since anyone around here has gotten laid."

Imbeciles. That's what I hated most about the fuckers I was surrounded by. They couldn't control their desires. Or their mouths. And yet, they walked around like they owned the place, when in reality, they were prisoners to it.

These men would all end up dead.

"You guys are disgusting," a third man—Leon, I was pretty sure—argued. He was the quiet type. Reserved. From what I'd witnessed during my time here, he was a decent man, but then again, he hung around these guys, so maybe I was wrong. "She's been through hell. Clearly, she's special, or Director wouldn't have bothered with that torture stuff."

He wasn't wrong.

"He's a tier three," Carter gritted out, "and he's wasting his claim on a powerless slut who will probably make things worse for all of us."

"She wouldn't be here if she was powerless," Leon replied.

Carter and his friend laughed. "Are you seriously defending her? You've gone soft for the new girl? Is that it? You're as desperate as he is, aren't you?"

I chose then to slap open the shower curtain and step out.

All three guys were now pissing at the makeshift urinal on the far side of the bathroom. The three of them snapped their heads in my direction, eyes widening when my identity registered.

Like I said. Imbeciles.

I kept my expression bored. "Something you'd like to discuss with me, gentlemen?"

They stuttered and looked at each other, as if wishing they could go back in time a good thirty seconds.

I cocked an eyebrow, silently waiting, secretly enjoying the way they squirmed.

"We didn't know you were in here, man." Carter quickly zipped up his pants.

I took a slow step in their direction. "I would seriously hope not. Though you do seem to be dumb enough to talk shit within earshot of the subject of your gossip."

"We only want the best for you, man," Carter pleaded.

"You've been down here a long time. You never know when a tier three woman is going to walk through those—"

The room darkened, and instantly, his eyes widened in horror and his words dried up. The phantoms—the dark tendrils of my magic that would destroy at my will—were only the beginning of my power. The way they surrounded us only skimmed the surface of what they could do. What *I* could do with them.

Especially when angry. And these men did not want to see me lose my temper.

All three went white and curled in on themselves. "Whoa, man," Carter said. "Relax! We were just messing around!"

"You think I'm messing around? You think I'm wasting my claim?" The ghosts of my emotions crept closer, almost grazing their faces.

Perhaps I'd allow them to kill the way the darkness urged me to. Perhaps the phantoms would remove the skin in a single breath.

Down here, with such little exposure, I could pretend it was difficult to control my power.

In reality, I could kill every person in this dungeon in one fell swoop. Most of the men imprisoned with me were tier ones, some twos. These idiots? They weren't worth my damn time.

The endless void inside me was irritated. Frustrated and full of pent-up energy. So I let my phantoms tease and taste, let them wallow in the fear of the jackasses cowering before me.

"No! Seriously. We didn't mean it, Sinner. We were

fucking around." If Carter hadn't already relieved himself, he'd be pissing his pants right there.

"You'd do well to keep your opinions about me to yourself. New Girl, too. She's none of your goddamn business anymore. Understood?"

"Understood," they barked in unison.

Cowards. All of them.

"And you." I turned my attention to Leon. "If you have an ounce of survival instinct left, you'll stop hanging around these morons. I won't think twice next time."

His nostrils flared, but he dipped his head in understanding.

Life down here had gotten so goddamn boring, though. It was nice to feel something again. My phantoms appreciated it, too. I let them take one last taste before I called them back and the black shadows recoiled into my body.

The void within me deepened as the monsters came back home. Most people would be disturbed by the endless emptiness my chest possessed. But not me. I preferred it that way, it was safest when I was devoid of all care, all hope, all love.

I turned away from the worthless gossips and returned to the dungeon that reeked of blood and desperation. Even monsters found no peace in hell, it seemed. But it was my fault for thinking that I had any chance of another type of reality.

Annoyed with myself for having to remember all the reasons I shouldn't give a fuck, I returned to my cot.

The stiff woven fabric creaked as I laid back, stretching

my legs until they hung over the edge and resting my head on my arms.

Sleep.

If only it were that easy.

Sleep was a trap, a sick, delusional cloud of comfort that would only bring me more pain. More nightmares.

No, sleep did not come easy for monsters like me. Sleep came like a punch to the face, unexpected and unwelcome.

Always unwelcome.

I would stay awake. This way I'd be ready for any errant thought that crawled back to me, torturing my mind with those voices.

And those damn memories.

I shook my head viciously. Thinking of the past wouldn't help me now. Thinking of anything at all wouldn't help me. I'd stick with focusing on the hatred and the anger. Those emotions, at least, allowed me to work on a path forward.

Mags and I were getting out of this place. I didn't give a fuck what I had to do to get there.

I glanced at the cot next to me, only to find big, warm eyes watching. They trapped me there, sucking me in and freezing each of my muscles so I couldn't look away.

And that pissed me off.

"The fuck are you looking at?"

She didn't even blink. For a second I considered that she might be sleeping with those pesky eyes wide open.

I knew better, though, when she said, "I'm trying to figure out what your plan is."

I scoffed. "Don't flatter yourself. It's not that deep."

She shifted slightly, her small body adjusting against the firm cot. *Fuck.* She was in a dungeon full of monsters and she had the nerve to move her hips like that, like she wanted everyone in the fucking place to stare at her.

They wouldn't, of course. Not while I was lying three feet from her. Not after I'd committed to mating with her.

The claiming was more than one night of sex under the blood moon. It meant that she was mine. It meant that none of these other useless imbeciles could touch her.

I was no better, don't get me wrong. I was not a man of morals or respect. I was someone to be feared. I was someone others ran away from, and for good reason.

A killer. A demon. A nightmare.

New Girl wasn't safe with me. But at least she'd be out of here in three weeks. That was more than any of the others could say.

She wasn't the innocent little new girl she pretended to be. I still couldn't place it, but I was working to dig out what she was hiding. Even being this close to her sent a primal shiver through my body. A warning, almost.

"You've been in this dungeon for months. Why are you suddenly so adamant about getting out of here?" she whispered.

"You're the first new girl we've had in a while. And Director thinks you're special. If she's right, then it's in my best interest to perform the claiming with you."

"Because you're a three?"

I clenched my jaw and pressed the back of my skull deeper against my wrist. "That's right. I'm a three. Do you know what that means, New Girl?"

"That you think you're better than everyone else?"

I had to bite back a sardonic laugh. "It means I'm more dangerous than anyone else in here. It means you should keep your distance before you get hurt."

"Says the man who wants to have sex with me."

"*Want* is a strong word, don't you think? Our survival could depend on far worse things." Fuck, even thinking about sex sent my dick twitching in my pants. I hated this woman, but she wasn't hideous.

And now that she was set to be my partner during the claiming, something had shifted. My power wanted her. It was desperate to be unleashed, to mingle with whatever it was she hid beneath that porcelain skin. Her power was hiding, too, likely longing for me in the same way.

Though the claiming was three weeks away, my power called for its equal. A force to entice it, to challenge it.

And for whatever reason, it was certain she possessed exactly what it craved.

"I won't help you. I won't become a slave to the government."

Despite my hardening dick, anger flared hot in my chest. This fucking woman. I pushed myself up and sat on the edge of my cot, facing her.

She pushed up, too, propping herself on her elbow and narrowing her eyes on me.

"Look around you," I bit out. "If you think you can get out of here on your own, you're wrong. You think Director will let any of us go, let alone a female?" I laughed under my breath. "Then you're dumber than I thought. The only way out of here is through the claiming. Get that through your thick fucking skull."

"And then what? You fight for them in the war you want nothing to do with?"

God, her flickering eyes annoyed me. She really thought I was above joining a fight in order to save myself?

"Who said I want nothing to do with it?"

She blew out a breath. "You can't be serious. It's no different out there. If you let them control you now, you're allowing them to turn you into a weapon, and they'll use you that way for the rest of your life. They'll use your power forever. They'll never let you go, especially since you're a three."

Chest heaving, I willed the anger coiling tight inside me to remain where it was. "I've spent months down here, New Girl. I've tried to escape a handful of times. It's all useless, there's too much at risk."

"You mean your sister?" She glanced over her shoulder to where my sister slept soundly. God, I hadn't seen her sleep so much since we arrived. It was New Girl's one redeeming quality. She made my sister feel at ease enough to let her guard down. "Because she can take care of herself. She doesn't want this."

I angled in until my face was inches from hers. "You don't get to talk about what she does or doesn't want. You know nothing about her."

"I don't?" She cocked her head to the side. "Because she and I are the only two women down here, yet not one of the rancid creatures has tried to touch her since I arrived. I don't see Director coming in here and trying to force her to pair up for the claiming. Suspicious, no?"

"Shut your mouth. Now."

"Why? Because you don't want her to hear what I'm about to say?"

A snarl escaped me.

New Girl *smiled*.

That's it. I stood, and before she even had time to flinch, I gripped her around the waist, threw her over my shoulder, and stormed away from the cot.

athena

"**P**ut me down!"

In the silence of the night, my words nearly echoed off the stone walls.

But Sinner only dug his fingertips into the backs of my thighs until I was certain they bruised.

He stormed to the front of the open space, just beside the barricaded door. I squirmed and kicked the whole way, but it was no use, he was freakishly large and inhumanly strong. He didn't loosen his grip until we had reached the very corner of the dark cavern, a place where even the moonlight didn't reach. Nobody slept this close to the entrance, leaving it wide open for Sinner to drag me here and—what? Kill me?

No way. Not when I was his one chance at getting out of this place.

He set me on my feet roughly, then cornered me against the wall with his arms caging me in place.

"Are you really so afraid that your sister will see the truth?" I pushed.

Head cocked, he loomed closer. "And what truth is that, exactly?"

Like this, I couldn't make out his features, but I could feel the heat radiating from him.

I hated it. I hated *him*.

"That you made a deal with Director to keep her safe."

I expected him to deny it. Instead, he glared at me, his dark eyes hard, his chest rising and falling with thick breaths as he pushed against the wall on either side of me, his muscles rippling. "If you ever say that shit again—especially around Margaret—I'll kill you."

Wow. More threats—surprise, surprise. Big boy was *mad*.

With a harsh breath out, he straightened a fraction, like he was going to turn away. I really should have let him go. But my ego wouldn't let him push me like this. Not when I was the missing piece of the plan he'd probably been working on for months now.

I lifted my chin, my lips curling up. "No, you won't."

He lowered his head so we were nose to nose. "You're right, New Girl. I won't kill you." He ran a finger down my cheek almost delicately, and my breath hitched, my traitorous body reacting in a way I hadn't given it permission to. "But I can make you so miserable you'll wish you were dead. I control everyone and everything down here. You think these men have left you alone because they're honorable?"

A shiver worked its way down my spine, betraying the defiant facade I'd created.

"Wrong. It's because they're afraid of me. Rightfully so."

His hand slid down to my neck, the touch electrifying me, and as he gripped my throat and squeezed, sparks flashed in my vision.

"You don't scare me," I gritted out with the little air remaining in my lungs. "I've dealt with far worse than men like you."

The breath from his laugh tickled my cheek, but he didn't loosen his hold. "You should be scared, New Girl, because when that blood moon comes around, when you willingly mate with me and complete the transformation, you'll see what a monster I really am. And I'll finally see what pesky powers you've been hiding under that innocent demeanor."

"I'll *never* willingly mate with you."

His grip tightened, and on instinct, I brought my own hands up and wrapped them around his thick forearm, fighting his hold.

He smiled. "We'll see about that."

Even in the darkness, the pure hatred in his deep brown eyes was clear. It emanated from him, like every single inch of his being was repulsed by my very existence.

Likewise, buddy.

He let go of me with one last push and stormed back to his cot.

My heart raced as he disappeared into the darkness. He

could threaten me, sure, but I was the one truly in control here.

He couldn't force me to mate with him. The claiming only worked if both parties were willing. Thank god for that tiny stipulation.

If he truly was doing this to save his sister, then his intentions were honorable. But Mags could take care of herself down here. She wouldn't support this plan if she knew what her brother was up to. And the aftermath would be catastrophic. Wouldn't it?

I rubbed the skin on my throat where his hand had been. Sinner had just slotted himself at the top of my list of enemies.

"Are you okay?"

I spun at the sound of the quiet voice, a hand over my once again pounding heart.

Leon—I think—stood a few feet away.

"God," I sighed. "I didn't see you standing there."

"Didn't mean to scare you. I'm just making sure you're all right. No matter how I look at it, I can't decide whether you're the luckiest person here, or the unluckiest."

One of those was certainly true. "And what makes you say that?"

With a shrug, he stepped closer. I'd been watching him the last few days, just like I'd been watching the rest of the men locked up in here with me. Leon was quiet. Observant. He didn't engage in the random fights with the other guys, but he could always be found nearby.

Never interfering.

I wasn't sure whether I could trust him, but in this

place it was safer to trust nobody at all than to take that risk.

Leon shrugged. He was good-looking in a reserved way. He kept his hair short, and though his shirt was baggy, it couldn't hide the lean muscle he was packing. "You're the newest person here, yet you'll be the next one to leave."

"Would it be better to stay down here with the rest of you?" *Seriously, would it?*

Leon's soft green eyes met mine. "That depends on what you're willing to do to survive."

I rolled his words around in my mind for a few seconds before I responded. "I think we'd all be willing to do all sorts of things to survive. The question is—which fate is worse?"

Lips tugged down in a thoughtful frown, he studied me. "You're smart. It's no wonder Director likes you so much."

"Gee, thanks." With a roll of my eyes, I turned toward my cot.

Before I made it more than a foot or two, Leon stepped in front of me. "Be careful, okay? Sinner may seem like he's on your side, but he's dangerous. Like you said, we're all willing to do all sorts of things for survival."

I nodded and brushed past him, doing my best to ignore the growing rock in my stomach. And when I dared a glance at Sinner, his dark gaze was locked on *Leon*.

⸻

"IT'S BEEN DAYS," Margaret whined. "I promise I won't let Sinner in. Just one shower, you'll feel so much better!" She tugged on my arm, as if she could physically force me into the bathrooms. I may not have been all that tall or muscular, but she was tiny.

We'd successfully avoided everyone all day. Margaret had kept me entertained by making up stories or talking to herself until I fell asleep. I was really, really glad to have her down here, however cruel and messed up that made me.

She made it a little less miserable.

"I don't really feel like being threatened while I'm naked again," I groaned. "It would just ruin my mood."

"That won't happen," she swore. "Sinner was just grumpy that day."

I rolled my eyes. "Right. Because his mood today is so much better." In unison, we turned and looked at her brother, who sat with his back to us. He and a few of the other guys were huddled together, talking about god knows what. The thought of him lounging around and talking about life or the weather made me cringe. It was so normal, and guys like Sinner were anything but normal.

"Look," she started, "I don't want to say that sleeping next to you is a form of torture... Someone else might say that. Not me, though." She held her hands up, her eyes wide. "I'm your friend, so I wouldn't say that."

This girl. "Fine." I bit back a grin and pointed at her. "But you're waiting outside the door for real this time. And don't let anyone inside."

Face alight, she yanked on my arm.

This time, I let her drag me over to the empty bathroom. Most of the guys were busy talking or working out, paying us no mind.

That was a relief. If they didn't know I was in here, they wouldn't harass me. That was the hope, at least. One glance over my shoulder told me Sinner was still sitting with his back to us, completely oblivious.

Perfect.

Though I probably should be disgusted by the way I smelled after going several more days without showering, I didn't mind it. The aroma made it easier to keep these men—Sinner included—far, far away from me.

"Go ahead." Margaret stepped aside and waved toward the showers. "I'll wait here."

First things first, I peered behind every curtain, making sure the bathrooms were completely empty. Once I confirmed we were alone, I enclosed myself in one of the stalls and quickly stripped. The less time I spent in here, the better.

I set my clothes outside the curtain where they would stay dry and turned on the water. And god, it was incredible. I'd forgotten how amazing hot water could feel when I fully succumbed to it. My stiff, tired limbs finally relaxed as I let go of all the tension and stress. That seemed to be my permanent state now—stressed.

It was better than dead.

Maybe. Honestly, death was starting to sound pretty damn peaceful.

I turned around and closed my eyes, letting the water hit my face.

My life had become unrecognizable since, one by one, everyone I loved had died. They would have protected me from this. They would have helped me figure out what to do. They'd have told these psychopaths that I didn't have any powers.

My chest ached as I thought about them. I missed them all. Ridiculously, I even missed the way Mother would nag me about wearing my dirty boots in the house. I missed the way Father would pretend to scold me over it, only to wink at me behind her back. I missed the way Kylar would try to talk me down from my temper tantrums, the way Katherine would braid Jasmine's hair before bed.

God, I missed all of it. Back then, I so often hated my life, the isolation, the way our parents sheltered us. Now, I realized how much they'd protected us. Had my parents known all along that this life was awaiting me? Had they known what would happen if the Ministry ever came for us? Is that why we'd lived in such isolation for all those years?

Tears stung my eyes, and for the first time since the day I buried Jasmine, I let them fall freely, allowing the hot water to whisk them away.

Even if I agreed to the claiming, then what? I wasn't a mystic, so the ritual would do no good, right? Then where would I be? Dead, I was sure.

My chest tightened again, and I took a few long breaths to relieve the pain.

I was doing the right thing, wasn't I? Resisting Sinner and defying the Ministry's order was the honorable way to go about this. Though a small, itching sensation in my heart flared to life every time I thought of Margaret, every time I thought of massive, evil Sinner moving atop me, inside me—the repulsive new girl—just to save her.

I couldn't forget that he'd also save himself by participating. The whole *protect my sister* thing could have been an act.

With a shake of my head, I cleared my mind of all those thoughts. Then I quickly washed my hair and body. I shut the water off, and when I reached for my towel and clothes, I nearly died.

Because they were gone.

"Margaret?" I shouted, my heart hammering against my breastbone. "Margaret, my clothes are gone!"

Silence.

I peeked through the gap at the edge of the curtain, looking for the culprit, but the bathroom was empty. Eerily empty.

"Margaret!" I called out. The usual stash of extra clothes and towels had been cleared out.

Someone had come in here while I was showering and taken everything.

Yeah, I was never showering again. I couldn't trust a single bastard in this dungeon.

Where the hell was Margaret?

Seriously. Stealing clothing like this? Were we *twelve*? I'd understand a dungeon full of depraved men trying to see me naked if—

It hit me then.

Those men wouldn't do shit.

Not with Sinner here, terrifying them all with his presence alone.

Not even if I walked into that dungeon completely naked.

Dripping wet, pissed off, and totally over my friendship with Mags, I stormed out from behind the curtain.

Out of the bathroom.

And into the dungeon.

I'd never been ashamed of my body. I was hardly curvy, but my body was strong. It had hauled me through more shit than any one person should have to endure.

I was proud of my strength.

So I held my head high as I stood in the middle of the open space, scanning the dark underground for the so-called *friend* who'd clearly abandoned me.

"What the hell are you doing?" Margaret darted over, her eyes wide as she scanned my body like she was concerned for my mental well-being. "I'm not sure if you know this, but you're, like, totally naked right now."

Fair.

"Where have you been?" I planted my hands on my hips and glared at her. "Someone came in there and took my clothes, Margaret! All the clothes, and the towels."

She glanced over my shoulder into the bathroom, holding her hands out in front of her as if that was really going to calm me down. "I've been standing here the whole time. Nobody came in or out. I swear."

A couple of men to my right snickered.

Fury sparking to life, I spun and took a step closer, ready to kill the next person who laughed. "What?" I yelled. Yeah, I was definitely losing my mind. "Does this amuse you? You all think this is funny?" Water dripped down my body, and if not for the anger burning through me, I probably would have shivered.

The guys continued to gather around, drawn to me like they hadn't seen a naked woman in years. Hell, maybe they hadn't.

Sinner barreled through the crowd, knocking men over left and right. "What the fuck are you doing?" he barked as he stopped in front of me. His dark eyes raked my body once, and I could have sworn he got even angrier as he looked at me.

Wow. Did I really disgust him that much?

"Someone took my clothes from the shower." I threw my arms out to my sides. "That desperate to see a naked woman, it seems." I propped my hand on my hip and lifted my chin. "Ground-breaking, I know."

A few more men laughed. One near the back even whistled, causing a round of cheers to break out.

Potent anger radiated from Sinner, each wave slamming into me more forcefully than the last. "Cover yourself. Now."

There it was. The possessive, arrogant asshole who thought he could control every person here, every situation.

"Why?" I stepped closer. "Not liking what you see? If that's the case, I have bad news for you. I don't think you'll be happy when the claiming ceremony comes around."

More laughter.

But not from Sinner.

A few painfully slow seconds passed. With each one, I became more and more aware of the fact that I was a naked woman standing in front of a group of depraved men.

With a curse, Sinner stepped forward and peeled his own shirt off his body.

"What are you—"

He cut me off by shoving it down over my head.

As the hem hit my thighs, I froze. I couldn't move if I wanted to. Not when his hands were on me. He let go, but he didn't back up, not at first. He stood inches away from me—shirtless—breathing so heavily his chest nearly touched mine. "You're coming very close to pissing me off. And you don't want to see me angry."

Right. Because so far, he's been nothing but cheerful since I arrived. "Why do you care if I stand here naked or not? It's none of your concern."

"It's *exclusively* my concern."

I scoffed, arms crossed under my breasts. "Because someone's finally disobeying your orders?"

Face reddening, he tipped his chin down until his sharp features were cast in shadow. If I wasn't so pissed, I may have been afraid. By the silence of the others, it was obvious they were.

Always so frightened of big, bad Sinner.

Even Margaret, my ridiculously chatty friend—*former* friend—was silent.

It was impossible to focus on any of them for more than a heartbeat. Not with the way his masculine scent flooded my senses, making my pulse race.

"You're mine, New Girl," he said, heat rolling off him

and soaking into me. "I agreed to claim with you, and as much as I wish I could change that, we're stuck in this situation."

"And what situation is that?"

He huffed, finally lifting his chin as if he'd only now realized how close we were. He turned over his shoulder, facing the crowd of eavesdropping men, and yelled, "Get the fuck away from us."

The crowd immediately dispersed, with only a few 'boos' from someone in the back.

"You're claiming with me," he said when he turned back. "That means our magic will be connected forever. It's you and me, New Girl. You don't get to walk around here and show all these other men what's rightfully mine."

I reared back. Was he joking? He was joking, right? "And you think my body is yours?"

He hooked a finger under the hem of my—his—shirt, something in his expression changing, shifting. "That's exactly what I think." Focus fixed on my face, he trailed that one finger higher until I gave in and clutched his hand to pull it away from my bare skin.

With a quiet laugh, he shook his head. "See, New Girl? You can put on a show all you want, but I see right through it. I see right through every mask you slip on. I know you're hiding something. I know you don't actually want fifty monstrous eyes looking at your naked body. You want control as badly as I do, but the difference?" Hand still clenched beneath mine, he leaned in until I could feel his breath on my face. "I'm still in charge here."

He ripped his hand from mine and turned away.

"Keep the shirt," he yelled over his shoulder.

I stayed frozen like that, like an idiot, watching him stalk to the far side of the dungeon. He'd been clear about his hatred for me since the moment I stepped into this hellhole, yet he had this freaky, possessive need to control me. *Me.*

I found myself tugging the hem of his shirt lower, making sure all the important parts were covered. As much as I wanted to whip it off and throw it at him, I knew better. And I knew Sinner wasn't going to sit back and watch me strip in a dungeon full of men.

But what did that mean? That he actually cared about me? Did he really think my body was his now that we were paired for the claiming? Now that *he* thought we'd be participating in the ridiculous ritual, that is.

My stance hadn't changed. I still had no intention of performing the claiming ritual with him. I had no intention of being controlled by anyone. Director, Sinner, *anyone.*

"Are you okay?" Margaret asked, drawing my attention away from the moronic shirtless man.

"I'm fine," I sighed.

"Really?" She tilted her head, her dark hair slipping over one shoulder. "Because a few seconds ago you were totally naked, having a standoff with the entire dungeon."

"Yeah, well, maybe I'm crazy. Who knows."

With a smile, she slung an arm around my shoulders. "Good. Crazy is good."

sinner

nger pulsed through my veins, igniting emotions that I tried very, very hard to keep locked in that little cage. *Don't let it go. Don't let it go. Don't let it go.*

Fuck.

She did this to me. She caused me to lose control, to nearly let my power loose.

And I hated to lose control.

So did she, apparently. That was clear tonight. She was testing me. Gauging how I'd react.

I ran my hands down my face, willing myself to cool off. She was talking to Mags now, which made calming down even more difficult. How could someone so insufferable become such easy friends with my sister? What did Mags see in her anyway? Or had they clicked so quickly because they were the only women here? Whatever it was, they'd been drawn to each other like two idiotic best friends.

Out of the corner of my eye, I saw one of the guys nearby lifting his mattress and shoving a dark bundle beneath it.

Feeling more out of control than I had in years, I stormed over to him. "What the fuck is that?"

He stood and spun, arms crossed, as if guarding his cot, suspicious as fuck. I knew his gift. He could cloak his own appearance for a few seconds at a time, which was likely how he got New Girl's clothes in the first place.

Anger simmered under my skin.

"It—it's not what it looks like. It was a joke. I didn't mean anything by it, I swear, it was just—"

"If you go near her again, I'll kill you." I angled in closer and wrapped one hand around his neck. "If you so much as look at her, I'll kill you. She's mine, and you are nothing. You shouldn't even be allowed to breathe the same air she does. Do you understand me?"

He thrashed and panicked beneath my tight grasp. As if that would save him. As if that would make me change my mind.

He should know better. They all should. I had no empathy. I was a monster. All humanity had long ago been scraped from me. Now I was an empty, cavernous void with nothing but death on my mind.

Pity? I had no pity.

I released him, and as he crumpled to the ground, I stepped over his useless body, barely burying the urge to give him a strong kick to the head to end his miserable life.

On second thought, maybe I was becoming a better man.

But I doubted it. I really, really doubted it.

I moved to a spot across the room, making sure I was as far away from her as possible. Even being close to her made me lose my damn mind. I couldn't think straight when she was near. I couldn't focus.

She did that to me. A venomous little snake infiltrating this dungeon.

My skin prickled with annoyance at the thought. I could barely stand the sight of her, and that was before she strutted out here naked. Every man here had now seen what was mine, what was owed to me by the claiming.

I hated her. I did.

Anger burned hot even as my dick kicked in my pants at the memory. It was the magic in my veins that clouded my senses, that caused these wicked thoughts of possessing her to flood me.

Wicked, wicked thoughts.

Thoughts about my hands gripping her small, perfect waist. Images of her writhing beneath me, impaled on my cock, moaning my name and begging me for more. Thoughts of her smooth, round breasts in my mouth.

I hated her for making me think these things. I hated my power for making me think these things.

Even across the dungeon, her toned legs glowed like a beacon in the moonlight, torturing me. She had pulled my shirt down to cover her ass, but the amount of skin still exposed was enough to make my heart take off at a sprint. And that wouldn't do.

With her clothes in my hand, I marched over to the cot where she and Mags sat, whispering to one another. I didn't even look at them as I tossed her clothes onto her lap and retreated to my own cot.

Their conversation stopped, and though I refused to look their way, I felt her eyes on me, burning holes into my back as I kicked off my boots.

"Do you want your shirt back?" she asked.

"Keep it," I forced out through gritted teeth. "You've probably ruined it with your scent, anyway."

"Hey!" Mags interrupted. "She just showered, and you're welcome for that, by the way."

I looked at my sister. At her guileless blue eyes and her good-natured scowl. She was still so...*her*. Like this world hadn't forced her to turn to stone. Like she was still unscathed. She was still whole. I was thankful she could still smile. Laugh. Play. But it was difficult not to envy her. To fight the bitterness, the constant ache I felt for the life I had to leave behind for the sake of survival.

I could no longer remember what it was like to be happy. To feel whole.

It was as if a time like that never truly existed.

"You think I should be grateful for the way she ended up traipsing around naked in front of the whole dungeon? Okay, then thanks, Mags." I looked away before her face crumpled in disappointment the way I knew it would. She looked exactly like Mother when she did that, and I was too close to unraveling to allow any kind of emotion to seep in.

"You don't have to be rude to her," New Girl argued. "We were having a perfectly fine time before you tramped over here."

"And delivered your pants? Put them on. I'm tired of looking at your legs." I was being harsh, I knew that, but I no longer remembered how to be anything other than brutal. Brutal was how I survived. Brutal was how *we* survived. If they hated me, good.

They should hate me.

After a few long seconds, fabric rustled behind me. *Thank fuck.* I fought the urge to turn, to watch her slide the trousers up those toned, pale legs. And then I hated myself even more for picturing the way her thighs would look spread open for me.

I laid back on the cot and turned on my side, putting my back to the two.

"He wasn't always like this," Mags whispered loud enough to ensure I could hear. "He used to be fun."

New Girl snorted. "I can't picture that."

"It's true! I remember when he used to put me on his shoulders and jump into the lake by our house. He taught me to swim by pretending to be a monster in the water. We had so much fun together before—"

"Shut up, Mags," I warned, my gut twisting. "Don't say another fucking word."

And by the grace of fucking god, she listened.

I loved Mags. I wanted to love her, anyway. I felt a deep urge to protect her. I *once* loved her. I was certain of that.

Now? I feared I lacked the ability. I felt nothing, not even happiness at the memory she mentioned. Because those memories only reminded me of how fucked up our world had gotten. How fucked up *I* had gotten.

It was my fault Mags was here with me.

And I would stop at nothing to get her out.

Eyes closed, I willed myself to sleep. It was nearly impossible. I was too attuned to the breathing beside me. The women settled into the cot, too, but though my back was turned, I could feel the way New Girl was assessing me, as if searching out my weaknesses. She wanted to break me. She wanted to control me.

But what did she know? I was a monster. An empty being with only one goal.

"CAN I talk to you for a second?" Mags stood over me with her hands on her hips. "In private?"

I closed my book with a groan and kicked my legs over the edge of the cot. "Good luck finding privacy in here, Mags."

She sat next to me and surveyed the area around us, looking for prying ears. "Are you really going through with this? The claiming, I mean?"

I swallowed. I'd been waiting for her to question me. "I'm not sure I have much of a choice anymore. If it's what will get us out of here, then yes."

Her shoulders sank a fraction. "You always have a choice."

"You, of all people, should know that's not true."

The way she flinched in response to my words made my chest sting. "I don't want you going through with this for me, okay? I know Director has spoken to you before, and I know you're trying to protect me."

Director did a hell of a lot more than speak to me about Mags. When the Ministry found us, they all but tortured her to get me to do what they wanted. And the worst part? It worked.

Mags was my weakness. And I'd never allow another person to have that kind of power over me. Because when it came to her, I would do anything the Ministry asked.

Even completing the claiming with New Girl.

"You don't need to worry about me. After the ceremony, I'll get us out of here. All three of us. We might not have another chance like this again."

Mags looked down at the hands she kept folded in her lap. "It's just that after what happened, you swore you'd never claim with anyone—"

"Don't." The word was harsh. Harsher than I meant. But the last thing I wanted to think about was that memory.

Memories wouldn't help us get out of here.

"I'm sorry," I said. "I appreciate your concern, Mags, I really do. But I'm okay. And as long as she is also willing, I'm going through with this."

Mags finally looked up from her lap, blinking away a tear. "Well, good luck with that, brother. She really doesn't like you."

I growled, my chest rumbling.

"What?" She huffed. "It's true! If you were a little nicer to her, maybe she wouldn't be so repulsed!"

I blinked. "Repulsed?"

"Her words, not mine." Margaret surveyed the

dungeon with a sigh. "We've been down here a long time. It would be nice to join the real world again."

"Yeah." I followed her gaze. This disgusting dungeon had slowly become a comfort to us—as depressing as that was. But we'd been down here in the darkness for so long, I'd almost forgotten what the outdoors actually looked like. Smelled like. "It'll all be over soon, Mags. I promise."

I zeroed in on New Girl, who was talking to Leon on the other side of the dungeon. I didn't like him. I didn't like anyone in this damn place. But she'd begun to relax around him over the last day or two. When she was speaking to him, her body lost a little of that constant rigidness.

With a grunt, I nodded in their direction. "What is she doing hanging out with that guy all the time?"

Mags straightened her shoulders beside me. "Oh, Leon? I don't know, he's nice to her. Something you should try sometime." With a waggle of her brows, she stood, then trotted over to join New Girl and Leon. The sound of the three of them laughing sent irritation coursing through me.

I didn't want her laughing with another guy. Looking at another guy. Speaking to another guy.

For now, I'd have to keep my focus fixed on what mattered. This would all be over very, very soon.

I just needed New Girl to agree to the claiming.

THE LOCKS of the dungeon clanged. It was too early to

be food. There were too many footsteps to be a supply check.

I was up before the door was even fully open.

One deep breath reassured me that my power was still in check, that I could control it for one more day. *One more fucking day.*

Don't lose it now. Not when you're so close.

It was a challenge to remain in control when Director walked through the damn door again.

The last time I saw her, she'd had one of her men drive a knife into New Girl's leg. So no, she was not on the very, very small list of people I could stand.

In fact, I spent a lot of my free time imagining how it would feel to strangle the last breath from her weak, brittle neck. It was one of the few things that gave me enjoyment.

"Good morning, mystics!" She entered the room, her shrill voice echoing off the damn walls.

My fists tightened, aching for the moment I would wrap my fingers around her throat.

As the girls stirred beside me, I stepped to one side, putting myself in front of them. I didn't give a fuck about New Girl, but Mags was in the same damn bed.

"What's going on?" a man a few cots down asked.

Director stopped in the middle of the dungeon, chin lifted and hands on her hips, surveying the group like she was about to give a damn speech, like she wasn't at all disturbed by the half-alive prisoners she kept locked away down here. "You've all been patiently waiting, and I applaud you for that. So much, in fact, that you are all being invited to a grand ball this evening! A celebration!"

"A celebration?" Carter asked. "For what?"

Director spread her arms out and scanned the space. "Our gifted team is making great strides. We've officially taken the eastern continent of Ashora."

The room was silent, the only sounds were the breathing of the guys around me and water dripping from the ceiling in the corner.

My chest tightened, my stomach twisted violently.

"Many of the mystics have returned from battle, and they've shown interest in meeting you. They'd like to show you what you have to look forward to. You'll all be sent appropriate clothing for the event. Try to look your best. Especially you two, ladies. I have something special in store for you."

They stayed silent behind me, thank fucking god, but every inch of my body tensed as Director peered around my frame.

"I'll see you all tonight!" She clapped twice, the sound nearly as fucking piercing as her voice, and then she was gone.

Great. As if it weren't bad enough that we were trapped in this lifeless dungeon to mate like cattle, she now wanted to parade us around her troops as if we were a grand prize to be won.

She wanted to play? *Game. On.*

athena

After the disturbing announcement from Director about attending a ball, the men killed time fighting each other.

Again.

"This is the stupidest thing I've ever witnessed." Margaret and I flinched in unison when Carter punched a man a couple of inches shorter than him directly in the nose.

Yep, I definitely heard a crunch.

This, naturally, resulted in a round of whoops from the men watching from the surrounding circle.

"I don't know," Margaret replied. "I once saw one of the guys strangle another over the last piece of bread after they forgot to feed us for a day. I mean, come on." She sighed. "It was only one day. One day is for rookies."

I gave her a sideways look, and in return, she arched a brow. *Okay*. She was definitely not joking about that last part.

"What's the point of all this anyway?" I asked.

Carter walked over to us, shaking his hands out, chest puffed up, clearly satisfied with himself. "Entertainment, mostly." Sweat dripped from his skin as he stopped a foot away. "But we like to stay in shape for when we finally get out of here."

"That optimistic?" I smiled sideways. Carter was easily my least favorite mystic in this place, always walking around here with an arrogant stride and annoying smirk.

"It wouldn't hurt you to learn some combat skills, sweetheart. Especially if you're getting out of here after the ritual. You ever fought before?"

I shrugged. "Here and there." *No. Not at all. Not physically, at least.*

"Great. Let's see what you've got, then."

"She is *not* going to fight you." Margaret glowered up at him. "We all know you can't behave yourself."

Carter laughed, his eyes narrowed on me.

Shit. With a grimace, I stepped into the semicircle and pulled one arm over in front of me, stretching, then the other. *This looks natural, right?*

"Leon, get in there," Carter ordered. "But go easy on her, all right?"

Leon smiled softly and stepped forward. He was lean and muscled and clearly strong, but he didn't creep me out the way Carter did. I could take him if he went easy on me.

Before he could make his way into the circle, Sinner stopped him with a hand on his arm. "No."

Leon froze. *Everyone* froze.

"You wanna fight?" Sinner let go of my would-be opponent and took his place in the circle a couple paces from me. "Let's fight."

My stomach sank. "You want me to fight you?" *God, please say no.*

He shrugged. "Sure. Why not?"

"Um." I glanced at Margaret, silently trying to communicate to her that her brother had lost his mind.

She only stared back with wide, amused eyes.

No help. I made a mental note to yell at her later.

"Great. Okay." I bounced on the balls of my feet. "Let's fight, then."

I swore as he took a step closer, the guys gathered around us took a step back. Yep. This was going to hurt.

He kept his arms relaxed at his sides as he moved in. It didn't matter. He was a massive wall of destruction. Everything about him was a threat, a warning.

My pulse sped up instinctively, and I stumbled backward. Behind me, hands landed on my back and shoved me forward.

"Well?" Sinner taunted. Was he *smiling?* "You want to fight so badly, let's see it."

"Fine. If you insist." I widened my stance and pulled my fists up to my face.

He didn't lift his arms to defend himself or step back. He didn't even act like he was concerned about me hitting him.

Rude.

Ignoring all the eyes trained on me, I rushed forward, aiming a fist at Sinner's face.

He stepped to one side, dodging me easily. But my momentum slung me forward, making me stagger.

And the guys around us actually *laughed.*

"Not bad," he teased. "You were saying you're a fighter?"

"I did *not* say that, I said I've fought *here and there.*"

Yeah, he was definitely smiling. "Well, try again."

So I did. And the room erupted in laughter again. I ignored the taunts, swinging at Sinner again and again.

He dodged each of my attacks—if they could be called attacks—without even trying. He let me go on for a few minutes before he ended my suffering.

As I tried to land another blow, he caught my wrist and pulled, spinning me around until he had my back pressed against his chest. He wrapped his massive arms around my torso and pinned me there.

I fought against him, but he only tightened his hold, making my struggle even more futile.

His heart pounded against my back, the heat of his body engulfing me, and his lips brushed the shell of my ear as he whispered, "You let any of these other guys touch you, and you're dead. Don't let me see you in this fight circle again."

With that, he shoved me lightly toward Margaret, who was watching me with the most amused smirk on her face.

My face was hot with embarrassment and confusion and maybe a little lust, but with any luck, the guys would think it had to do with my horrible athletic abilities.

This place was getting weirder every damn day.

"Athena, wow! You really are a great fighter. You showed him. Totally badass." Margaret could hardly contain her laughter.

I punched her lightly in the arm as I passed her. "Your brother has some serious issues. I hope it doesn't run in the family."

We spent the rest of the day ignoring the fights and pretending like we weren't killing time until the strange event took place tonight. Every time I thought about the ball, my stomach dropped. Something wasn't right, but I wasn't exactly in any position to fight back.

So the two of us laughed and we told stories and we pretended we weren't in a terrible, dark dungeon as the hours dwindled by.

But reality came around soon enough, and all the shit that was dragged along with it.

I HAD NEVER WORN a dress like this before.

My dress and Margaret's were similar in style. They were both made of a thin, silk material that hugged our curves and fell to the floor. I'd be lucky if I made it through the night without tripping over the hem. The slit that came to just above my knee helped make walking easier, at least.

The straps were thin and wrapped around my upper arms. The fabric of my gown was a shimmering blue, reminding me of the blue veins beneath my skin. But Margaret's was a beautiful pale pink.

I smiled as I looked at her. She was gorgeous in a way that reflected her soul, that radiated in her deep blue eyes. She was a pure, good human.

Sinking my teeth into my lip, I turned away, busying myself with pulling the rest of my hair into a braid over my shoulder. A person like her shouldn't spend her time with the likes of me. Even my simple presence in her life could be damaging. Especially if she knew the real me.

"What? What is it?" she asked, her tone uncertain. "Do I look that hideous?"

"No, no. It's stunning." I spun and forced a smile. "You are an absolute gem, Margaret."

Cheeks going pink, she shook her head as if she didn't believe me. If I had a heart, it would've broken right then. Because it was always the purest souls that could not see the beauty they harnessed just by existing.

"You're not half bad yourself," she replied. "I can hardly believe you're the same girl who refused to shower! Twice!"

With a roll of my eyes, I tied off the end of my braid, then turned and followed Margaret out of the bathroom.

The men had already been taken out of the dungeon, all of them dressed like Director's little playthings.

As we stood in the empty room, dread coiled in my stomach. There was no way Director would pull all of her mystics from the dungeons and expect the night to go peacefully.

I didn't have the first clue what powers these men possessed, but I was smart enough to know there was a reason we were hidden underground, enclosed in an inescapable cage.

Letting monsters out of their cages was never a good idea. Even if they were dressed up and told to play nice.

I had only been in hell for a handful of days, and I was ready to climb the walls. The rest of the population had been here much longer. Surely, they had to be itching to break free.

"All right, let's get this over with," I said, more to myself than to Margaret. Let's somehow manage to survive the night, even though every single bone in my body told me death was very close.

As we approached the group of guards waiting for us by the door, Margaret buzzed with an alarming level of excitement. I couldn't really blame her, I guessed. If I had been down here for months like her, I might have been excited, too.

I'd never been to a ball or anything like it. I'd never even worn a dress like this. I never had any reason to. Until the day I was brought here, my life had been quiet and simple. We'd spent most of our time taking care of the land, feeding the animals, and cooking. I couldn't begin to fathom living in a world where people dressed up like this to—to what? Mingle? Pretend to like one another?

Sounded absolutely terrible.

"Get moving, ladies." The guard who hurried us along sounded equally as robotic as he looked. As robotic as they all looked, dressed head to toe in black tactical gear. "You're expected at the ball in five minutes."

With a huff, I followed their lead, my arm linked with

Margaret's. As we traversed the tunnels and hallways that led above ground, I did my best to remember every twist and turn. Though I quickly discovered the guards were purposely backtracking, walking us in circles, doing their best to confuse us. On top of that, I was half certain my brain had shrunk while I'd been rotting away in the damn dungeon.

"What's this ball for, anyway?" I asked.

For a long moment, not one of the five guards responded. I was ready to accept that I wouldn't get an answer when one finally spoke up. "Think of it as a celebration for the mystics."

Real freaking rich. "And why would the gifted be celebrated? All we've—they've—done is sit in the damn dungeon for months."

Without looking at us, the guard scoffed. "You know nothing of what's happening in the world, mystic. But you're about to learn."

When we approached the stairs that led above ground, my heart nearly stopped. The scent of the outside air ignited my senses like a distant memory. It tasted like freedom. Like hope.

"Do you smell that?" Margaret asked, sniffing the air. "It smells like...like..."

"Like fresh air."

Her face lit up, eyes sparkling as she looked up to where the leading guard pushed the door open. "Let's go."

She scurried up the steps first, and when she hit the top, laughter bubbled out of her. When I stepped onto the dirt beside her, I found myself choking down my own excitement.

We were outside.

Outside.

"Don't even think about trying to escape," one of the guards barked as the five of them surrounded us. "Director isn't stupid. She's taken precautions to ensure the mystics don't try anything."

Curiosity piqued, I scanned our surroundings, noting the dense trees and the dark sky above. "What type of precautions?"

"The type you don't want to have to discover."

Vague. Cryptic. If I had power, I would blast this whole place to the ground, being sure to take everyone with it. Aside from Margaret, of course.

The music caught my attention first. It flowed through the thick forest, ricocheting off the trees and vibrating through the crisp leaves. The tune was surprisingly uplifting.

And as we were led through the dense foliage to a white tent in a clearing, my stomach nearly dropped. All around, twinkling lights had been strung through branches and crisscrossed above to look like stars.

This was a real ball. A real party. With people wearing formal suits and gowns, not military uniforms. They were eating and drinking and chatting as if life was completely normal. Surrounding the white tent, of course, was a perimeter of armed guards. Surely, they'd recruited mystics to work with them. Otherwise, they would be no match for the gifted that had gathered here.

Margaret waved at a group of men from the dungeon and went as far as to try to tug me in the direction of the dance floor, where a few women were dancing and laughing.

"You go," I insisted. "I'll be over there getting a drink."

"Oh, come on!" she argued, still clutching my elbow. "Give yourself permission to have a little fun. You might not get another chance."

"Same goes for you. Don't let me stop you from letting loose." I shooed her off. "Go!"

With a roll of her eyes, she backed away, but there was no fighting the smile that overtook her as she turned. She weaved her way through the bustling crowd, dragging a helpless man—one of the quieter mystics from the dungeon—with her as she spun to flow with the rest of the dancers.

I lingered toward the edge of the party, trying my best to identify the mystics and the...well, whoever had shown up. Regardless of their magical status, I couldn't trust any of them. They were all here for her, for Director. Any of these people could be soldiers, the force that killed on her behalf. There was no way to tell whether they'd only just washed the blood from their hands before donning the elaborate garb and showing up here to indulge.

Sickening.

To my right, I found a quiet spot where only a few guards lingered, not paying much attention to the party. I took a few steps in that direction and crossed my arms over my chest, doing my best to look somewhat normal.

"You're scowling." Leon approached, holding two glasses of sparkling wine.

I accepted the flute he held out like a peace offering, but rolled my eyes to fortify my stance on the matter. "This is just my face."

He shoved his free hand into the pocket of his trousers as we watched the crowd. Regardless of what he had to say, I was ready to argue. In a mood like this, it was my default setting. But he just...stood there. Silent. Watching.

I'd allowed my muscles to relax a fraction and had taken a few sips of the wine when he finally spoke.

"They're all acting like we actually have something to celebrate here." He huffed. "They're also very aware of the conditions we're being kept in, but nobody seems to give a shit about any of it."

Anger flared to life in my chest once more. "Why would they care? They claim to be winning the war. According to them, they're doing the right thing. Their absurd mystic matchmaking plan seems to be working just fine."

"You don't actually believe that, do you? They'll say anything to keep the mystics fighting. They'll even make up this story about how we actually stand a chance."

He made eye contact with me, but his attention was caught by something over my shoulder. Instantly, his expression fell, his eyes shifting quickly from flirtatious to stone cold. Then, without so much as a goodbye, he turned and left, bumping shoulders with another man as he scurried back into the crowd.

What the hell?

I felt him first. A cold, solid presence behind me,

making my heart beat faster, as if telling me to be alert, then lighting up the rest of my senses. The hair on my arms stood, and my stomach flipped over itself.

Sinner.

"What did I tell you about talking to other men?"

I stiffened. "And what did I tell you about giving a shit?"

I didn't give him the satisfaction of turning to look at him. I kept my gaze straight ahead and gulped the rest of my drink.

He stepped up beside me, his shoulder brushing mine as he settled much too close. In heels, I was still a head shorter than he was. It was hard to scowl at him when I had to look up to see his face.

"Shouldn't you be out there celebrating with the rest of the mystics?"

In my periphery, he shoved both hands into his pants pockets. He wore a black suit, similar to the rest of the men, though if I didn't know any better, I would have sworn it was tailored to his exact measurements. It fit his lean body perfectly, drawing my eyes to his large biceps and toned chest before—

Shit. I was staring.

"And leave you here sulking by yourself, pretending you're not actually one of us?"

A spark of annoyance ignited and burned hot. "I don't have to pretend."

"Bullshit." He angled in until his lips were at my ear. "I see through your facade, New Girl. I know you're hiding something. Whatever gift you have will come out soon enough." He lingered there for a moment, sending chills down my arms, before straightening and returning his focus to the crowd. "This game you're playing is growing old."

"And what game is that?" I finally turned to face him head-on. "Exactly what would be the purpose of hiding a power? You better believe that if I had power, I'd be using it to get out of here, unlike the rest of you."

Jaw clenched, he gritted his teeth. "If it were that easy, don't you think we would have done it by now?"

"Unless you're not as powerful as Director thinks you are. Which would make plenty of sense, actually."

His low laugh floated on the air around us, low enough that it felt more like a vibration than an emotion coming from Sinner. A single dark shadow spun out of his chest and twirled up the side of my neck.

I sucked in a breath as the darkness grazed my skin, sending chills down my entire body.

He smirked at my reaction but said nothing as the shadow twisted around a loose strand of my hair and tugged lightly.

The space around us disappeared. For a second—for a long, torturous second—it was just the two of us and Sinner's shadow. His dark eyes lured me in, trapping me within their depths.

And when he lowered his focus to my lips—

"Am I interrupting something?"

At the sound of Director's voice, I yanked away from Sinner and spun, expecting to be punished for his minuscule show of power.

Instead, all the air was knocked from my lungs.

Because standing next to Director was a tall woman in a pristine ball gown. She had long black hair and a familiar tight smile on her face.

If I had the capacity to breathe, I'm pretty sure I would have screamed. Instead, I wobbled, but before I could fall, Sinner clutched my arm roughly and steadied me.

"Hello, sister."

sinner

Oh, this was golden. New Girl's sister was here, indulging in food and wine with the rest of Director's prized mystics.

Was this what she'd been hiding?

I wanted to think so, but based on the shock in her expression, I wasn't so sure.

When she swayed on her feet, I begrudgingly kept her from falling. No use making a scene. She stood with her mouth agape and her brown eyes wider than I had ever seen. In another life, I might've felt bad for her. Might've even wanted to help her.

But not in this one.

"You two are sisters?"

The woman—New Girl's sister—couldn't have been more different. Her hair was done up elegantly, not a strand out of place. Nothing like the constant mess of her sister's mane. She had a softer face. A softer smile. Softer everything. People like her instantly put me on guard. It was clear she hadn't suffered in this life.

And those who hadn't been truly damaged didn't understand what it was like to get shit done for survival and survival alone.

Not that I trusted New Girl, either. She was a whole different type of disaster.

"They are," Director answered for them. "And they have plenty to catch up on. Let's leave them to it, shall we?"

I immediately sought out New Girl's gaze. Her deep brown eyes flashed to mine, too. A silent plea. This shit wasn't right.

But here, we were simply pawns, pets of the Ministry. Bound to obey their every order. So, like the good little pets we were, we listened.

Director looped her cold, boney arm through mine and pulled me from the sisters.

I fought the urge to look back. To strain to listen to what they were saying. If I did, that would mean I cared, and I certainly did not.

I cared about nothing. Especially not that girl.

"I couldn't help but notice your small show of shadows, Three." Her voice was polite, casual even, as we veered through the crowd and toward the other edge of the clearing.

"It was nothing."

With a tsk, she shook her head in a way that made me want to rip it off. "You know the rules. No powers, for the sake of your sister." She lifted her chin and zeroed in on something in the distance. I followed her gaze, instantly recognizing Mags. She looked ridiculous in that pink dress, laughing with her head tossed back and glowing as if we were really here to enjoy the party.

Of course I knew the rules. It would be impossible to scrape the insides of my mind free of the memory of those men putting their blades on Mags's skin. Of her screams ripping through the dungeon until I thought my ears would bleed.

That was the aftermath of my first and only attempt at escaping. The Ministry did not make idle threats, not when it came to powers. Not when it came to keeping the mystics contained.

My chest tightened. She was my one weakness, the one fucking string Director could pull. I would give my life for Mags. There was nothing I wouldn't do if it meant keeping her safe. And now that we were both here, now that Director could clearly see how willing I was to protect her, I was fucked.

"I'd be willing to overlook your breaking of the rules, of course." She brushed a hand down my arm.

I swallowed a gag. "Cut the bullshit. What do you want?"

Brow furrowed, she sighed. "So angry. So defensive. Your claimed may not like that, you know. Has she agreed to mate with you yet? You are aware that both parties must be willing, aren't you?"

A surge of anger rushed through me. "I am very aware, yes."

"And yet, it looks as if she's not on board with your plan."

"She'll get on board."

"Yes." Director eyed me carefully.

Since the day her disgrace of a fucking army found Mags and me, I'd been dreaming up all the ways I might eventually kill her.

She underestimated Mags. Thought so little of her. Saw her as nothing.

But me? She looked at me like I was her ticket out of this fucking war.

I'd yet to figure out why. Surely she had dozens if not hundreds of threes fighting in the war. There were probably several here tonight, all waiting for orders from their beloved Director.

I hated her. I hated everything she stood for. She wasn't a mystic herself, I'd never sensed even the tiniest amount of power coming from her morbid skin, yet she walked around here like she was the most powerful person in the world.

If it weren't for Mags, she would be dead already.

But Director knew that.

"She will get on board. And if you fail at convincing her, I'll have backup measures in place."

My gut twisted painfully at the malice in her tone. "What is that supposed to mean?"

She smiled, possibly the ugliest sight I'd seen all day, and I lived in a shithole with way too many disgusting men. "You'll find out soon."

With a wink that sent a disgusted chill down my spine, she turned and disappeared into the crowd.

I checked on Mags again, making sure she was still laughing and having the time of her life with whoever the fuck she was talking to, before searching for New Girl again.

She was still talking to her sister, her shoulders drawn back, her chin lifted—she had to be a good four inches shorter than the dark-haired woman she was glaring at—and her brown eyes were fierce. Dark. Angry.

Her sister's posture was much more poised. She kept her anger mostly hidden behind a feigned smile. Though now that I'd seen a hint of it, it was easy to make out the flush of red on her pale cheeks and the spark of fury in her eyes. She was equally as angry at New Girl, even if she didn't show it.

My interest was officially piqued.

I stood my ground at the edge of the party, though, waiting. Watching. New Girl didn't strike me as the family type. She certainly didn't strike me as the *my sister is a mystic and is already working for the Ministry* type.

Full of surprises, wasn't she?

The music around us grew even louder, adding to my growing agitation. I'd always hated music. My father loved it. Mags, too. They would play it all hours of the day, singing along and laughing ridiculously.

But for me, music was never simply music. It came with memories. Vivid ones. Each song like a fucking time capsule.

Here, there was nothing I could do as the melody washed over me, washed over my senses.

"Attention!" Director announced loudly, yanking me from the painful memories and ceasing the horrid tunes. "Attention, everyone!" She stepped up onto a small, raised platform on the far side of the room. "I have a few things I'd like to say."

The crowd fell silent.

I glanced one more time over to New Girl. Her sister grasped her arm harshly, fingers digging into the skin, but New Girl yanked away and stumbled backward.

Thankfully the people around them were all focused on Director and paying the squabble no mind.

I was half tempted to interfere. Half tempted to drag her sister aside and ask what the fuck her problem was.

But soon, she, too, was watching Director.

"Today," she said, her voice ringing out clear and strong, "we were victorious."

All over the clearing, people broke into applause.

"It wasn't long ago that mystics were considered lesser in Ashora. They were once forced to hide. To suppress their talents. To lie about their true abilities." She took a long, shaking breath. Were people really buying this shit? "But because of you, because of the hard work the Ministry army puts forth every single day, we are freeing those who live in fear. We are freeing those who have been put down by their own communities. The earthlies cannot control us anymore, not when we stand together in our power!"

The crowd roared.

I fought the urge to vomit.

"I can say with true pride and honor that every single mystic in attendance today will help save the rest of the gifted population from the fate that they were destined to succumb to!"

More applause echoed off the trees. This was all so, so wrong. *This* was the fate we all feared. Being forced to merge our powers under the claiming was what we should be fighting against. We should be rallying to stop the entity forcing us into slavery.

"Today," she continued. "I present our new mystics with honor. These are the next fighters of our cause. The next soldiers in our army of freedom. With pride, they step into their true strength so that we may one day know peace. So that one day, we'll no longer have to live in fear."

Predictably, she had to pause for applause once again.

"Dance," she insisted. "Indulge. Enjoy yourselves this evening. The mystics who have not yet claimed, please take the time to speak with our army." She scanned the crowd pointedly. "I'm certain they'll inspire you to become who you were truly born to be."

More cheering. More clapping and stomping and hollering. Had these people all been fucking brainwashed? Had the Ministry figured out how to control the minds of the masses? Maybe the entire fucking army was being controlled by a few of the mystics, forced to obey their commands. Forced to fight for the Ministry. It was the only solution that made sense. There was no way in hell this many would willingly fight for the Ministry. Not when they had seen firsthand how mystics were treated under Director's rule.

Still. They danced. They smiled. They seemed to be enjoying this pathetic excuse of a life they'd been given.

All the while the pit in my chest grew.

And grew.

And grew.

athena

"I thought you were dead," I whispered as soon as Sinner and Director were out of earshot.

Despite what I'd assumed, Katherine looked very much alive and healthy, apparently in the good graces of the Ministry, too.

Her smile did not waver an inch. "Disappointed to see me, sister?"

Disappointed? A million emotions flooded my body. When Katherine left, I was pissed. How could she leave her sisters when we needed her the most?

And all that time, she had been here. With them. Disappointed in her? Maybe. But to see her alive and in the flesh... I swallowed down the anger and panic rising in my throat and forced a curt smile. "Just surprised. I was sure I'd never see you again after you left us."

Her brown eyes sharpened. "Yeah, well, things change. And change isn't always a bad thing, Thena."

I clenched my fists so tightly my nails pierced into the

skin on my palms. "Oh yeah, it's been real peachy for me so far. You know Jasmine is dead, too? I had to bury her by myself while the crows circled in the sky above me. A real pain, dragging a body with no help."

For a split second, Katherine's smile faltered. "What?"

I shrugged. "Not like you'd care about her, or any of us. When you left, it was pretty damn clear you wanted nothing to do with our family."

Inwardly, I cringed. I'd planned to take the high road. But the warm buzz from the wine was infiltrating my senses, making me forget why my behavior mattered at all.

Hell, I'd all but forgotten why *anything* mattered.

"Are you working with them? Did they take you, too?" My words came out in a rush, a mix of curiosity and hurt and panic.

"I'm here to help you." She stepped even closer, her sweet perfume wafting over me and making me dizzy. "When Director told me they found you, I could hardly believe it. But here you are." She looked me up and down, her expression scrutinizing.

"Considering they came and kidnapped me from our *home*. They found me, all right. Suddenly, it makes more sense. For our whole lives, we lived in peace, without the threat of the Ministry, yet you wandered off, and within weeks, they'd discovered our home. Now look at us."

Darkness overtook her expression for a heartbeat. "You're hiding your powers from her and you need to stop. It's only going to hurt you."

There was no stopping the scoff that escaped me. My

sister had definitely gone nuts. *They had gotten to her, too.* "I have no powers."

Her laugh shook my bones. "We both know you're a mystic. You're not helping anyone, least of all yourself, by lying."

Yep. She'd lost her mind completely. Had she been indoctrinated into the *Athena-has-powers* club?

"Lying? You've known me my entire life, Katherine! Are you seriously telling me you think I'm a mystic?"

"Look around you," she ordered.

Over her shoulder, I scanned the room of soldiers dressed and playing nice. People were laughing. Dancing. Probably getting way too drunk.

"Everyone here is a mystic," she said, her tone harsh. "Including me. Including you."

Oh. My. God. This conversation had gone from concerning to entirely deranged. "You're a mystic?" I breathed, unease coiling in my stomach. "Exactly what type of power do you have?"

"That's not important right now. They don't want mine nearly as much as they want yours. That's why we're having this discussion." She sighed like she was already tired of this conversation. I despised it when she acted like even speaking to me was below her.

Standing tall, I locked eyes with her. "You're lying."

"About what?" She held her arms out. "What reason would I have to lie?"

"If I were a mystic, don't you think I would have used my power to get out of here?" I threw a thumb over my shoulder. "You know where they're keeping us, right? Do you know what they want me to *do*?"

"*Of course* I know. I'm a lot closer to you than you think, Thena. You're being detained in the dungeons with the rest of the mystics until the claiming. But it will all be over soon, okay? I promise you this is the worst part."

A silent beat passed between us while my mind raced with all kinds of ridiculous thoughts. Who was this person? She'd never been overly kind to anyone, but she was absolutely frigid now. "Did you go through this, too, Katherine? The claiming?"

She stepped closer to me, lowering her voice. "Yes, and you better do it too. If you cooperate and perform the claiming with that man, they'll get you out of that dungeon."

My heart pinched painfully. My sister, the one person left in this world who should care about my well-being, was here forcing my hand just as Director had been. Where had we gone wrong? When had things gotten twisted enough to send her running to the enemy?

"How could you say any of this? How could you *support* this? You know how awful this is! This isn't right!"

Her only reaction was a deep inhale and a lift of her sharp chin. "There is no place for right or wrong here, Thena. Just survival. You want to survive, don't you? You've always been quite the survivor."

My heart raced at her proximity. *My sister.* After all this time, she was alive. And she was with them. I could barely believe the words coming out of her mouth. She wasn't here to break me out, to help me. No, her purpose was to ensure my compliance.

I looked to where Sinner and Director were speaking near the edge of the party, talking in hushed tones like Katherine and I were.

Always so secretive.

I'd been dragged here with nothing. Nobody. I had no intention of giving them anything they wanted. But the deep pit in my stomach told me the tides were shifting. There were more forces working against me than I'd realized, one of which, it turned out, was my heinous sister.

"If I agree to go through with this—which is still pretty damn unlikely—you need to do one thing for me."

She stiffened. "What?"

"There's another girl in the dungeons. She barely has any power. Margaret. You have to let her go free."

Katherine's mouth fell open in disbelief. "Are you kidding? You really think Director will agree to let a mystic woman walk free?"

"She's a low level, probably a one. I think your bitch of a boss would be more concerned about Sinner and me participating in the claiming than about keeping a low-level mystic around. If Director really wants this to happen so badly, she'll let her go."

She studied my face, lips pressed together and eyes narrowed to slits.

For a moment, I considered asking her more about what she did for the Ministry, how she'd ended up here, how long she had been with them and what power she was using to assist them.

Before I could, though, she exhaled loudly, pulling me from my thoughts.

"You'll claim with him willingly on the next blood moon?"

God, this felt so wrong. Everything in me was telling me to run, to lie, to hide.

But if I was really being forced into this fate, maybe one good thing could come of it. "If you let her go, yes. I'll do it."

A few seconds passed, but eventually, she nodded once. "Fine. I'll see what I can do, but I make no promises."

Rather than walk away like I expected, Katherine lurched forward and gripped my forearm, her expression full of fear. "You'll die if you don't go through with this. I know you. I know you've been trying to fight, trying to find a way out. But there is no way out. Bond with him, use your power, and fight the battle you were born to fight."

I yanked my arm free from her anyway. "I don't trust you."

"Good," she whispered. "Don't trust anybody. It's the only way you'll make it out alive."

Director was on the stage now, garnering the attention of the crowd. Katherine—like the good little dog she was—looked proudly toward the stage.

Disgusting.

Director rambled on about the war, spitting lies and claiming false victories while the crowd blindly cheered. As soon as it ended, I turned to find Margaret.

Before I could locate her, a piercing sound split through the air, stopping my every thought in its tracks.

"I'll see you soon, sister."

A breath later, the world went black.

WATER. I needed water. My mouth was caked with thick saliva and my eyelids felt weighed down. I pried them open eventually, though my vision was blurry. What the hell happened? And how long had I been asleep?

"Finally." A deep voice echoed off the walls and ricocheted inside my skull.

Fuck. Sinner's voice tended to do that.

"What happened?" The words were barely audible. My lips were cracked, my head pounding. As my vision cleared, I pushed myself to sitting and quickly assessed my surroundings.

From the look of things, the two of us had been locked in a smaller cave-like room. It was large enough to fit one of those tiny cots from the dungeon, but not much else. There were only a few feet of stone floor between it and a padlocked prison door. At least this door was made of bars, and we could see the hallway lit with exposed hanging bulbs, but nothing else.

Sinner pushed a cup of water in my direction with his foot. He sat on the ground with his arms crossed over his chest and his back resting against the wall. And, of course, he looked as annoyed as ever.

"I know just as much as you do. Someone must have used their power to incapacitate us. Couldn't tell you why, but now we're here."

"Only us? Why would they separate us?" I downed the water in two gulps.

Sinner cocked his head to the side like that was the stupidest question I could have asked.

"Oh, right," I answered for him. "Because we're supposed to be doing this stupid claiming ritual in two weeks."

"I'd say that's a decent guess." He rested his head against the wall behind him and closed his eyes. His throat bobbed as he swallowed.

His lack of general concern for our well-being was seriously starting to concern me. "And you're...what? You're letting them?"

A second passed. Then another. Rage built inside of me with every lingering moment of silence. How was he not absolutely freaking out right now?

"It's not like we have a choice, New Girl. We never did."

"Don't say that." I stood and immediately swayed. My vision darkened, and for a moment I was sure I'd pass out. I breathed through it, willing myself to stay conscious, and when my vision returned, I made my way to the cage door that secured our new little prison. I yanked once on the bars, rattling them loudly, but it didn't budge. That was unsurprising, of course, but damn. At least I was willing to try.

"Can't you use your magic? Have you tried? You could... You could—"

"I could *nothing*," he whispered, sounding far too serpent-like for my liking. His eyes locked on mine. "You forget who we are down here. We are pawns. Toys. We are powerless."

I shrugged, annoyed. "You didn't look powerless earlier tonight. That's all."

"You truly believe I haven't thought about using my power to escape?"

I gave up on the bars and kneeled in front of him so we were eye to eye. "Why not? You could do it. We could get out of here!"

He assessed me, his lips tugged down in an expression that appeared to be annoyance but then morphed into sadness. "There's too much at risk. It's not only my life I'm worried about. Fuck, if it was, I would've burned this place to the ground and taken myself with it."

Then I remembered the sad realization of Sinner's situation. "You comply because of your sister."

He dipped his chin, then rested his head on the wall again. "Bingo."

"You think she'll get hurt if you try to leave."

"Trust me, I don't just think it. Director has made her intentions very clear to me."

I sat back on my heels, my heart rate picking up, and cleared my throat. "I guess this is probably a good time to tell you that they're freeing her, then. If they haven't already."

He eyed me like a predator assessing its prey, searching for every one of my weaknesses and finding them with ease. "What are you talking about?"

"My sister, the woman I spoke to at the ball. She told me she would release Margaret."

He scoffed, his lip curling in disgust. "And why would she do something like that?"

"Because she wants me to perform the claiming willingly."

Sinner straightened and inspected me, the intensity in his eyes so fierce I swear to god he made time stop. I nearly crawled out of my skin as he sat, silently shooting daggers at me.

"You agreed to claim with me in return for Mags's safety?"

"I did."

His chest rose and fell with a heavy breath. "I don't trust your sister. I sure as hell don't trust Director. Whatever they told you, they're lying."

A wave of unease washed over me. "She wouldn't lie to me."

My sister had her flaws, yes, but she was a woman of her word. If she made me a promise to free Margaret, then she'd be free. Especially if they wanted me to claim.

And for reasons I had yet to understand, they were dead set on my participation.

"What makes you think I'd believe that?" he gritted out. "You seemed awfully surprised to see her. A mystic. At the president's ball. You're hiding something, New Girl. Don't think I can't see it."

"I'm not hiding anything." I heaved a breath out. "I didn't know my sister was mystic, and I sure as hell didn't think I would ever see her again, let alone at Director's ball. Forgive me for being shocked."

"Does she know?"

"Know what?"

"That you're hiding a power Director wants."

God, she was the *reason* Director was under the impression I had power. She had been the one whispering about me, as if I were some sort of pawn that would save them all from this war. She believed it all, too. She believed she was a mystic, and she believed I was, too.

Had they tortured her? Had they locked her down here and brainwashed her until she'd broken? It was the only explanation, because my own sister thinking I had magic?

No way.

I crawled away from Sinner and sat against the opposite wall, arms crossed over my chest in hopes that I could retain a little of my body heat. I was still wearing the dress from the ball. Sinner was still in his suit as well, though he had stripped down to his undershirt and trousers.

It was colder here. Darker. Before this moment, I couldn't have imagined missing that dank, dirty, crowded dungeon, but this made that place look like a haven.

Sinner was still staring at me, waiting for my reply.

"I'm not going to argue. I don't have any power, but clearly you've chosen not to believe me."

"Correct."

"Enjoy being disappointed, then."

I waited for a quip, for a scathing response, but none came. Only silence. Silence and the thick tension that suffocated me with every passing hour.

It was going to be a long freaking night.

sinner

I couldn't help that initial wave of relief that hit me when New Girl told me she'd negotiated for Mags's release. Was it possible she really did care about my sister?

It was hard to say, because I didn't trust her for a damn second.

She slept sitting with her back against the wall, her legs stretched out in front of her with one ankle crossed over the other. Her head was slumped to the side as her chest rose and fell with each deep breath.

The dress was fucking ridiculous. They would have to bring her new clothes eventually, and thank god, because there was no way I could live in this tiny-ass room with her dressed like that.

A deep, all-consuming annoyance crept up the back of my neck. I hated her. I really did. I hated that she was sleeping like that. I hated that she actually seemed to care about my sister.

And that she was actually willing to perform the claiming with me.

That part surprised me the most.

Despite my hope that she would so we could get out of here, I'd assumed she'd never agree. Why would she? She had been kidnapped and dragged to a dungeon full of men she didn't know. The last thing on her mind was probably having sex with one of them.

Especially me.

But maybe she'd finally realized the truth—that the claiming was her one and only ticket out of here. Or maybe she was finally accepting the fact that somewhere buried deep inside of her, she was a mystic.

New Girl had power.

I could feel it down in my soul. What was left of my soul, anyway.

Her eyes fluttered beneath her closed lids as she slept. She was probably cold. Exhausted. Starving.

I shouldn't give a shit about any of those things.

But the damn claiming changed things. We were still a while away from the actual ceremony, but it was as if my body knew she was mine. My power knew it, too. The shadows under my skin sang, pulling me toward her.

Pressure built in my chest as I tried to focus on anything but her.

But it was no use. Trapped down here, forced to be so close to her, my thoughts consumed me.

Slowly, silently, I climbed to my feet. Fuck, every muscle ached. Whatever they'd used to knock us out at that ball had done its job and much, much more.

Not that I'd ever really known comfort. Maybe that's why I'd survived down here for as long as I had. This life wasn't all that different from the life I'd come from.

Breath held, I scooped her up from the floor, one arm under her knees and the other behind her back. Her head rolled onto my chest as I stood, causing me to inhale sharply. It was a mistake, because I was instantly engulfed in her addictive scent.

I laid her on the small bed in the corner of the room and as she shifted, I stepped back. She murmured nonsensically as she adjusted her body to the new position but fell still again quickly.

I picked up the jacket I'd tossed to the floor when I'd first woken up in here and covered her with it. As much as I didn't give a fuck about whether she was cold, my power damn near insisted I take care of her. Like it would disobey me for her if given the chance. It was more of an annoyance to me than anything.

But at least this way I didn't have to stare at her every time I opened my eyes.

I gave her one more glance, then returned to my spot on the floor.

It was quiet here. Lonely.

My chest ached for Mags. Wherever she was, I hoped to god she was safe. The dungeons? This place? It was the farthest thing from it. The only reason Director hadn't used her in the claiming ritual yet was because she was more interested in my power than my sister's, and I would have never agreed to participate if anyone had even looked at Mags the wrong way.

But with every day that passed, my control dwindled and the Ministry's grasp on me grew tighter. It was fucking suffocating.

Less than two weeks until the blood moon. Until the claiming. Less than two weeks until this was all over, and we were out of the dungeons for good.

"HELP ME, *help me, somebody help me!*"

I bolted upright, my senses on full alert as my eyes adjusted in the dark room.

New Girl thrashed, arching off the bed. *"Help me. Help me. Help me."*

Before I was aware that I'd moved, I was hovering over her, shaking her shoulders. "Athena! Athena, hey! Wake up!"

Her eyes popped open, her lips parted, and for a moment, all she did was blink up at me in confusion. Sweat beaded on her pale skin, glistened across her chest. "What happened?"

"You were screaming."

Her eyes went wide, becoming the deepest, darkest pools. I could have fucking swam in the depths of deep brown. It was rare to see her this way—defenseless, unassuming.

"Sorry," she muttered, her voice hoarse. "Did I wake you up?"

"Did you screaming 'help me, help me' wake me up?" I bit back a smirk. "A bit, yes."

She sat up, and I stepped back. She took a few long breaths, slowly calming herself. Like this, she reminded me so much of my sister. I'd seen Mags go through this same kind of shit far too many times.

I didn't care about New Girl, but I couldn't let her scream in her sleep.

"You called me Athena."

"Excuse me?"

"When you woke me up, you didn't call me New Girl. You called me Athena."

Fuck. I fought the urge to smack a palm to my face. "Yeah, well, I assumed using your actual name would be more effective. Don't worry. It won't happen again."

A weak laugh escaped her. "You don't have to do that, you know."

"Do what?"

"You don't have to be the big, scary tier three who hates everyone. It's just us now. You don't have to pretend anymore."

Her words were like a knife to the gut. "I'm not pretending. I called you by your name once, you don't have to worry about that becoming a habit."

"Right." She sighed, shoulders sagging. "And what about your real name?"

I bit back a growl. She was awfully fucking talkative for someone who'd just woken up from a nightmare. Though I supposed maybe that was the point. She was distracting herself from whatever had scared the shit out of her.

But turning the conversation on me? Wasn't going to fucking work.

"What were you dreaming about?"

The smile slipped from her face. "I can't remember."

"You can't?" I hummed. "It must have been bad. Otherwise, you wouldn't have been screaming for help."

She swallowed thickly, her eyes so wide another version of me might've felt bad for her in the past. But that version of me was gone. Dead. Forgotten.

The man I was now didn't give a fuck that those big doe eyes were locked on me.

"It was only a nightmare." She lowered her head, focusing on her lap. "It wasn't real."

I scoffed. "We both know nightmares are very, very real in this world."

Even drenched in sweat and clearly still recovering from the battle she had been fighting in her mind, she looked at me in defiance, her jaw set, ready to wage war.

All the more reason I knew she was hiding something. People like that—fighters—weren't simply born. The world made them that way. The world had shown New Girl here that for whatever reason, she had to be tough. She had to fight.

Fight what? Director, sure. The Ministry, of course. But what else? What was she fighting in that pretty little head of hers?

I leaned in, loving the way she flinched slightly as I approached her space. "I'm going to ask you one more time, New Girl, and you're going to answer me. What were you dreaming about?"

"Dying." The word was so quiet I barely heard it.

My stomach sank. "You have nightmares about dying?"

She finally broke our electric gaze—thank god, because I never would have—and dipped her chin. "I have nightmares about dying, and I have nightmares about being alive. I can't quite decide which ones are worse."

No fucking shit.

"I don't buy it."

"Don't buy what?"

"A girl like you seems to have very little fear of dying. You don't seem too concerned with your safety here. Unless you're an expert at hiding all that behind that mask you're always wearing."

Her expression lit with anger. Good. I liked her angry.

I liked it a little too much.

"I know you think I'm an idiot, but I do possess a basic need for survival. If I didn't, then I would have left this world a long, long time ago."

Her words created a pit in my stomach I didn't want to examine.

"There are always reasons to fear death. Even if you don't know what they are in this moment." It took me a second before I realized I said that aloud.

New Girl only shrugged. "Sometimes they're hard to figure out."

Footsteps echoed off the stone walls, growing quicker and closer with every second.

We both froze, watching the door to our cell, waiting for what came next.

A woman dressed in black tactical gear approached. She was young, with her hair pulled away from her face in a way that made her look almost innocent.

But she was one of them. Regardless of her looks, she was far from innocent.

"Here," she motioned, passing a glass jug through the bars. "More water. You're going to need it."

"Why are we here?" I asked. "What are you doing with us?"

Her eyes softened a fraction as she looked from me to New Girl. "Prepare yourselves. Drink the water. I'm sorry, I tried to stop this."

Then she was gone, retreating as quickly as she'd come.

"Okay," New Girl said. "That was suspicious. I'm going to try really hard not to panic right now."

"Don't worry," I said, even as unease wormed its way through me. "She probably has no clue what she's talking about."

Silence fell between us, though New Girl studied the door, then me, as if dying to ask more questions. Questions I didn't have the answers to. I tried to relax, and I tried to forget about the strange woman who had come to warn us.

If she was one of them, why would she have bothered? And what were we supposed to prepare ourselves for?

A few hours later, after we'd both pretended to relax, our questions were answered.

It started slow—a tendril of smoke creeping down the hall and into our cell, but before long, the smoke grew thicker and filled the room.

I scrambled away at first, but it was no use. Whatever this fog was, there was no escaping it.

"Oh my god," New Girl gasped. "What is that?"

"Stay calm," I said, not that I felt at all calm. "We don't know what this is yet."

"*Stay calm*? Are you kidding me? There's a strange gas filling our cell, and you want me to stay calm?" She scrambled back onto the bed.

It was pointless. Within minutes, we were completely engulfed in the gas. We had no choice but to breathe it in, to move in it, to become part of it.

"They're trying to kill us, aren't they? This is how we die!"

"You are really not helping right now." Panic crept into my voice, regardless of how I tried to hide it. They wouldn't kill us like this, would they? With gas pumped into the room while we were trapped here like fucking dogs?

They were cowards, yes, but they needed us.

I held my breath for as long as I could, then covered my nose and mouth with my hands and tried to keep that gas out of my lungs, but it was no use.

We were pawns in the game of the Ministry, and there was nothing we could do about it.

"Oh, god," New Girl groaned from behind me.

Heart racing, palms sweating, I turned to her. Fuck, was I imagining it, or were my senses heightening?

"It's them," she said. "They're drugging us."

athena

My heart pounded, my pulse beating in my fingertips and all the way down to my toes.

First, I thought their plan was to incapacitate us again. Kill us, maybe. Clearly, I was wrong.

Sinner stiffened, the broad shoulders beneath his shirt tensing as he too realized what was happening. "Why would they do this? It isn't even the night of the blood moon!"

I scooted back on the bed until I was pressed up against the cold concrete wall. *Slow breaths. Slow breaths. Lower your fucking heart rate, Athena. You're not going to let a heart attack take you out. Not after everything you've been through.*

In front of me, Sinner shuffled to the front of the cell and gripped the bars so tight that his hands shook. "This isn't right."

"Obviously." I choked on the fog and fell into a coughing fit. My eyes watered, my throat stung. "Gas invading the room is typically *not* right."

He growled again, igniting the tiniest spark in my chest. I didn't fear him, but sometimes I was reminded that he was a monster. He was one of them—a mystic. A powerful one at that.

And now I was trapped in this tiny room with him, and he was getting angrier by the second.

At least, that's how it looked. And I could practically feel the fury simmering inside him as he stood with his back to me, tense as a freaking rock.

I pulled my legs up to my chest and wrapped my arms around them, still willing my body to calm down. Sinner had draped his jacket over my shoulders at some point, which was a blessing considering I was still wearing the very thin dress from the ball.

I didn't want to die wearing a flimsy dress. It would be a real shame.

My racing heart slowed a fraction, but the pounding changed from panic to something wholly different. Heat emanated from my chest and rolled through my extremities. I took a few long breaths, silently begging the warmth to dissipate.

Instead, it settled in and morphed into something else. Something...deeper.

Sinner pressed his head against the bars as he shook them with abandon. "They want us to mate. That's what she warned us about. They're drugging us so we'll willingly mate. I'd bet they're using tonight to test us before the blood moon comes around."

My heart lurched painfully. "What? That's crazy! They can't do that, can they?"

He tilted his head to the sky, back still to me, and laughed. It was a laugh to whatever god had cursed us with this fate.

"We have to fight it," I said. "A drug can't make us do anything." On cue, the heat that had worked its way through me began to pool between my thighs. Okay, maybe a drug could make me feel things, but it sure as hell could not make me willingly touch Sinner.

Absolutely the fuck not.

"As long as you stay over there and I stay over here, we'll be fine." His voice was rough and strained, his knuckles white as he clutched the bars. "I'm not touching you."

"Feeling is mutual."

The fog started to dissipate, the hazy cloud lifting a little. I focused on my breathing. That was a good sign. Maybe it would clear out as quickly as it had settled in here. There was no way this tactic would work. If it did, then the Ministry was taking the free will aspect out of the claiming.

Or would it be successful? Was there some sort of loophole? *Shit.* If that was the case, then the Ministry could pair whoever they wanted, whenever they wanted to. Hell, they were already pretty much doing that.

This would simply speed up the process.

Every second that passed was more torturous than the last. *Breathe in. Breathe out. Focus on the cool air, focus on it cooling your body.*

I sat up and pushed Sinner's jacket off my shoulders, tossing it onto the edge of the bed.

"You're taking your clothes *off?*"

"Only the jacket! You want me to burn alive back here?"

"If it means remaining clothed, yes!" His shoulders rose and fell, rose and fell.

Without my permission, my eyes trailed down his back, lingering over his waist. He was too damn attractive for his own good. Why couldn't he be hideous?

I'd never been a big fan of men. Not like I'd spoken to that many outside of my family, but from the few interactions I'd had, I'd learned to be wary.

Though none of the men I'd ever met looked like him. And none of them pissed me off while also making me want to beg them to touch me.

No, only Sinner had that privilege.

And right now, emotions like anger and frustration and desire were all mixed up.

I stretched my legs out and ran my hands down my face, wiping the sweat that now glistened across my skin. The heat was only getting stronger, only pooling deeper in my belly, so deep I had to clench my thighs together.

My breath grew more shallow as the feelings compounded.

"Whatever you're thinking right now, stop it."

"I'm not thinking anything," I panted. "Except for how much I hate this. And how much I hate you. And how much I wish I was in here with literally anyone else."

"Is that right?" He finally spun around, pressing his back against the bars. His cheeks were flushed, his eyes darker than usual. "You'd rather be trapped in a tiny cell with a sex-drugged man with less restraint?"

I coughed on a laugh. "You really think you're the only mystic here with restraint?"

He rolled his eyes. "I think plenty of men in that dungeon would be more than happy to be in this situation with you."

That stung. I didn't want any of them to touch me, and I sure as hell didn't want any of them trapped in here with me. Yet it hurt, knowing Sinner wasn't one of the men who'd gladly be stuck in this situation with me.

Was I that appalling?

I eyed him, only to find him drinking me in, his focus lingering over my exposed legs.

I took it back.

This was much, much worse than thinking he was repulsed by me.

I pressed my head against the wall until it hurt, clenching my thighs together even harder.

A broken sound left Sinner, one that forced me to dig my fingernails into the skin of my legs so I could think of literally anything but how badly I wished he'd move closer.

"It'll pass. It'll pass, right?" My voice cracked and my next breath came out as a rush of air.

Sinner clenched his jaw. "Either that, or they keep pumping the gas in here until they get what they want." He trailed off at the end, taking another long, shuddered breath. From this angle, his chest looked wider than I remembered. He was strong as hell, that much was obvious. He was easily the biggest man in the dungeon, the biggest man I had ever seen, actually.

So when my eyes drifted down to his waist, below his belt, I shouldn't have been surprised.

But I was very, very freaking surprised.

And before I could stop myself, a soft moan left my lips.

His bulge grew even thicker in his pants, and like me, he pressed himself against that wall like it would save his life.

I relaxed my thighs, letting them fall apart slightly, causing the slit in my dress to ride a little higher. God, I needed a little cool air. That would stop me from doing the very bad things I was imagining.

Sinner started to pace, mumbling words I couldn't make out.

"Sinner." I meant for it to be a warning, but my voice betrayed me, turning the two syllables into a plea. God, my body needed him. I needed him to touch me.

Right. Now.

I spread my legs farther as he paced the tiny room. Even farther still, until one slipped off the edge of the bed.

My nipples ached beneath the thin fabric of my dress, no doubt on full display. My restraint was quickly dissipating.

This is what they want. They want you to give in.

I was beginning to wonder why I'd bothered fighting it at all.

We were going to participate in the ritual eventually, right? What was to stop them from pumping this gas into the air again if we didn't give in now? They'd try again tomorrow, and maybe the next day, until they could ensure that we would actually claim during the blood moon.

And I was very close to giving in.

I arched my back and closed my eyes, clutching the mattress on either side of me in order to resist touching myself, because right now, I'd give just about anything to relieve the pressure coiling and building and tightening inside me.

Though, if this feeling didn't start to fade in the next five seconds, that was looking like a good option.

I squeezed my eyes shut, but when the mattress dipped, I flung them open again.

Sinner sat dangerously close, wearing a wild, disheveled look. He'd situated himself between my legs, his hands planted on either side of my hips, the warmth of him lighting my entire body on fire.

"They want a show? We'll give them a fucking show."

sinner

This was a very, very bad idea. But if New Girl didn't get off, I'd have to sit here and listen to my name on those lips over and over again.

And if she touched herself? There's no way I wouldn't lose all control.

Neither of those were good options.

This close, I could feel the heat simmering off her body. I pushed her legs farther apart so I could move closer to her, getting a peek of her black underwear through the slit in her dress.

Fuck, it took more strength than I would like to admit to fight the urge to rip them off.

"What are you doing?" she breathed even as her body arched toward me, begging me to touch her.

I obeyed, sliding my hands up her thighs, pushing the blue fabric out of the way as I went. "They want to know their drug works. So we'll show them that it does, then they'll put an end to this."

Her eyes widened, her mouth opening for a split second, like she was going to argue. To tell me to stop.

I froze, waiting for exactly that. *Please for the love of god tell me this is a terrible, terrible idea. Tell me to get my hands off you before I do something we'll both regret.*

"Please, Sinner," she moaned.

I had done something very wrong to deserve this, because this was my personal form of torture.

"Help me."

I caught myself leaning forward, inhaling her sweet scent and getting drunk off the proximity of her. This was a bad, bad idea. "Help you how? Tell me how to make it better, and it'll all be over."

She pressed the back of her skull against the wall and arched, her perky breasts fighting against the ridiculous fabric caging them in. "I need you to touch me. Now."

I trailed my hands past her hips, up to her thin waist, and like a fucking idiot, I hovered close and let myself taste the skin below her collarbone.

She moaned, arching further into my touch. My cock throbbed against my pants, but I refused to press myself against her. No, I'd keep at least that much space between us.

I'd have to make her come without ripping all her clothes off and burying myself inside of her, no matter how badly every ounce of me screamed for it.

My tongue trailed the sharp bone, then I kissed her skin softly, savoring this moment, letting the heat pull me under.

She wanted me to touch her. It was for the greater good, right?

I wrapped an arm around the back of her waist and dragged her down the mattress until she was lying flat on her back beneath me. God, she was so small. So submissive under my touch.

She brought her hands to my chest, then slid them lower. I tensed immediately, unused to being touched, especially like this.

And not when I was this close to losing control.

"You don't want to do that," I warned.

"Yes, I do." Her fingers trailed lower.

Sweat beaded at my temples as I fought the desire to roll my hips against her. "You aren't in your right mind right now."

She sighed. "I don't care. I want you."

A very pathetic sound left my lips. One I was certain I would beat myself up for over the next few days. Weeks, even. Years.

Before she could unleash the monster resting deep in my soul, I snatched her wrists and pinned them above her head in one swift motion.

While I held them there with one hand, I gripped her thigh with the other, hard enough to make her gasp.

She arched into me. "More," she begged.

The heat emanating from her thighs was so torturously tempting. Fuck, did I want it.

I shoved her dress up and ran my hand down her center. She jerked as I touched the sensitive apex, but eventually relaxed. "Oh, god."

"Tell me what you like."

Her eyes fluttered open. "I don't—I don't know."

"You don't know? You don't know what?"

"I don't know what I like. I like this. Keep doing this."

I stroked her pussy through the outside of her thin underwear. Fuck. The way she reacted to me... "Have you been with anyone before? Or are you a perfect little virgin begging to be ruined." I punctuated that last part by slipping one finger beneath the fabric.

She whimpered, eyes squeezed shut. "No."

She was soaked already. Fuck, I wanted to tear every stitch of clothing from her body and sink deep inside her. "No, what?"

"No, I've never been with anyone."

Like this couldn't get any worse. I bit my tongue to stop another ridiculous moan from escaping me. I was a fucking man. I was in charge here. I did, in fact, have some ounce of self-control.

This untouched woman lying beneath me, begging me to touch her, would not make me lose control. I had more strength than that. *You hate this girl, remember? You absolutely despise her.*

But as I slid a finger inside her, I forgot all the reasons why. I forgot why this was such a bad idea. I forgot everything except how absolutely perfect she was.

She arched even further, grinding into my hand. "Sinner, please."

I moved down the bed and kissed the sensitive skin on the inside of her thigh. Yeah, I was definitely going to regret this.

She squirmed beneath me and tightened around my finger. Fuck, that sensation alone nearly made me come undone.

"Come for me, Athena." I added another finger and pumped faster, using my thumb to circle her clit.

She was utterly at my mercy, and knowing that I was the only one who had ever touched her like this?

That thought was fucking addicting.

She was seconds from climaxing. Her body was wild under my touch. Undone. Relaxed. Fucking primitive.

My name on her lips was a sound I would never fucking forget.

I licked the inside of her thigh, closer to her apex than before. Her breath hitched and her body tightened like a bowstring. And then she was flying over the edge. She shattered beneath my touch, coming on my fingers and ruining my entire fucking life.

At the height of her pleasure, I registered an unfamiliar sensation in my mind, in my being. Like a whisper against the inside of my skull.

The drugs. It had to be the drugs.

Only...

The way my own power reacted to it, nearly catapulting out of my control, told me it was not the drugs.

It was Athena and her big, dirty secret.

Before I could catalog the sensation and what it was doing to me, though, it was over.

Slowly, her trembling body relaxed. When her muscles were languid, I pulled my fingers out of her soaking pussy and braced myself above her, not ready to leave yet.

She finally opened her eyes and stared up at me in awe, like she was waiting for me to make the next move. So naturally, I did something very, very stupid. I put my fingers in my mouth and tasted her.

It might've been the lack of any tasteful food in these damn dungeons for the last few months, but she tasted like everything I had ever needed in my life.

She swallowed as she watched me, equally as drunk on the sight of it as I was.

For a moment, we were frozen like that. My heart pounded as my mind whirred, trying to assess the last few minutes. I was still drowning in my own need, but it would pass. I'd gotten a taste of her. That was enough to satisfy me for now.

"What just happened?" she whispered.

I hovered closer, only stopping when our noses were an inch apart. "I fixed our problem. You're welcome."

With that, I pushed myself off the bed and returned to the very, very cold bars of the cell that felt more like a torture room than before.

athena

S inner said nothing to me for hours. He stayed on his side of the tiny cell, as far away from me as he could get.

I didn't blame him. I'd literally begged him to touch me last night. Could I be any more pathetic? Clearly, I had no restraint. The same could not be said for Sinner. He'd gotten me off quickly, then extricated himself, obviously not affected at all by the drugs they pumped into the cell.

Drugs or not, he had more self-control than I expected. That, or he didn't think I was half as attractive as I thought he was.

Now that the haze of those drugs had lifted, I was regretting every choice I'd ever made in life.

Nobody had ever touched me like that. Nobody had ever made me tremble under their grasp. And the scariest part? A sensation I'd never experienced before sparked to life in that moment—one that had nothing to do with his hands on my body. And part of me suspected he felt it, too.

Especially when he finally broke the silence.

"You're telling me you've never used powers before? Even by accident?"

He sat with his knees drawn up to his chest, his back against the bars. I couldn't even look at him without picturing the way he literally licked my slickness off his fingers.

If only that drug had killed us.

It would've saved me this misery.

"No," I answered on instinct. "Never."

He eyed me skeptically. I wanted to ask him what we were both thinking. *Did you feel that, too?*

Instead, I kept my mouth shut.

"And your family? Your sister? What tier is she? What's her gift?"

I squeezed my eyes shut. Seeing my sister here had obviously been a surprise. One I had done all I could to avoid thinking about.

"I don't know," I sighed. It was a weak lie, one he would see right through. But how did I tell him the truth? How did I show him the pieces of myself that I hadn't even taken out and looked at on my own? "We weren't that close."

I lowered my head and picked at my nails, unconcerned that I'd already caused them to bleed.

He watched me with such intensity, his attention bored holes into me and blanketed me with an invisible weight.

And there was nowhere I could go to hide. Not this time.

"Hm," he started. "So you have a sister. Anyone else crawling around in the Ministry I should know about?"

I forced myself to keep my breath steady. "No. Everyone else is dead."

One beat. Two beats.

"Your whole family is dead?"

I nodded.

"How?"

"Different things. Accidents. Illness. My younger sister died right before the Ministry found me and brought me here. I had just finished burying her with the others."

A long silence fell upon us. Long enough that I dared glancing up at Sinner.

When I saw the pain in his expression, I immediately regretted seeking him out.

"You buried your own family?"

I shrugged, averted my focus again. "I had help. Until Katherine left and Jasmine died. Then it was just me."

"Why did she leave? How did she end up with the Ministry?"

I shifted, no longer caring about what he could read in my body language. Let him see the discomfort. "You're awfully talkative today."

He scoffed. "And you're awfully secretive. I can tell when you're hiding things from me, Athena."

Athena. That was the third time he'd called me by name.

I hated the way my body reacted at the memory of my name falling from his lips last night.

"You're hiding things, too," I asserted. "You think I

can't see the concrete walls you've built around yourself? People don't do that when they have nothing to hide."

He swallowed, but held my gaze. "Be very, very careful with what you say next."

"Why?" I asked. "What'll happen if I don't? You'll kill me?"

Few things made me shiver the way his smile did. "We both know I could do things far worse than that."

"What else can your power do?" I pushed.

He wanted me to talk about a power I didn't possess, but he wasn't willing to give me information about his own power or his life. "When did you discover it?"

"Conversation is over," he barked, his eyes sharp. "Let's just sit here in silence. It's much less painful."

Agreed.

We sat like that for hours. Time and time again, I had to bury thoughts of how his fingers had scoured my body deep into the shadows of my mind. I tried to think of literally anything else, forcing myself to consider where Margaret might be and what might have happened to all the other people at that damn ball.

Were they back in the dungeon like nothing ever happened? Was Margaret with them, or was she miles and miles away from here by now?

I was seconds away from losing my mind entirely when guards finally approached. Sinner was on his feet in an instant.

"Let's go," one of the men dressed in head-to-toe black ordered. He fumbled through keys and inserted one in the lock.

Sinner stepped to the side in a way that, if he were anyone else, would make me think he was shielding me with his body. "Go where?"

"You're going back with the others. Make it fast or I'll drag you both there myself."

I bit back a scoff. *As if he could.*

The cell clanked open with a loud bang, then he waved an arm, impatiently motioning for us to exit. Sinner didn't move. He didn't even flinch, actually, until I stepped forward and put a small hand on his back.

He snapped to life and stepped forward, breaking our connection, without bothering to give me a glance.

I followed him out of the tiny cell.

Back to hell.

At least we wouldn't be trapped in a four-by-four space any longer.

We were led silently through the tunnels, and within minutes, we stood outside the massive, fortified door that led to the dungeon.

The dungeon that was slowly starting to feel like home.

"Welcome back," the guard sneered.

It took every ounce of strength I had—which, admittedly, wasn't much—to control the urge to punch him square in the face.

As the door opened and several familiar faces turned our way, I was hit with a strange sense of relief.

But Sinner was as tense as ever.

A few steps in, he stopped in his tracks, nearly making me run directly into him.

Hands on my hips, I glared up at him. What the hell was his problem?

Carter and Leon, walking side by side, approached. "Where have you been? We thought you were dead!"

"Director wanted to run some tests on us," Sinner said. "But we're back now."

"Tests?" Carter crossed his arms over his chest, chin tilted up. "What kind of tests?"

I kept my focus fixed on a spot on the floor between us, hoping the guys wouldn't ask me directly. Sinner could handle it.

"Tests you don't need to concern yourselves with."

Carter laughed. "What? You two fuck or something? Did Director send you back here so you could finally share?"

Between one blink and the next, black smoke erupted from Sinner's chest and wrapped around Carter's neck, then his torso, until his entire body was bound tight.

Shit. Sinner had *officially* lost his cool.

sinner

I was in no mood for games.

Leaving that incredibly small room was a blessing, yes, but returning to the place where dozens of men could look at what was mine?

Especially so soon after I had her squirming for me?

Call it an absurd protectiveness triggered by the upcoming claiming. But I had no intention of sharing anything.

And Carter clearly hadn't learned his lesson.

"Sinner, stop!"

Oh, Athena. She thought she could stop me, but the sound of her voice only made me squeeze harder. I called on more of my magic—the dark demons crawling within me—and pushed them toward Carter. I had only one motive.

Destroy him.

I would have, too. I was drinking up the way his eyes widened with panic until they nearly burst.

But when a strong hand fell to my shoulder, accompanied with another scream from Athena, I startled and pulled my magic back a fraction.

Leon stood beside me, doing his best to rip me away. "Don't do this, man," he pleaded. "She's going to make you regret it. You know she will. He isn't worth it."

Athena stood beside him, hair wild and alive.

Fuck. Leon was right. Director hated it when we used our magic down here. She'd made that clear to me on more than one occasion.

With a grunt, I released Carter, letting him fall to the ground, where he writhed, gasping for air.

"Fine. But keep your friend in check," I said as I stormed away. If I didn't put space between us, I'd end up finishing the fucker off. "I won't show mercy like this again."

Athena stumbled after me, grasping my bicep with both hands.

I stopped and spun around so fast she lost her balance. "Fuck." I steadied her. "I can't have these men thinking they can put their hands on you whenever they want."

"Why?" she pushed, shaking loose of my hold. "Why do you care?"

Instead of brushing her off like I should have, instead of storming off and cooling down in the showers for a fucking change, I closed the space between us and cupped her face, tilting her chin up.

I could have kissed her. Fuck, I *would* have. I hated her, but I wanted her. And that made me hate myself more than anything.

"I care because you're mine. And now that I've had a taste of you, I don't think I can let you out of my sight for a second. So do what I say. It took all my willpower to keep myself in check the last time. I'm not sure I can do it again."

Her mouth opened and closed, but all that escaped her was a tiny squeak. I loved it when she was speechless. I loved it even more than when she was annoying the living shit out of me with her words.

"They already think we're together," she finally breathed. "Nobody is going to try anything."

Every mystic in this place was watching us now. They really did think we had fucked, and maybe that misconception would benefit me. Maybe that would make the others think twice before doing anything stupid.

I wanted to believe it. But I didn't trust it. Not for a second.

So I took advantage of the situation. I lowered my head and moved in until my lips were only a breath away from hers. She didn't argue or pull back. Maybe she understood that this was for her protection, too. "Good," I whispered. "Let them think that."

Before I could do something really stupid like actually brush my lips against hers, I pulled away and stormed to my cot.

It was empty, thank god, but when I realized Mags's was too, my chest tightened, making it hard to breathe. "Hey," I called to Leon, who stood near the wall. "Have you seen Margaret?"

He shrugged, his expression morphing into one of pity

that made me want to unleash my shadows again. "She never came back after the ball, man. I don't know what happened."

My stomach sank. I still didn't trust Athena, but all I could do now was hope that she really had made a deal to get my sister out of here. I couldn't consider the other option—that they had gotten rid of her. That they no longer saw her as useful.

"All right. Thanks." I sat on the stiff bed—thankful I wouldn't spend a third night on the cold floor—and kicked my shoes off. I needed a shower. I needed food.

But right now? Right now, I needed sleep.

Before I allowed my eyes to close, I waited until Athena slowly—sheepishly—made her way to the bed she'd shared with Mags. She didn't look at me, but she didn't look at anyone else, either.

Smart girl.

She mimicked my movements, obviously also exhausted by the excursion we'd taken from hell. I tried to wait until she fell asleep. Tried to wait until her breathing slowed.

But somewhere in it all, I drifted into the darkness.

"WAKE UP."

I jolted awake, covered in sweat. My nightmare only got worse when I discovered that I was surrounded by four armed guards.

Fuck. I didn't even hear the dungeon door open.

And when I found Athena in front of me strapped—once again—to that damn torture chair, my nightmare took a sharp nosedive.

"What's going on?" I forced out, my tone hoarse.

The guards parted, and Director approached my bed, a cocky smile on her face.

I looked from her to Athena. Her chest rose and fell with strong breaths, but her hands were bound behind her. Her pale skin was covered in a sheen of sweat. "Don't tell them anything, don't—"

The guard on one side of her smacked her across the face. Hard.

I had to physically restrain my phantoms. If I didn't lock them down tight, they'd have his head ripped off in a matter of seconds.

Whatever Director was playing at now—it was a test. It was always a test, always part of some twisted game.

Even knowing that, I'd do whatever the hell she wanted if it meant she'd let Athena go. And *that* was an issue.

"It seems we have a problem. Two problems, really." Director took another step forward.

My instinct was to leap out of bed, but the guards on either side of me held their arms out, silently signaling me to stay put.

The rest of the men in the dungeon were wide awake, watching the damn show. Guess this was the best entertainment we'd had in some time.

"What the hell do you want?" I asked.

"You broke the rules," Director said with a tsk. "You

think we don't know about your little outburst last night? Your show of power?" She tilted her head to the side, eyeing me like I was a damn toy to be played with.

Fury ignited in my chest. "I didn't do anything wrong."

She shrugged. "Wrong or right, you broke the rules. And you know as well as I do that there are consequences."

I stared her dead in the eye. Of course I knew. She'd used Mags to keep me in line all these months.

But now? Now she thought she could use Athena in her place? Is that what this was?

I surveyed Athena, who didn't struggle against her restraints but whose eyes lit up in defiance.

"If you're going to punish me for defending my claimed, then go on. Get it over with," I spat.

Director laughed, the sound causing my power to push against the inside of my chest. "Not so fast. After our little experiment, you have information I want. You both do."

My gut tightened. The hell was she talking about?

"This close to the blood moon, and with the chemicals we administered to you, you should have sensed it. So tell me, Sinner, what is the power your claimed has been hiding?"

Even from a few feet away, I felt Athena stiffen. The air shifted, the room grew still. She knew. She knew I'd brushed up against her power last night—even if I didn't entirely understand it.

I cleared my throat and forced myself to look Director in the eye. "I have no idea what you're talking about."

"Of course you do. You were closer to her power than

you even realize, Three. Tell me what you felt, and I'll let her go."

My heart raced, pounding wildly against my rib cage, my power simmering beneath my skin and pushing the edges of my control. Even if I could explain what I'd experienced with Athena last night, there was no way in hell I would tell Director.

"Tell me where my sister is," I demanded instead. "Where did you take Margaret?"

The bitch straightened, one side of her lips tipped up in a smirk. "Your sister is fine. She'll be fine as long as you cooperate with us."

What the hell was that supposed to mean?

Athena pulled against her restraints, clearly wondering the same thing.

"The girl is *fine*," Director huffed, as if annoyed by our concern. "You wanted her out of the dungeons? She's out. So start talking."

I said nothing.

"Really?" she pushed. "You're willing to risk not only your sister, but the well-being of your soon-to-be claimed? All I'm asking for is a tiny piece of information."

My teeth ached from grinding them so hard. "I already told you I don't know. There's nothing I can tell you."

"Right. Well, maybe this will change your mind."

The guard at Athena's side pulled a knife from his belt and jammed it into her thigh. Athena screamed until the sound echoed off the dungeon walls.

I gripped the edge of the bed, seething, fighting the urge to rip Director's head from her shoulders. It would do me no good. They'd incapacitate me before I could touch her, and that would only make matters worse for Athena.

The guard pulled the dagger out, positioning the tip near her neck below her ear. "Shall I go again?" he asked.

Director glanced between us, a brow cocked. "That depends. Sinner, shall we go again?"

I was going to kill her one day. And I'd make her death slow and torturous and fun. "Touch her again and I'll refuse to claim with her."

Her eyes widened. "See, that's not how this works anymore. You'll claim with her because your sister will die if you don't. This?" She pointed to Athena. "This is just for fun. We want information about her powers, and you're going to give it to us. You want to make life difficult until the blood moon? Fine. But we *will* get what we want."

My breath came out in pants like I'd already gone ten rounds in a fighting ring.

"But to make sure you're getting the message..." Director stomped over to the guard and pulled the blade from his hand. Then, with a grin in my direction, she dragged the tip down Athena's arm until a trail of blood stained her pale skin and dripped onto the floor.

"So far, we've been relatively nice to you, Sinner. You refuse us much longer, and you'll see what we're really capable of." She turned toward the door. "Bring the healer in. And clean this up. You know where to find me when they change their minds."

A hooded figure stormed in and fell to their knees in front of Athena. The feminine hands hovered over Athena's body, pouring magic into her, and her skin literally mended itself.

Athena watched, brows pinched in a mixture of confusion and pain. Delusion morphed her features, and her eyelids drooped as she fought against them.

Half the guards followed Director out of the dungeon, but the others stayed with the healer. When she was finished, she stepped back, and the man with the knife sliced through the rope tied around Athena's wrists, then tipped the chair until she crumpled to the ground. He stormed out, dragging the bloody chair behind him.

The healer was the last to go, hesitating, head bowed, focused on Athena. Eventually, she left as well, though her steps were hesitant, like maybe she wanted to stay and help. Like maybe, like the rest of us, she was tangled in the ropes of the Ministry, forced to do this work for her own survival.

The moment the door clanged shut, I jumped out of bed and rushed to Athena's crumpled body on the bloody floor. Her thigh gash was healed entirely. In its place was nothing but a light scar that matched the others. I quickly wiped the blood from her thin arm to make sure the healer had finished that one, too.

"Athena," I whispered, pulling her onto my lap. "Can you hear me?"

Her eyes fluttered open and she trembled in my arms. "Thank you," she breathed.

"Don't thank me for anything," I replied. "They stabbed you."

With a grimace, she straightened and tugged at my hold. I refused to let her go.

Instead, I picked her up and carried her to her bed. "Rest, okay?" I pulled back. "You'll feel better in the morning."

"Wait—" She gripped my arm. "They can't know."

I froze, willing my heart not to take off again.

"Did you really feel it?" she asked.

Swallowing past the lump in my throat, I forced myself to hold her gaze. "Feel what?"

"Did you feel my power?" Her eyes widened, enticing me to dive into their depths. She looked...hopeful, maybe. Or scared? I couldn't entirely place it.

"Sleep." I placed a hand on her cheek and rubbed my thumb across her sharp cheekbone. It was stupid. I didn't care about this woman. But this was for the best anyway. Every man here was watching us, and this would convince them otherwise. "We'll talk about this later."

I stayed by her side until her eyes fluttered closed.

Athena had a secret all right. And now I was holding tight to it right along with her.

athena

Everything hurt and I was dying.

Okay, maybe I was still alive, but honestly, dying might be preferable to this pain.

And whatever softness I imagined Sinner showing me last night was long gone. We'd been training for two hours now. He'd woken me up and forced me to eat. We'd been doing this ever since.

I needed to work my muscles and gain strength so the next time the cowardly guards who worked for Director decided to impale me—his words, not mine—I could fight them off.

"You're not even trying," he complained.

I wiped the sweat from my brow. "I can assure you, I am trying. But thank you for that constructive feedback."

I turned my back to him and gulped in one lungful of air after another. God, he wasn't even fazed by this. Since I'd arrived, he'd done nothing but lie in bed and read that damn book, yet he blocked punch after punch like I was nothing more than a pesky bug.

Or maybe I wasn't any stronger than a damn fly. No. I refused to believe that. I'd hold tight to my dignity and keep trying.

But it wasn't looking good.

"These guards are powerful, and they've been training their magic for years. You have to be smarter than them, Athena."

Athena. Every time he used my name, it sent a chill through my body. But I shoved my reaction down and turned to face him.

"I was *stabbed in the leg* yesterday, remember? Why are you insisting on turning me into a soldier today?"

"You were healed, weren't you? This is for your own good. Now, try again."

Yeah, I was healed. I vaguely remember the warmth of the healer, the same warmth I felt the first time.

And again, something about them seemed so *familiar.* After Sinner laid me in my bed, I'd had the dream again, the same one I had after the first time I'd been healed. That the person healing me was my sister, not a mystic from the Ministry.

But then I woke up, and any soft memories of sisterly love vanished.

Sinner and I worked in silence after that, other than when he'd laugh at my weak hits. For hours, he pushed me. He didn't ask me about my power, and I didn't ask him about what happened last night with Director.

If he thought he'd discovered my alleged power, he lied

about it. Why? If Margaret's life was on the line and he really had sensed something, wouldn't he be itching to spill what he knew?

I hoped with all that I had that Margaret was far, far away from the Ministry's grasp. But deep down, I knew better. Director would never let her escape when Sinner was still here. Not when she could be used to bend him to the Ministry's will.

So, I numbed my mind, focusing on the physical pain. I let my muscles ache, let my bones scream at me until I couldn't hear my own thoughts.

Again.

And again.

And again.

TIME MORPHED into one long stream of eating and sleeping. Director did not come back. The guards did not return to torture me. That was the tiny perk in this ongoing hell.

Sinner barely spoke to me outside of our training sessions. After a few days, my muscles started to get used to his tactics.

But it wasn't like that would ever be enough. Time was not on our side.

I had three days. Three days until the claiming cere-mony. Three days to decide whether I'd really go through with it.

The sinking feeling in my gut answered that for me. I

was in too deep. This was happening.

I sat on the edge of my bed and ate the dinner Sinner had kindly brought me. I'd argued at first, but like he'd been doing since I woke after being stabbed, he reminded me that I needed all the energy I could muster. We never knew what the Ministry would do next. Return with their blades? Pump sex drugs into the dungeon again? Yeah, eating this strange meal would definitely help in that situation. *Not.*

For reasons unknown, the air in the dungeon was thicker, more tense than usual. Everyone was on edge. As if we were all very, very aware of the ticking clock.

Sinner included.

I wanted to ask him about his magic. I wanted details about the extent of his abilities, what he was really capable of. But I couldn't bring myself to speak to him about anything meaningful after our night in that cell. I couldn't look at him without seeing the way his lips had been pressed to my thigh, without feeling his hands on my body. God, even thinking about it made me blush. I was constantly very grateful that this dungeon offered very little sunlight.

Sitting alone on my bed seemed like a much better idea.

When I wasn't sleeping or thinking about the doom looming over my head, I thought about Margaret. I missed her. I missed her so much that I actually hated myself a little for letting her worm her way into my cold heart.

She had to be okay. My sister would have upheld her side of the bargain. Right? Chest tight, I set my plate on the floor and fell backward, staring up at the ceiling with a sigh. I used to think I could trust Katherine, but doubt was slowly infiltrating my thoughts. The reality was, I didn't trust anybody.

I hadn't for a very, very long time.

Katherine had been my friend once. Really. But throughout our teenage years, we hadn't gotten along. The four of us siblings had always had our issues, but more so Katherine and me. We fought. My parents had been the type to sit back and watch the chaos rip us apart rather than step in, but I was fine with it.

I was a fighter. Always prepared. Always ready for conflict.

Katherine, though? She was sneaky. She wasn't the type to get angry and roll her sleeves up. No, she was the type to harbor a grudge for months. Years, even. One time, I'd accidentally ruined her favorite sweater, and she refused to speak to me—even look at me—for an entire winter.

When she disappeared, I assumed she was dead. It was easier that way. Though after seeing her—gifted with powers I never knew she possessed and working with the Ministry—I questioned everything. And now she, too, thought I was harboring some secret magic.

Was she right? Did she know more than she was letting on? Had she left so she could find the Ministry? Could she have really believed in what they were doing? Could she have known about the magic I possessed? Maybe she'd seen it, sensed it, and so she'd left to find the Ministry so she could turn me in.

My heart raced as I stared at the underground ceiling, my blood hot with betrayal.

My only living family member.

No. I was getting ahead of myself. Surely my sister felt some sort of loyalty toward me. I had to believe that Margaret was somewhere safe, being taken care of, being protected. At least she wasn't here.

Margaret was safe for now. And soon, Sinner would be out of here.

I would be, too.

The dungeon seemed so quiet now. Almost...empty. Now that everyone believed that Sinner and I were together, no one even looked in my direction. Mags would be proud. The last time I saw her, I was still terrified to even turn my back for a second.

If she were here, she would tell me to take a fucking shower.

I had traded the ripped ball gown for a pair of pants and an oversized T-shirt the night we were tossed back in here, but I still hadn't showered. I was no longer afraid that one of these guys would assault me. No, now the idea of being alone was too painful to bear. Lying in bed was all I had energy for these days.

But as silence grew in the dungeon, I knew this might be my only shot. The showers would be empty, so I might as well get it over with.

So I shoved myself up off my creaking cot and made my way to the showers for the third time since being kidnapped.

They were completely empty, just as I expected. I padded through the dimly lit space to the shower at the end—the one I liked the most—and pulled the curtain closed behind me.

I didn't leave my bra and underwear on this time. Either I had ultimately decided to give no shits, or my confidence had grown to a slightly stupid level. At this point, I didn't bother questioning myself.

Instead, I closed my eyes and savored the way the hot water slid down my body. I didn't even realize how cold I was until the steam filled my lungs and the heat brought my limbs back to life.

See, Athena? You're alive. You're breathing. You're even showering. Things could be much, much worse.

I repeated those words to myself as I washed my hair, then my body, scrubbing my thighs extra hard in hopes that the memory of Sinner would swirl down the drain with the suds. I didn't want to think about his body against mine.

But no matter how hard I tried to drown those images, there was no forgetting that we would be mating in three days.

Three freaking days.

There had to be more to the claiming, facets unseen that lingered between Sinner and me. Because ever since the other night, I could feel him. I thought I was losing my mind at first, but my chest actually fluttered when he was around. My body ignited, my senses alert to his every move.

It had to be his power. There was no other explanation.

That had to have been what I felt the other night, too, because it sure as hell wasn't mine.

I had no power. I was nothing. Nobody.

And these feelings for him? The desire to be touched by him? The need for more than just that touch? They were part of his magic, too.

Because I hated him. And he hated me. End of story.

Footsteps approached, followed by low male voices. I froze. Surely they'd seen me come in here. Surely they wouldn't try anything stupid.

They continued to talk as they entered, at least four voices that I didn't recognize. Then Sinner's joined in the conversation, sending an unwanted spark of excitement up my spine.

One curtain after another was dragged along its rod, the metal rings scraping in a way that made me cringe, then one after another, showers turned on.

Okay, maybe they didn't know I was here.

I wasn't sure which was worse.

How come every time I stepped into the shower, shit went down?

I held completely still, afraid of what a group of men would do if they stumbled upon a wet, naked woman all alone.

As I held my breath, they chattered on, clearly oblivious to my presence. "Seven fucking months I've been in here," one of them said. "If I'd known there weren't any women for me to claim with, I never would have agreed to this."

Another guy laughed. "Did they really lure you here by telling you you'd get to have sex?"

"Hey! It sounded much more convincing than that, okay!"

Laughter echoed off the dank walls and ceiling.

The noise drowned out the sound of my curtain being eased back.

My heart stuttered painfully as Sinner entered.

If I hadn't been holding my breath, I would have screamed. But before I could force the air from my lungs, Sinner shut the curtain and stepped under the stream of hot water, one hand cuffing my neck and the other covering my mouth, stifling any scream I could have mustered.

"Scream and they'll all come running, wanting a look. Stay quiet, be patient, and they'll leave in a few minutes." He said into my ear, his words barely audible over the falling water.

As the fear that gripped me when his big figure appeared finally dissipated and my body slumped, he removed his hand from my mouth. Instead of backing up, he splayed both hands on the wall behind me, caging me in.

"You have a serious problem with showers! And privacy!" I crossed my arms over my chest and squeezed my thighs together. Did he not have any respect for boundaries? Any class? I was completely naked!

Water beaded off his thick blond hair and rolled down his bare chest. He was shirtless—of course—his sculpted torso larger than life this close.

He bowed his head, water clinging to his lashes, and slid his attention down, down—

A laugh rumbled out of one of the other guys. He made a joke about the Ministry, then another man asked Sinner a question.

His eyes continued to wander my naked body.

For the first time since my visitors arrived, the room was silent save for the water pounding against the stone floor.

I shoved him lightly in the chest. "Answer them!" I mouthed.

As if pulling himself out of a fucking trance, Sinner blinked. "Of course." He cleared his throat. "Why else would I be here?"

His words echoed through my bones. He was a quiet man, he really was, but when he spoke, he commanded the whole room.

Shower curtains and all.

I didn't take my eyes off him. Not like there was anywhere to look, really. Aside from the very small space between us and his bare chest, it was just us.

"Two days and you're out of here," one of them said. "Are you really going through with this?"

Sinner brought one hand to my bare waist, letting his fingers brush the skin there.

I sucked in a breath. Damn my body for reacting this way. *Get a grip, Athena.* He was just waiting until the shower was over and then leaving.

He only acted like this because he was a possessive asshole. He'd committed to claim with me. That meant he didn't want to share. Nothing personal.

"Yeah, I guess I am," he answered as he zeroed in on the apex of my thighs.

In response, my muscles clenched tighter. Dammit.

He knew exactly what I had been thinking about before they entered. I was sure.

Because it's what he'd been thinking about, too. I could see it in the way he drank me in. I could feel it in the tiny tug below my belly button.

When he grasped my wrists, I didn't resist. Nor did I when he pulled them away from my chest.

I was at his mercy, and I didn't bother to fight him. I was a damn fool.

I waited for him to laugh or make a crude joke and leave. He did hate me, after all. It would be on-brand. But he did neither of those things.

He took a long breath, and I swear to god I heard his chest rattle.

The water was hot, but the cool air against my skin made my nipples peak. That, and, well, the few inches that separated Sinner's body from mine.

And when Sinner's massive hands caressed my body, I bit my lip to keep from making any noise. He clutched the curve of my waist with one hand, while cupping my breast with the other, teasing my nipple with his thumb.

Chest rising and falling, breaths coming fast, I watched his face, desperate for his reaction. I wanted to see how intoxicating it was for him to see my naked body like this.

Because I was sure as hell drunk on his touch.

As he palmed my breasts, hot water ricocheting off his

body, his friends remained completely oblivious. This was very wrong.

We should stop.

I should stop him.

But before I could find the wherewithal to do so, he lowered himself to his knees, and all rational thoughts fled my mind. He was tall enough that like this, his face was level with my naval.

If I'd felt vulnerable before, it was nothing compared to the sensation rippling through me when he was so close to my naked body.

Though he'd had his head between my thighs before, I'd still been wearing clothing. Hell, I'd even been wearing underwear, even if it hadn't been entirely in its place.

Here? I was fully exposed.

Nobody had ever seen me this way before.

And he knew it.

"Stay quiet," he whispered against my belly.

That was the freaking plan.

"Let me take care of this."

When he pulled my right knee up and over his shoulder, I nearly cried out. And when he kissed my lower belly, just below my belly button, my legs shook.

He held me up, his strong hands at my waist, supporting me, as he trailed his lips down my hip, moving from my stomach to my thigh.

God, I was so completely at his mercy.

I was so distracted by his hands that it took a moment to realize his friends had fallen silent again.

"Trust me," he muttered against my flesh, "she'll be willing."

Arrogant asshole. I lifted my head off the wall and scowled at him.

He didn't notice. He was too busy diving into my center. He licked me slowly at first, making my body jerk.

With a hand splayed over my abdomen, he did it again. His movements remained slow, restrained. He was torturous. Delicate, almost. He devoured my core with his tongue, sending me into a state that could only be described as euphoric. Each lick lit up my insides, and my body quaked. Thank god my leg was still draped over his shoulder. Otherwise, I would have fallen straight to the ground.

And then he added a finger.

Instantly, the building pressure sent me soaring. In seconds, I was ready to hurdle over the edge. But I was jarred from the sensation by the sound of shower curtains being pulled open.

His friends were turning their showers off and moving toward the stash of clean towels outside our stall.

Sinner didn't stop. As if completely unbothered, unconcerned about being caught, he curled his finger inside me and licked my apex again and again.

"You haven't had sex in so long, you've probably forgotten how it works," one of the guys said.

Sinner paused and smiled against my inner thigh until I shivered. "I think I can figure it out."

"Be careful," one of the other men grunted. "Who

knows how many guys got a piece of that while she was outside. She doesn't exactly look like a virgin."

Another scoffed. "That girl is insane! Of course she's a virgin! Who would come near a mystic like that?"

"An *alleged* mystic."

Heat rushed to my face and all the desire that had built washed down the drain.

Who the hell did they think they were?

I expected Sinner to lash out, to get pissed and attack the guy for his brash statement. But when I looked down at him and his water-covered lashes, he was still smiling. *Smiling.* He had never looked more dangerous.

"She's mine, now, boys," he said. And my entire fucking heart tightened. "Nobody else gets to touch her."

And then he returned to his feast, devouring me until I was ready to scream his name, ready to let it echo off every stone wall.

My heart raced in my ears, but I was still vaguely aware of the guys making jokes as they shuffled out.

Then, blessedly, the footsteps were gone. The voices too.

Until it was only us.

And when my pleasure reached its peak, I did my best to suppress the scream that ripped from my lips.

I was sure I failed.

Sinner didn't try to shush me that time. What was the point? We were the only ones left in the shower rooms, our breaths filling the small space around us like a privacy blanket.

"You still have issues with personal space," I added,

trying my best to regain some semblance of control over the situation.

He rose from his knees without taking his eyes off me, the water beating down on him as he loomed over me. "You think I couldn't feel you? Your need practically screamed at me."

My heart lurched. "It did not."

"It did. How else would I know you were in here?"

I opened my mouth to argue, but words escaped me.

"Right," he sneered. "This claiming is already changing us. It started the second we were both in agreement. Once it's over, I'll go back to staying as far away as humanly possible. But for right now, I have to handle these things when they arise because my power literally does not let me ignore it."

I grimaced at his words, wishing I could escape him. That stung. It didn't surprise me that he'd want to go back to avoiding me, but at some point during the last few days, I'd begun to think—stupidly—that something had changed between us.

God, I was growing soft.

"Fine by me," I retorted, forcing my expression to morph into one of apathy. "And next time you feel the need to join me in my shower," I leaned in so my lips almost brushed his, "don't."

I pushed past him and grabbed a towel. Yes, he'd seen me naked, but now that the rush of the moment had passed, vulnerability was creeping back in. Heat, confusion, and an annoying level of pain swarmed my mind, making me dizzy. Yes, this was all part of the claiming. That made sense.

But why couldn't my stupid heart understand that? What was happening between us wasn't personal. But it *was* our ticket out of here, so it had to happen.

As I dried off, I could feel his attention on my back. "What?" I snapped.

When he didn't respond, I spun to face him. He watched me, his eyebrows pulled together, his fists clenched at his sides, his every muscle coiled tight.

He shook his head and straightened to his full height. "Nothing. Not important." With that, he stormed out of the showers, finally leaving me in peace.

If only peace was what I felt.

sinner

Powerless? What a load of shit.

I could have been convinced that I'd imagined it the first time, but as she came undone in the shower, it was unmistakable. I could feel her. Her magic. Her...whatever the hell it was that pulsed within her.

Did she know? Could she feel how close she was to exposing herself to me? Or was she oblivious to the magic? Blind to the reality that it was seeping into me, becoming part of me?

Either way, I had to keep my distance from her. I nearly asked her about it in the shower, but she was too flustered, too...damn, I don't even know. I had fucked this all up by touching her. She hadn't been with a man before, and I was the last one who should be touching her, tainting her. Someone like me would ruin her forever.

And the more time I spent with her, the more I didn't want her to crumble into ruins.

That was a deep personality flaw I would be assessing

later. For now, I had to clear my head. My power buzzed under my skin after being so close. Still soaked, I stormed out of the bathroom, uncaring of who saw me.

All I cared about was getting control of myself. We were too close to the end to lose it all now. Though, now that Mags was gone, I'd considered turning the entire underground to rubble, taking all of these monsters out with me.

I'd considered it for a very, very long time.

But we had two days left. After that, I could make a new plan. Find a new path. Maybe I could even get the rest of them out of here before the next blood moon, before anyone else was forced to—

I stopped myself before the thoughts continued.

How many times would I have to learn that lesson?

I laid on my cot, soaking it in the process, and shut my eyes. I stayed like that until Athena's presence forced my eyes open again.

She was minding her own business, yet she commanded my attention. Controlled every ounce of it.

"You're staring," she whispered. She dropped her boots on the floor and lay on her back with her fingers intertwined over her stomach, head turned so she could effectively glare at me.

I glared right back. "No, I'm not."

"You are. It's weird."

"I'm not staring and it's not weird. I'm watching you so I know what you're doing."

"I'm lying in bed doing absolutely nothing. So you can stop watching me now."

God, she was infuriating. Even the taste of her on my lips irritated me, but it drove my power absolutely mad. I choked it back, pushed it deep, deep down, funneled away with the darkest parts of myself where I locked it up tight.

But Athena made those locks crack. Made those chambers of my soul slowly crumble, made the walls shake with a need for release.

And it was very, very dangerous.

I pulled my book from under my pillow and flipped it open. It was the same ragged paperback I'd pretended to read for months. The pages were torn and rippled at parts, but I scanned the pages anyway, memorizing the shapes of the letters. I'd never learned how to read. I wouldn't dare ask anyone here. But at least it gave me something to look at when every part of me wanted to look at *her*.

My attempt to ignore her backfired within seconds.

"What's that book you're always reading?"

At first, I ignored her. It seemed like a reliable plan. But when she shifted in her cot, propping herself up on her side so it was clear I had her full attention, it was nearly impossible to tune her out.

I tried. I swear to fuck I did. But she waited, her gaze burning into me.

"Nothing."

"Oh, come on. What's it about?"

I ignored her again for a few seconds, but she wouldn't let it go.

"It has to be more entertaining than laying here and staring at the ceiling. Please?"

"It's about people doing things." I flipped a page for emphasis.

She flopped back. That was fine with me. As long as she quit pushing. "You really are an asshole, you know that?"

"Trust me, I'm aware."

I scanned each line, wishing, not for the first time, that I knew what the story was about. I imagined it was a historic record. An account of a time before the Ministry corrupted the world, ruining everything it touched. It could have been a book about peace. A book about love. It could have been about any number of things.

Maybe I would've told Athena what the book was about if I could have actually read it. But, then again, maybe not.

Getting close to her would only make things harder when we went our separate ways after the claiming. My powers were already seething over the thought of it, pulling at my skin with the shadows that pulsed in my veins.

But she would never be safe with me. She would never be happy if she were chained to me.

It was better for both of us if she stayed far, far away.

A SOFT WHIMPER WOKE ME, and instantly, I was ready to fight, ready to kill if I had to.

But there was no imminent threat looming over my head. The dungeon was dark, and all its occupants were still asleep.

Including the woman writhing on her cot beside me, her head slicked with sweat. Her eyebrows were drawn together, and she mumbled words that sounded like *it wasn't me.*

"Athena," I whispered.

She didn't respond, only continued whimpering.

"Hey, wake up." I considered tossing my book onto her cot. Surely that would wake her up. But a pull in my torso urged me to go to her, to do more than simply wake her. It was the stupid claiming causing my power to want to comfort her.

Through the connection we'd established, I could feel her. Though this wasn't like before. This time, the desperation coursing through her was palpable. I could feel a chaos, a dark, looming energy that might have frightened me if I hadn't felt that exact darkness every day of my life.

So I did the exact opposite of staying away from her.

Silently, I pushed myself off my bed and made my way to hers. She was curled on her side, close to falling off the edge, leaving plenty of room for me to slip in behind her.

She was oblivious to my presence at first, still jerking against visions I couldn't see. But when I wrapped an arm around her torso and pulled her body to mine, whispering her name, she stilled. She wasn't fully awake, but the move distanced her from the nightmare. "Athena," I repeated. "It's just a dream."

Her heart thundered as she slowly made her way to consciousness.

"Sinner," she breathed.

"Sleep. I'm right here."

It was stupid. It was fucking idiotic. A girl like her didn't need the likes of me anywhere near her, but it put my power at ease to think that she was safe.

Almost instantly, she relaxed against me. The summoning feeling of the darkness that slept inside of her started to fade. I kept my arm wrapped tightly around her, my hand splayed across her stomach. *Sleep*.

She didn't speak again. Didn't ask any stupid questions. Didn't respond with a quick remark or give me shit about crawling into her bed.

She just adjusted her body against me until she was comfortable.

And for what felt like the first time in a long, long time, I slept soundly.

athena

I couldn't breathe as I sat on my cot and waited for the massive door to open. Our jailers would be here any minute now. The sun was setting, and tonight was the night.

The blood moon.

I'd never paid much attention to the moon before. But tonight, it felt as if the moon itself was making her presence known to every single person in this hell.

My body buzzed with anticipation. I had never been with anyone before, and Sinner was...he was surprising. When I met him, when he first volunteered to perform the claiming with me, I had been livid. I'd wanted to punch him in the face for daring to take away my autonomy. For daring to assume I'd be a willing partner in whatever he had planned.

Back then, I'd refused to let it happen. Because I'd always believed that all men were monsters, taking what they wanted by force. Like they deserved it. Like it was all owed to them.

Sinner, though, had shown nothing but...a strange level of respect for me. Yes, he ripped open my shower curtain from time to time and had a serious issue with personal boundaries. But the experiences we'd shared? The way he had pleasured me when I was drugged? When he could have done much, much more? It was hard not to be hopeful. Every instinct inside him had probably screamed for him to control me, to do with my body what he wanted.

Yet, he'd held back.

Was he entirely disgusted by me? Maybe.

But he hadn't once boasted about the claiming, he hadn't celebrated what would happen tonight, how he'd be given the opportunity to fuck me. How he'd be given the chance to get the hell out of here.

No, instead, he paced the dungeon near the door, ignoring us all. Not even acknowledging the men who tried to speak to him. Something else was on his mind. Something big.

I stayed on my cot, reminding myself to breathe.

There was no stopping this. No words we could use to convince the powers that be to reconsider, no deals we could make now.

We agreed to perform the claiming. Tonight.

In the crack of moonlight that filtered into our underground prison, I took in every sight, trying my best to sear every detail into my memory. Not because it had been a luxury or even a comfort, but because one day, when I was free, I would come back here and burn this whole place to the ground.

"Are you ready for this?" Leon asked as he approached, hands shoved into his pockets and his shoulders practically resting at his ears. His voice was quiet, but in the rare silence of the place, it nearly echoed.

"Is that a serious question?"

With a soft smile, he took a seat on the edge of Sinner's cot. If it were anyone else, the owner of that particular bed would've marched over here and punched him in the face.

But even Sinner had a soft spot for Leon.

"It's normal to be nervous." He cleared his throat. "I don't have any advice or anything, but I have a sense for these things. Tonight will be different."

"Of course it'll be different. It's the mysterious blood moon, and apparently, it's going to change my life forever."

Head shaking, he lowered his forearms to his knees. For a moment, he watched me silently. Then, with a quick look over his shoulder, he angled closer. "No," he said, his voice barely audible. "This'll be different from any other blood moon. Something is up. You and Sinner, I don't know exactly what will happen, but be careful. Tell him the same."

I wasn't exactly one for superstition, but the concern in his eyes made me second-guess my decision to agree to this. "I'll be careful. You know I will."

He nodded. "Be prepared for anything, okay? They might be the Ministry, but they aren't as strong as we are. They aren't as strong as *you* are. That's why they keep us locked underground."

I scoffed, my heart pinching. "We both know they're stronger than I am. This entire mess has been a huge mistake. They'll find out tonight that they were wrong about me."

His jaw tightened. "I wouldn't be so sure about that. I see it in your eyes—you really don't think you possess any power. But Sinner?" He peered over his shoulder quickly. "He sees something in you," he said when he turned back, his lips turned down. "He saw it the moment you stepped into this prison. That's never happened before, and we've seen a lot of ones and twos come and go since we've been here."

Adrenaline pulsed in my veins. "You think I have power?"

He gave me a smile so genuine it pulled at my stupid, stupid heart. "I know you have power. You just have to believe you do. Your survival is on the line here."

One lock on the massive door at the front of the dungeon clicked, then another. As it creaked open, the floor beneath our feet shook. Straightening, I squinted against the sudden influx of light.

Leon stood, and I did the same, trying my damnedest to be ready for what came next.

Eight guards—maybe more—stood at the entrance. Sinner faced them head-on, fists tightened at his sides.

I gulped once.

"Sinner. Athena. Time to go."

With a harsh breath in, I forced my feet to move.

I'd only made it a single step before Leon caught my arm. "Athena," he whispered.

"What is it?"

"If you get out of here, and you have the chance to fight them…" He swallowed audibly, his face darkening. "Make them all regret it."

Sadness washed over me, but I nodded. That was the best I could do. I couldn't trust myself with words. How selfish had I been? I was getting out of here. I actually had a chance to survive this mess, to live life outside of this disgusting dungeon.

Could these other guys say the same? Monsters, I had called them. But could I blame them? They were trapped like animals down here. Stuck. Forced to do whatever it took to survive.

When death stared a person in the face, it was a hell of a lot easier to face it as a demon than as an angel.

"Hurry up!" the guard yelled.

Sinner glanced over his shoulder and locked eyes with me, his expression one of grim determination.

Good. He hadn't given up yet, either.

If Leon was right, if something more than a typical blood moon claiming ceremony was going down tonight, we had to be prepared.

Sinner had to be prepared.

I gave him a tight smile and followed the guards out of the dungeon.

***

"IS THIS REALLY NECESSARY?" I asked. Not even ten minutes after being whisked away from the dungeons, Sinner and I were being shoved into the back of a van.

I really hated vans. Along with the men who hand-cuffed me and forced me into them.

This time, thank god, the guards didn't make any flirty, disgusting comments at my expense. They kept their wandering hands to themselves, and they sure as hell didn't look in my direction unless they had to.

I assumed I had Sinner to thank for that. He towered over every one of them, his broad shoulders and massive biceps making the trained soldiers look like teenagers.

He might not have noticed, but I did. They were afraid of him.

"If either of you try to use your powers, we'll shoot you both. No questions, no exceptions."

Sinner growled as he was shoved into the back of the van beside me. The two of us were positioned on a cold bench, and across the van, three guards sat, weapons at the ready.

The doors slammed shut, and the space darkened. "Well, this is cozy." *Yeah, humor was my coping mechanism, okay?*

None of the men in the van responded. *Tough crowd.*

We maneuvered through the forest, the van bouncing violently for what had to be thirty minutes before the path smoothed out. My shoulder bumped against Sinner's, and either of us could have moved at any time, but we remained that way. I was silently grateful for his presence, a tiny reminder that tonight, I wasn't totally alone.

We might've hated each other, but our motivations

were aligned. Survive, and fight like hell when this was all over.

Survive so we could come back here and kill every last one of them.

"Where are we?" I asked as the van came to a stop. "If you wanted to kill us, you know you could have done it back in the dungeons, right?"

As if in response, the van doors swung open. "Welcome to Director's mansion."

Holy. Shit.

"The ritual is at Director's mansion?"

Sinner let out a low groan, probably annoyed by all my chatter.

I ignored him as I was unceremoniously yanked from the van. He was shoved out after me, nearly face-planting on his way out. I hated seeing him like this. Restrained. Defeated, almost.

It helped, though, knowing he had a hell of a lot of fight left. Someone like him wouldn't go down easy.

"The ceremony will be at midnight. First, you'll be dining with Director and a few others. Now get moving. It's gonna take a miracle to make you two look presentable."

Strange. She hadn't had a problem with our appearances the dozens of other times she's seen us.

But I digress.

I'd never seen anything as beautiful as the mansion before us. Granted, in my twenty-three years on this earth, I hadn't seen many things outside of our small cottage in the woods. But this was...this was otherworldly.

The massive home was lit up, the white columns along the front showcasing the power that resided inside. The floor-to-ceiling windows added elegance, the tall peak at the center only making the structure look taller. There had to be thirty rooms inside, maybe more.

People seriously lived like this?

Sinner and I were guided—or shoved, rather—toward the front doors. Ten white stone steps—way too large to be useful at all, by the way—led to a set of doors that had to be two stories high and required two guards each to open.

If Sinner was impressed at all by this house, he didn't show it. I, on the other hand, caught myself literally drooling as we stepped inside.

"Oh my god," I whispered.

Sinner elbowed me gently in the ribs to shut me up.

The grand entrance was flanked by two spiral staircases. Everything was white. *Everything.* Statues and white stone masterpieces littered the edges of the large, open space. Once the guards funneled in behind us and those massive doors shut, all I could hear was the sound of my own heart beating, my own breath slowly fueling my lungs.

Two older women approached from the back of the house. "Sinner. Athena. Welcome to the Directorial Mansion!" Both wore modest clothing, a white apron, and a smile—which was the strangest part of it all.

Sinner and I stood and stared, neither of us speaking. I mean, were we supposed to say thank you?

"You'll be dining in the grand hall this evening, but first, we'll need to get you cleaned up. Come with me." One of the women stepped forward and grabbed me by the shoulders, ushering me to the staircase on the left while the other woman guided Sinner to the one on the right.

For the first time all evening, Sinner spoke, his voice rough with disuse. "Where are you taking her?"

The woman escorting him laughed softly. "She's going to bathe and change before dinner. You'll be reunited shortly, she's in good hands."

My chest tightened. Did he really care about where they were taking me? Or was it his magic making him possessive again?

Either way, I forced myself to give him a small reassuring smile.

We could survive this. We *would* survive this.

We didn't have another choice.

<hr>

MY FEW ATTEMPTS at conversation with the woman fell short. She was nice enough, but even that made me oddly uncomfortable. How could anyone working for the Ministry be this kind?

She bathed me first, insisting that she help scrub the grime off my body, before drying my body and hair with a thick towel. She laid out a few dresses for me to choose from, but they were barely distinguishable from one another. They were all much, much too fancy. Even fancier than the one I wore to the ball.

"I don't know," I groaned. "Does it even matter? This is all a big game to her, anyway."

Ignoring my comment, the woman picked up the dress in the middle and held it up to my naked body. "What about this one, miss? I think it suits you."

It was thin. Very thin. The slim silhouette was made of a single white layer so light it was nearly sheer.

But none of the other options looked any more modest. "Okay," I sighed. "I guess that will work."

She helped slip it on, oohing and aahing as it fit me perfectly. *Okay, maybe this was why she was so happy.* She got to look at pretty clothes while she played dress-up with prisoners month after month.

I supposed there were worse jobs in the world.

"Are you sure this is it?" I asked. "I feel naked."

The woman laughed as she twisted my hair into a loose bun at the base of my skull, leaving a few strands free by my face. It looked...effortless. I actually didn't hate it.

"You look beautiful," she whispered, her eyes on mine in the mirror. "Your body is a tool, miss. You must wield it as a weapon, no?"

"Hm. I don't exactly feel like a weapon. More like a rag doll."

She straightened behind me, placing both hands on my bare shoulders and angling in close to my ear. "You can be a rag doll if you wish. But you are a woman. You are smart. You are sneaky. They will underestimate you. If you act weak, they will see you as weak. But perhaps that is your greatest advantage."

She smiled again. This time, rather than creepy, her expression was a little rebellious. The twinkle in her eye ignited a fire in my chest.

"What was your name again?" I asked.

Focused on smoothing my hair back, she said, "My name is Lauren."

I dipped my chin, watching her in the mirror as she straightened my dress. "Thank you, Lauren. I suppose tonight could be a lot worse than it is."

She didn't meet my eyes as she kneeled in front of me with a pair of white heels. She grasped my ankle gently and guided my foot into one. "It could be worse, miss. You're alive. It could always be worse."

When she opened the door and gestured for me to step through it, I did so with my head held high.

I was nobody's rag doll.

But a weapon? I rather liked that.

sinner

I hated being touched. I hated being looked at. I hated being perceived in any meaning of the word.

The woman silently bathed and dressed me, ignoring every one of my arguments and grunts of refusal.

Finally, *fucking* finally, I was dressed in a loose-fitting white linen suit, a thin shirt, and soft white shoes that matched the ridiculous outfit.

All white? Wasn't that supposed to signify purity or peace?

I was neither of those things. As I surveyed myself in the mirror, it took effort not to laugh.

Who the fuck was the asshole looking back at me?

The woman in charge of dressing me might have seen a big man with too-long hair. Or maybe she saw a guy who'd elevate the Ministry's magic by performing the claiming ritual under the blood moon.

But I saw a monster being held in chains. A demon decaying under the surface.

A man drowning.

"You ready, sir?" She motioned toward the door.

No. I would never be ready for this. I sure as hell wasn't ready for what I knew would come after this.

Regardless of how much I dreaded what would happen after this preposterous dinner, Athena had to feel worse. She was good at masking her emotions, almost as good as I was, but instead of shutting down, she covered her emotions with humor and attitude.

I'd been convinced by the act at first. It took weeks to finally see what was truly beneath the surface. And like me, she was hiding plenty.

Not just secrets I hadn't pulled from her yet, but true, genuine fear.

"Let's get this over with." I sighed as I strode across the pristine floor in my ridiculous white shoes.

In the hallway, I was stopped in my tracks.

Athena stood in front of me, having just stepped out of her room as well. And my god...

Like this night wasn't already going to be painful enough. She wore a white dress—no surprise there—that slouched off her shoulders, exposing her collarbones. The fabric fit her slim body perfectly, like a second skin, as the almost sheer fabric drifted to the floor.

And her hair was pulled back. I had never seen it pulled entirely off her neck before.

She looked incredible, her face clean of any unnecessary makeup, thank fuck. She didn't need it. Never would.

She stared back at me, too, focus drifting up and down, probably cataloging my ridiculous outfit.

I made my way to her, forcing myself not to fawn over her as I approached.

"The grand hall is this way," one of the maids said as they shuffled slowly ahead of us, giving us a few feet of space.

In a move more than a little uncharacteristic for me, I held my arm out to Athena.

Her eyes widened. "You choose now to become chivalrous?"

"There aren't exactly many other opportunities to be chivalrous around here, Athena."

She inhaled sharply at the sound of her name. I loved it when she reacted like that. Like she was excited, almost.

People were rarely excited by me. Afraid, maybe. Disappointed, absolutely. But never excited.

"All right, then." She looped her arm through mine and we slowly followed after the maids. "I guess the only way out of this is straight through it."

"It'll all be over soon." I kept my posture as stiff as possible as the heat of her body radiated from her. "As long as there are no surprises at dinner, anyway."

"Can't you feel it?" Athena whispered as we continued through the ridiculous maze that was the mansion.

We came to halt in front of massive doors that I could only assume led to the grand hall. "Feel what?"

Brown eyes wide, she peered up at me, and I saw it again. The fear. "Something isn't right."

Before I could ask her what the hell she was talking about, the doors were opened, and we were suddenly the center of attention.

The grand hall was the first thing I had seen in this place that was not white. Not even close.

The entire room—walls, table, chairs, floor—was gold.

Director rose from her seat at the head of the long table. Behind her, several guards were stationed. A man I didn't recognize sat toward the other end of the table, and then—

My heart stopped beating.

Mags.

It took everything in me to remain calm, to keep my composure. She stood from her chair, too, just as Director did. She wore a modest white gown that made her look younger than she really was. Her cheeks were pink and her skin was clear, not covered in dirt like she had been the last time I saw her. She looked... She looked healthy.

The woman beside her stood, catching my attention, and my gut clenched. Athena's sister. The one from the ball.

Beside me, Athena froze, her lips parted and her focus scouring the room. Like me, she was taking it all in. Assessing the situation. Waiting for the other shoe to drop.

"Welcome, welcome!" Director waved, ushering us inside. Athena tightened her hold on my bicep. "Come in! Sit down! You're just in time. The food will be served momentarily."

I led Athena to the two open chairs directly across from Mags and Athena's sister. I took the seat closest to Director, leaving my counterpart to sit next to the man I didn't recognize.

Every cell in my body told me this was wrong.

As soon as we were seated, the rest of the group settled as well.

"Margaret," I said as my sister shifted in her chair. "What are you doing here?"

It was impossible to keep anger from dripping from my words. She was supposed to be gone. Safe. Very, very far from here.

She cleared her throat. "Since Director pulled me from the dungeons, I've been staying here in the mansion. It's beautiful, isn't it?"

I scanned my sister's face, looking for any sign of trouble. She was a ball of fire when she needed to be, but she was smart. She would play any part if she needed to.

The question was, was this a role? And if so, what was the point?

When I didn't respond, Athena spoke up. "I thought you would be long gone by now. That was part of the deal, wasn't it?"

Her eyes were not on Mags, but on Katherine.

Katherine's fake smile tightened, the thin skin around her eyes crinkling. "She's out of the dungeons, isn't she?"

Director's shrill voice echoed off the gold walls as she interrupted, "I was surprised when Katherine told me of the deal you made. You'd perform the claiming willingly if it meant this girl could go free, do I have that right?" She assessed Athena, her expression calculating.

I choked back the trepidation trying to crawl its way up my throat. My sister was not a toy to be played with. She sure as hell did not belong to the Ministry.

"It was a tempting deal," she said. "It really was. But

you're a smart girl, aren't you, Athena?" Director leaned forward until her elbows were resting on the table.

I clenched my fists to keep from punching her in the mouth.

"I'm sure you can understand why I need Margaret here to stay with us."

Anger and panic radiated from Athena, soaking into me the way her power had the other night, as if our connection allowed the easy transfer. It only compounded my own fury. Betrayal. Resentment.

"You lied to me," she whispered, turning her attention back on her sister.

"No, I didn't. I told you I would try, and I did. This is a much better arrangement for her than—"

"I'm fine, Athena!" Mags zeroed in on her. "I'm fine here. It really has been nice. Much nicer than that dark place." She swallowed audibly. "But I did miss you two."

Director smiled, though the expression didn't reach her eyes. "Yes, she did. It's why I wanted us all to share this meal. Now, I assume we can all behave ourselves long enough to do that, can't we?"

Athena took a shaking breath. Mags's eyes were still on mine, a silent message playing beneath her small smile. *Behave.*

Yeah, I wasn't much for following rules.

But they still had my sister. *They still had my fucking sister.*

"Well." I cleared my throat. "It is nice to see you again, Mags. I suppose this is a nicer arrangement. How long do you plan on staying?"

Staying. As if she had the choice.

Mags shrugged, eyes darting between me and Director.

"She'll stay until we know we can trust you."

Hackles rising, I stared Director down. "You can't trust me?"

She gave me a condescending smile. God, I hated her. "No, I can't. You say you'll perform the claiming tonight, but as the only unclaimed three in our arsenal, measures must be taken. You understand, right?"

Thank god the guards chose that moment to pour wine into our glasses. Without the interruption, I might have actually exploded.

I forced myself to look at my sister. If I looked at Director any longer, there's no telling what I'd do with the knife on the table in front of me. Then I continued to survey the people around the table. When I stopped on the unfamiliar man, I frowned. "And who is he?"

Next to me, Athena picked up her wine and gulped, her whole being radiating tension.

"This is Benedict. Katherine's claimed. The two of them are here to walk you through the ceremony."

I tried to bite my tongue. But I'd never been good at keeping my opinions to myself. "We need teachers? Really? I think we can figure it out for ourselves."

Director did not look amused.

"It's actually more complicated than you think," Katherine added.

The woman was so clearly nothing like her sister. She was the kind of woman who instantly made me put my guard up. I wasn't exactly sure what it was that made me distrust her. It could have been her smile—clearly fake. Clearly rehearsed. What the fuck was there to smile about here?

Or maybe it was the way she looked at Athena.

They were sisters. I would die for my sister. Literally. But her expression was full of calculation rather than fondness when she looked at her sibling.

I didn't know Athena well. But I knew she wasn't the type to be this cold to her own blood. Especially the only family she had left.

"More complicated?" I repeated. "How so?" I fought the urge to reach for my own wineglass.

Katherine cleared her throat and looked down to her lap.

"That's what we'd like to talk to you about, actually," Director spoke. "It's more than simply being together physically. There's an aspect of magic sharing that you'll need to be prepared for."

"Magic sharing? What are you talking about?" Athena asked.

"Since you've agreed to perform the ritual, that means that when the blood moon reaches its apex, you will feel a pull. A summoning of your magic, of your partner's magic. It's so the powers inside you can combine."

"And what if I don't have any magic?" she asked.

Mags's lips kicked up for a fraction of a second. See? I wasn't the only one confident that she was hiding something. Something powerful.

"Whatever magic you do or do not possess, it will open

itself to him, but only if you willingly merge. Your magic will not betray your intentions."

That was a fucking lie. My magic had betrayed my intentions twice already, and it had come damn close on many other occasions. Even seeing Athena in that dress had my power ready to betray my every command.

"Then what?" I asked. "When it's over, we'll be normal again?"

Director's gaze hardened. "You will never be normal again, Sinner. This ceremony will make you unstoppable. You will unleash a new level of power within yourself. Your abilities will be stronger than you ever expected they could be."

"But I'm already a tier three. How could I possibly become more powerful?"

"You are an *unclaimed* three. A claimed three could tear you up on the battlefield."

The words fell across the table, making my heart lurch. "And the battlefield? That's where we'll go next?"

One servant after another appeared, each with a tray of food. The smell immediately had my stomach churning.

"We'll discuss all that later," Director said, waving to the group of people hovering near the door that likely led to the kitchen. "Once it's all done."

Done. Like it was that easy. I would be stealing Athena's innocence tonight. There was no end to that.

It would haunt me forever.

"May I use the bathroom?" Without waiting for Director to reply, I pushed my ridiculous gold chair back and made my way to the door.

The guards reached for their guns as I approached, but Director said, "Let him go," and they parted for me.

One of them pointed to a door on the left side of the hall, and as I shuffled that way, he followed.

I scoffed. It's not like I could escape. There were at least a dozen guards here, and my sister was seated next to the woman pulling all the strings.

I wasn't going anywhere without her.

What I needed was a new plan.

Just as I placed my hand on the bathroom door, a high-pitched voice called out.

"Elijah, wait!"

I turned and frowned at my sister, who was running down the hall. "What are you doing?"

She stopped in front of me, panting, her cheeks flushed. The smile she'd been holding since the moment I saw her fell. "I know what you're worried about."

"Really? Aside from this fucking claiming bullshit, I now have to worry about getting you out of here. You were supposed to be gone, Mags! Far away. Somewhere peaceful! Happy!"

"You worry about me too much," she said, chin lifted. "I'm fine. I'll *always* be fine." She glanced over her shoulder at the guards standing a few feet away murmuring to one another. "I know why you don't want to do this. But Athena's strong, okay? She can handle it."

My chest tightened, and I turned away. "I don't know what you're talking about."

She gripped my arm, stopping me. "Yes, you do. Just like I know what used to happen with you and Father."

Head hanging, I cursed. "You weren't supposed to know about that, Mags. You were never supposed to know."

"I understand that you love me and you're trying to protect me. But I want to protect you too, okay?" She took a deep breath. "Athena is different. And if it helps at all, I think she likes you."

Her words were like a knife to my chest. "No, she doesn't. And even if she did, it wouldn't make what I have to do to her tonight any better. It's vile."

"It's survival. She'll see it that way, too."

Fuck. Survival? I didn't want to make my first time with Athena about surviving. I wanted it to be about...about literally anything else.

I blew out a breath, my entire being deflating. "Go back to dinner. I'll be out in a few minutes."

Mags frowned at me, her deep blue eyes glassy with concern. It wasn't the least bit surprising. She always worried, and it fucking gutted me. I was her big brother. I was supposed to be the one worrying.

She cared too much. It was why she had been so damn nice to Athena when she showed up in those dungeons. It was why she cared about our parents. Why she still thought there was even an ounce of me that was worth redemption after what I'd done.

I stood in the white bathroom for a minute or two, slowly willing myself to rein in my power. If my phantoms took over tonight, there would be no turning back.

I had to control myself. For Mags. For Athena.

When had I become so damn sensitive?

Once my breathing was steady and my heartbeat had slowed, I made my way back to the dining hall.

As I approached, the guards were all rushing forward.

And when a scream tore through the air, it took everything in me to keep my phantoms from exploding out of me. Because that scream. Fuck.

It was Athena.

Though, as I breathed through the panic, I realized it was more of an angry howl. I shoved past two of the guards and burst into the dining hall.

Just in time to see Athena throw her knife across the table at her sister.

Shit.

athena

"YOU LIAR!" The small golden knife left my hand before I could even consider choosing peace in this situation.

It impaled her thin bicep instead of her chest. I'd have to work on my aim next time.

"Liar, liar, liar!"

She was lying. It was all fake. This was some sort of trick to get me riled up before the ceremony, so they could control me.

"Athena!" Director yelled.

Margaret sat frozen in her chair, lips pressed together like she was holding back a laugh.

I stood, hands splayed on the golden tablecloth, watching blood drip onto Katherine's white dress.

"You *bitch*!" she yelled. "I am not lying, and we both know it! I've *seen* you use your power!"

I picked up Sinner's knife, ready to throw that one, too.

What the hell had gotten into me? It was like a deep hatred I had buried for Katherine had suddenly unleashed itself.

And I was ready to fight.

Two seconds before the knife left my grip, a strong pair of arms banded around me and hauled me backward.

"You don't want to do this," Sinner whispered in my ear. "Not now. Not here."

"Trust me, I really do!" I reared back, fighting against him. But he effortlessly lifted me off my feet, restraining my arms against my own chest until the wave of rage had passed.

Director was standing now, holding a hand up to her guards.

Why? I had no clue. They could've taken me out easily, with the sheer number of them in attendance. Apparently throwing knives wasn't cause enough for concern.

"Calm down, Athena," she said. "Your sister is only trying to help."

Katherine was crying now, gawking at her arm and the knife still inside it. She had always been a wimp.

"My sister has never in her life tried to help me. Everything she's done has been for her own gain. Her apathy for her own flesh and blood has never been more evident than it is now, considering she's willing to help the Ministry destroy her own sister."

"You have this all wrong," Katherine said through gritted teeth. "The Ministry are not the monsters you thought they were. They're the only ones who can help the mystics!"

"And how would you know that, Katherine? What is your gift?"

She yanked the knife from her arm with a grunt. Then, as I stared at it in stunned silence, the wound began to heal itself.

Within seconds, the gash on her arm had closed.

Healing. My sister was actually healing her own damn wound.

Blurry memories of the healer who visited me in the dungeon flashed through my mind. The woman who'd always seemed so familiar, yet had never allowed me to see her face.

"Oh my god," I whispered. "You're the one who's been healing me in the dungeons! You were there!"

She'd seen me the day I arrived, yet she hadn't shown herself to me. And how many chances could she have had to—

"I was doing what I could to help you," she replied. "I'm *still* doing what I can to help you."

My heart sank. I should have seen it coming. "So, you really are mystic, then." *You really are one of them.* It was like looking into the face of a stranger.

"I am. And you're a mystic, too. After all that happened to our family, I can't understand why you'd try so hard to deny it. Open your damn eyes, Thena!"

Sinner had loosened his grip on me, though his hands still hovered over my body, waiting for my next move.

It was a smart plan. That gold knife was still looking mighty appetizing.

"My eyes are open. If I had used magic, I would know!"

"I've seen it!" Her voice cracked as a sob left her. It wasn't about the pain anymore, I realized, because her wound had completely healed. She wiped the blood away with a clean cloth. "I've seen it! You're...you're powerful. Just accept it!"

My heart pounded and blood rushed in my ears. What the hell was she talking about? She had seen it? That was impossible. *I had no power. I had no power. I had no power.*

"See?" Director said, her tone exaggeratedly calm, like she was talking to two wild animals. "Like I said, she's only trying to help."

"What is it?" Sinner asked from behind me, each of his words vibrating through his chest and into me. "What is her power?"

Katherine looked from Sinner back to me before she glanced down at her hands in her lap. *Don't say it. Don't say it. Don't say it.*

She was lying. Whatever it was, it wasn't the truth.

I had no magic. This was all so, so messed up.

"Did she tell you about the rest of our family?" Katherine asked softly, focus fixed solely on Sinner.

"About how they're dead?"

She nodded, her lips pressed together. "Yes. They're all dead."

"What does that have to do with anything?" I asked. "I was there when they died. I know what happened."

I was there when Mother drowned in the lake.

I was there when Kylar was bitten by the snake.

I was there when Father's heart attack stole him from us.

And when Jasmine's fever wrecked her body.

I remembered every damn second of the agony. And I had *nothing to do with it.*

"Of course, you know what happened. Considering your magic is what killed them."

If Sinner hadn't been holding my arms, I would've collapsed. *Liar. Liar. Liar. It wasn't true. It couldn't be true.*

I would know if I had used powers against them. I didn't have powers. I didn't. I couldn't have hurt them.

My vision tunneled. I tried to fight the pull of unconsciousness. I opened my mouth, desperate to tell them all that Katherine was wrong, that I hadn't killed my entire family, but the room spun—

And everything went black.

<hr>

MY HEAD POUNDED as I shook like the rag doll I feared I'd become. "Athena. You need to wake up." More shaking. Harder this time.

I blinked up at the ceiling. No, not the ceiling. There was no ceiling.

I sat up, my hands sliding across white silk sheets. Beneath it, a soft mattress. Sinner and I were in a bedroom, but...not.

We were outside. The bed had been placed in a small clearing surrounded by thick pine trees. And if I wasn't mistaken, there was an illuminated film where the walls should have been, where the roof should have been.

I watched as a single glowing butterfly fluttered across the open sky above.

"Where are we?" I asked, struggling to wake completely. "What is this?"

Sinner let out a sigh. "We're outside in the woods, but her mystics have enclosed us in some kind of magical room. We have to be under the full light of the moon for the ritual to work, apparently. These walls will stop us from leaving or running away."

A piercing pain radiated through my skull as I took it all in.

"Oh my god." As I rubbed at my temple, the reality of the situation hit me. Yes, I'd known what would happen tonight, but being here made it all too real. The moon was nearly at its apex, and we were sitting on this bed that was made for, what? For a fake, stupid romance that was supposed to merge our powers?

My heart took off at a sprint. Shit.

Don't freak out. You've already freaked out way too many times tonight.

"Oh my god," I groaned.

"I know," he added, his head lowered. "Stay calm, okay? Can you do that?"

His hair—the thick locks that had been perfectly slicked back for dinner before—was in a disheveled mess. His shirt hung loosely off his body now, the ties across his chest almost entirely undone so I could see a large portion of his torso. His ridiculous shoes were gone, too, and so were mine.

I nodded slowly and forced air into my lungs. "I can stay calm. I can do that. Panicking won't help anything, right?"

"No. It won't."

I closed my eyes for a few moments, and when I opened them, Sinner was watching me intently.

"What?"

"I need you to tell me the truth, Athena."

My stomach sank at the seriousness of his tone. "What truth?"

"Is it true?"

I stumbled over my words, unable to summon an answer.

"Is what your sister said about your power true? About your family?"

I shook my head, giving him a pleading look. "I don't want it to be true." The words were a whisper. "It can't be true. I couldn't live with myself if—if—"

"But if she's right..." He leaned in until I could feel the heat of his breath. "If it's true, then you're even more powerful than me. Powerful enough to get us out of here. Powerful enough to get my sister out of here."

I was already rejecting his words, head shaking. "I can't do it." I tried to match his whisper, but the words were too loud in the silent forest. Desperate for him to understand me, I clutched his arm. "If I could do what my sister says I can do, don't you think I would've done it a long time ago? Like when I was first captured?"

"Fear could suppress your—"

"I am *not* scared!"

He flinched at my words. He'd never reacted to me like that before.

I crawled off the bed and scrambled away from him. The forest floor was cold under my bare feet, and the cool night air that soaked through the barely-there fabric of my flimsy dress didn't help, either. "I just need…I need time to think about this."

He stayed where he was on the bed, head tipped back. "I'd assume you have twenty minutes. Maybe less. The second that moon reaches the apex, they'll force us to claim."

"I know. I know." *It was impossible to freaking forget.*

"And they'll hurt Mags if we don't. That's why they kept her. That's why they—"

"I know!" I spun around with a roar, my heart cracking wide open. "I'm very aware of what is at stake here, okay! You don't need to remind me!"

He put his hands up in surrender. God, he was only trying to help. I knew that. He'd been forced into this shitty situation just like I had been.

"You said you had a plan." I stepped closer, my voice lowered in case there were guards nearby listening to us. Spying on us. Surely someone was watching. "What is it?"

His eyes flickered with a rebellious light. "I've felt your power before, Athena. I know I have. When we were drugged, and again in the shower. They say we have to perform the claiming in order to share our magic, but…"

Holy shit. "You think you can do it without completing the ritual?"

His dark eyes locked on mine, his expression earnest. "Yes. And I think if you truly accepted the gift you wield, it would be even stronger."

My heart stumbled. "How would that help us, though? Even if I did have power, I can't summon it at will. I have no idea how to use it, how it works, anything."

"That's the thing about the claiming," he whispered, standing and stepping closer. "You won't have to know how to wield your power. I can wield it for you."

It hit me then. The most terrifying emotion I could possibly feel in a situation like this one.

Hope.

"That could work."

"And they still have no clue what your power can do. Sure, your sister prattled on about it, but they won't take her word for it. They have to see it to really believe it exists."

I lifted my chin and swallowed past the lump in my throat. "Can you feel it now?" I asked. "My power?"

He stepped closer and placed a hand on either side of my face. I shivered at his touch. My nerve endings lit up, urging me closer. My every cell was pulled toward him. Whether because of the blood moon, the ceremony, or the chaos of this day, I didn't know.

But I wanted him closer. I wanted more of him.

The sound of a mallet striking a large gong rang out across the forest, bouncing off the trees and startling me.

Sinner's eyes widened, but he didn't release me. "It's time."

"We have to do it." I gripped his forearms. "They'll know if we don't. If you try to pull on my power without the actual claiming, they'll know."

His smile matched the fight in his eyes. "I'm an excellent actor. Do you trust me?"

sinner

The plan was risky. If this didn't work, we would be punished for it, and Mags would be in danger. That alone made me consider ditching the plan entirely.

But if I gave in and did what they wanted, where would that put us? Would we ever be free of the Ministry's grasp?

Mags was tough. Far tougher than she looked. She would be okay. And Athena was a fighter. I would *not* be the one to take that away from her. Especially not like this. I couldn't fucking live with myself if I forced her to give any part of herself away.

I could already feel my magic reacting to her, the influence of the blood moon kicking in. This plan would work.

"We have to make them think we're being intimate, okay?" I kept my tone low, ducking closer so we wouldn't be overheard. "But I need you close so I can access your full power. Last time..." I cleared my throat. "I didn't try to touch it, explore it. But it would have been easy. I'm sure of it."

Hands still cupping her face, I ran my thumbs over her sharp cheekbones. Instantly, she softened. She always did, and it made me want to never take my hands off her.

"Okay," she breathed. "But I don't know how—I've never—"

"Don't worry." I bowed my head, moving in until our lips were almost brushing. "I'll take care of it. I just need you to open your power to me so I can access it. No more holding back, New Girl. No more hiding."

She swallowed, averting her attention. "What if you hate it? What if it kills you?"

Oh, Athena. My heart pinched painfully in my chest. There was so much she had to learn about me still. So much she would learn very quickly if what I had planned worked the way I thought it would. "I'll tell you a secret." I lifted her chin, forcing her to look at me. "Nothing can kill me."

When I kissed her, my entire being roared to life. I held her face gently while I moved my lips against hers. Guiding her. Coaxing her. She was shocked at first, still, but eventually she kissed me back.

And nothing could have been more perfect.

When she'd relaxed in my hold, warming up to the sensation, I slid my tongue along the seam of her lips, urging her to open. She did instantly, melting for me.

Fuck, I wanted her.

I had wanted to kiss her for longer than I could even

admit to myself. I had touched her, I had seen her completely naked in the shower, but this?

This was more intimate than sex. More personal than any orgasm I could give her.

Open up to me, Athena. Let me in.

When I bent down and picked her up by the waist, she wrapped her legs around me effortlessly.

Bed. We needed to get to the bed.

I shuffled that way, all the while reveling in the feeling of having her entirely wrapped around my body. She slid her arms around my neck while she kissed me back, growing more and more confident with each second.

When she pulled away to take a breath, I laid her gently on the white silk sheets.

Chest heaving as she caught her breath, she watched me, her dark eyes wide and her pupils dilated as I stood over her and pulled my shirt up and over my head.

I pulled the sheets back and waited for her to slip under them, then joined her, making sure we were covered. We deserved at least a small amount of privacy.

Athena spread her legs for me, and I notched between them, fitting perfectly, bracing myself with an arm on each side of her head.

Phantoms slipped out of my control, flickering around us.

She gasped, her attention darting behind me, but rather than fear, her expression was full of awe, just like it had been the last time she saw my shadows.

My power liked that. My power really, really liked that.

I kissed her again, more urgently. My power needed

more of her. I needed her full surrender if this plan was going to work, and she was still hiding behind walls. I didn't blame her. We were supposed to have *sex* in the middle of this forest while god only knew who watched. It was fucking creepy.

Then there was the bomb her sister had dropped on her. It was no wonder she tried to hide.

I pulled back, resting my forehead against hers. "Do you trust me?"

She whimpered at the sudden distance between our mouths. 'Yes."

That's my girl. "Good. Because I don't want you to think about anything else right now, okay? Just me. Just us."

She sucked in a sharp breath but nodded.

It was all the response I needed. I ran my hand down her body, then, ensuring the white sheet covered her entirely, I pulled her dress up her thighs slowly. Torturously.

That's what my power liked. It liked the way she sucked in a sharp breath the second my fingertips touched her thighs. It liked the way she arched against me, her body begging for more. "That's it," I whispered. "Close your eyes."

She did, her thick lashes fluttering.

"Now think about my touch and nothing else. Can you feel the way your body reacts to me?" I brushed my finger-tips higher, pulling her dress along with me until I had reached her bare hip bone.

A low growl escaped me when I found no material in my way. Of course they hadn't given her underwear.

Athena whimpered, which only made things worse.

Or, in this case, better. This was exactly what I needed to unleash my power. To set me on edge so I had no choice but to consume her, devour her.

"Yes," she breathed. "I can feel it."

"Good." I leaned down and kissed her neck, sucking gently on the skin.

She moaned, her back arching.

My stomach dipped as my magic purred.

More phantoms filled the air around us.

As I sensed them, I nearly pulled them back, afraid I would lose control. But I fought the urge, knowing I still needed more if I was going to help Athena and Mags.

I needed everything. My power *and* hers.

Fingers digging into her flesh, I moved my lips down her collarbone. She pulled herself against me, slipping her bare leg around my hip, pressing her exposed core to my groin and holding herself there.

Holy. Fuck. The heat of her seeped through the fabric, and I almost lost all control. Jaw clenched, I pulled back and inhaled deeply.

She kept her eyes closed, trusting me to do what I told her I would. The thought grounded me, brought me back to myself. I brought my lips down against her collarbone. I wanted to rip that dress right off her body, but that was definitely *not* part of the plan.

With a squeeze of her hip, I relished the way my fingers dented her flesh. Fuck, I loved the feeling of her bare skin under my touch. And apparently so did she, because a pulse of her magic shot through me, causing my power to jerk back.

"More," she breathed. *My god.* "More, Sinner."

"Open up to me. Let me in. I can feel you." I brought my hand down to her bare pussy, barely brushing across her skin.

Eyes snapping open, she sucked in a harsh breath and hooked her arms around my neck.

I pressed my forehead to hers and rubbed my fingers through her slit. She was already so fucking wet. Her body wanted this just as badly as I did.

But no matter how much we wanted each other, it wasn't right. She would regret it afterward. I probably would, too, though I was starting to think regretting anything to do with Athena would be damn near impossible.

I pushed a finger inside her and swallowed down the moan that rolled off her tongue. My dick was so hard in my pants it fucking hurt, but this wasn't about me. It wasn't about what I wanted.

This was about her.

More of her magic filled my chest. It warmed me, but there was something sinister there, too. A facet that reminded me of my own magic.

A darkness.

I choked back my shock as I curled a finger inside her, watching for cues as to what she liked, reacting to every whimper or squirm.

My power loved every minute of it.

"Oh god, Sinner."

"It's working," I whispered, my face buried in her neck. "It's working, Athena. Keep opening up for me."

She whimpered again, spreading her legs even wider and tightening her fingers in my hair. "Take it," she said. "Take it all. It's yours."

Though she was talking about her magic, a deep, primal part of me responded when she arched her back and pressed her breasts against me. She was mine. *All fucking mine.*

"That's it, Athena, that's it." Without slowing my movements, I brushed her clit with my thumb. I wanted her to drown in pleasure. To be overcome by it.

"I've got you," I said as more of her magic crawled into me like it was finding its home. My power stirred and shifted, shadows now filling the room.

Athena didn't seem to care. I had been pushing my powers down for so long, this finally seemed like freedom. *She* finally seemed like freedom.

And the power she was giving me, holy shit.

It was like nothing I had ever felt before. My phantoms roared, and I realized I had let out a roar, too, as the warmth of her magic pumped through my fucking veins.

She pumped through my fucking veins.

It wasn't until she reached her climax, wasn't until she was writhing and arching against me, telling me it was all mine, that my power reached into her chest, too, and gave itself over to her.

"ATHENA, CALM DOWN."

It took the space of a heartbeat or two to realize I was no longer in the forest. No, I was in Athena's mind. Her memories. She stood around with what had to have been her family. I could sense the familiarity, just like I could sense her emotions and her thoughts.

And they weren't good.

Darkness surrounded her—a darkness she couldn't see.

Katherine screamed at her to calm down, to relax, but Athena couldn't hear. Her attention was locked on her mother.

"Tell us the truth!" she yelled, her hands clenched into fists at her sides. "Why can't we go into town? What are you hiding?!"

"I'm not hiding anything!" her mother responded. But her voice was laced with fear.

Her mother was afraid of her? Why?

The small kitchen where we stood would be cozy, if not for the anger that poisoned the air.

"It is for your own protection," the older woman said.

"That's what you and Father have been saying for years, but it isn't true, is it? There's something else. You hide us here like fugitives! You can't keep us here forever!"

Her mother—fear and all—slammed her small fist onto the wooden counter. "I am your mother and you will obey me, dammit! I say you don't go into town, so you don't go into the damn town!"

Athena's chest rose and fell rapidly with each breath, her pulse racing in her neck. Rather than calming like her sister continued to urge, she was more worked up.

But her mother took a long, shaking breath. "I'm not going to sit here and listen to this nonsense. I'm going to cool off in the stream." She paused in front of Athena, eyes glossy. "If only you were more like your sister. Katherine has never had a problem following the rules—"

"Well, I'm sorry I can't be the perfect daughter that Katherine is, I'm sorry I—"

"That is enough," her mother interrupted.

"No," Athena spat. "No, I'm not going to shut up and sit down anymore. I want to know the truth!"

"I can't do this." Her mother waved a shaking hand, then stormed off, leaving a fuming Athena behind with Katherine.

Two silent beats passed. Then Katherine lifted her head. "You work her up on purpose. She's done nothing but provide for you all her life. Calm yourself down before you do something stupid."

If only it were that easy. Athena's anger was uncontrollable, unstoppable. It buzzed with something more than a simple emotion. It buzzed with something thicker, something tangible.

"She wishes I was never born. I know she does. Maybe I can't blame her, because sometimes I wish she were dead."

My eyes flew open, and all I could see was Athena. She was panting beneath me, her grip still tight in my hair as she came down from her climax. As I slid my fingers from her warm channel, her eyes locked on mine, and her body finally relaxed.

"Sinner," she whispered. "Did you feel that?"

Okay, so she had the strange visions, too. I didn't want to ask what she'd seen. We didn't have to go there.

"It worked," I said. "It worked, Athena."

"Okay," she breathed, though her brows pinched. "What now?"

I closed my eyes and rolled my hips, though I didn't allow my pelvis to connect with hers. But we had to continue the ruse. We had to make it look as though we were still continuing the ritual.

She got the hint quickly and tossed her head backward, moaning slightly. My cock throbbed again, but I ignored the sensation.

Instead, I focused on my power. It felt uncontrollable. Undeniable.

So I sent my senses out, like before, and urged my shadows to search.

This time, they easily slid through the magical barrier.

With the power of the claiming, I was made new. And with Athena's power now pounding in my chest, I was unstoppable. Outside the barrier meant to keep us contained, my phantoms immediately found the mystic using his magic to enclose us in this room and strangled him without a sound.

The luminescent walls disappeared. Athena noticed this, too.

"Did you just—"

"Get ready," I teased as I tugged her dress back down her thighs. "Now, we fight like hell. Let's go get my sister."

athena

Still crashing from the best orgasm of my life, I shot to my feet and followed Sinner off the bed. He was seemingly unfazed by the connection we'd just experienced. For now, I couldn't worry about that. We had far bigger issues to focus on.

His power...his power had literally burst through the barrier that held us in this room. I watched in awe as bodies fell from trees around us, guards who had been hiding in the darkness plummeted to their deaths.

Sinner was using his magic. Each time he did, there was a slight pull on my chest, like an awareness of his every move.

I understood it so clearly now. I understood *him* so clearly. What I had seen in those few seconds of euphoria...

It was nothing but death. Destruction. Pain.

Maybe we really did belong to each other.

He sprinted through the woods at a ferocious speed, not bothering to make sure I was following him. He wouldn't need to anymore. If he felt even a fraction of what I felt, he would never need to look for me again.

Considering the way he had practically consumed me with his own phantoms, he had absorbed much, much more of my magic than I had of his.

Shadows slashed out around us, shielding us from prying eyes like dark clouds covering the moonlight.

We were new. Stronger. Faster. *Fearless.*

I was not afraid as we stormed through the forest. I was not afraid for my safety or Sinner's. There were mystics all over these woods, yes.

But they were no match for us.

The Ministry had underestimated us. They underestimated how powerful we would be after we claimed.

From here on out, I'd never be used as a pawn again.

I was a weapon now. My own weapon.

As the mansion came into view ahead, Sinner's shadows brought every guard we encountered to their knees. I didn't have to fight anyone, I wouldn't have to. Sinner's power flared out around us like an animal with a mind of its own. If I didn't have so much adrenaline pulsing through my veins right now, I might have been shocked by it. Mesmerized, even.

But we didn't have time for that. The farther we ran, the more violently my bare feet screamed in protest. The rough forest floor tore at my soles, but I pushed away the pain and channeled the determination coursing through me. The strength. Power.

We were saving Margaret and getting the hell out of here.

My lungs burned as I pumped my legs, pushing to catch up to Sinner.

When we reached the small clearing around the house, he screeched to a halt. I nearly plowed into him as my feet slid against the damp grass.

The dark clouds around us tightened, as if they could shield us from weapons that may be pointed in our direction.

In front of me, Sinner glared at the balcony on the second floor, where Director held Margaret in front of her chest, a dagger to her throat.

"You make one more move and she's dead!" the bitch yelled. "One more move, and I'll slit her throat!"

Sinner held his hands out in surrender but the shadows around us did not weaken.

I was starting to think he couldn't have made them disappear if he tried.

"Let her go," he shouted. "She belongs with us."

"And you two belong to *me*."

My heart thundered so violently, I worried it would explode. I was awash in wave after wave of Sinner's hatred and anger and darkness.

I wanted nothing more than to slip all those sensations around Director's throat and squeeze. Tight.

Sinner snapped his attention to me, eyes wide in shock. For a moment, all I could do was watch him, confused by his expression.

Only when movement in my periphery caught my attention did I realize what had caused the reaction. His shadows had crept over the railing of the balcony and were slipping around Director's throat, hauling her backward, away from Mags, and squeezing until her face turned purple.

"Oh my god," I whispered.

"Athena," Sinner said slowly, clutching my forearm. "Whatever you're doing right now, don't stop."

My heart lurched. *My* magic was doing this? My powers were controlling his phantoms this way?

Margaret stumbled forward, away from Director and the shadows. "Sinner!" she yelled. "Help me get down!"

He took off at full speed for the front door. She couldn't jump from where she was. It was too risky. She would have to go inside and—

A body slammed into me from my left, my guardian dark cloud shattering as I was rocked to the forest ground with a thud.

"Stop!" Katherine's voice was shrill and desperate. "You don't know what you're doing!"

My concentration slipped, no doubt freeing Director. Shit. Shit. Shit. *Run, Margaret. Run.* I could only hope that Sinner would get there in time.

I rolled to my back, fighting for power over my sister. She had always been strong, but she'd only grown more so since becoming part of the Ministry. Her movements were sharp and fierce, but predictable.

She clawed at my bare arms and chest, but no physical pain would stop me. Not when so much was on the line here.

"Get off me!" I bucked my hips and shoved her off, then crawled on top of her and pinned her down with my body weight, pressing her hands into the grass so she couldn't scratch me. "Why the hell did you do that?"

"You're making a big mistake. You can never come back from this!" She thrashed under my grip but it was no use. She wasn't going anywhere.

"Good!" I spat. "How can you stand this? I know we've never gotten along, but working for them? How could you do it so willingly? Have you been brainwashed? That's the only freaking explanation for how you could possibly be complicit in what they're doing! Do you not see how insane this is? They're forcing people to mate so they can harness the power in war!"

An angry growl escaped her. "You have no idea what you're talking about!"

"Don't I?" Sinner's magic tugged deep in my chest, signaling that he was wielding more shadows. *Get her out alive,* I pleaded. *Get her out and run.*

"You're either with the Ministry, or you're against them. And do you understand what happens to anyone—mystic or not—who is against the Ministry?"

Fury boiled in my veins. "I don't care! There's nothing you could say to me to make me agree that kidnapping innocent people and forcing them to live like this is okay! NOTHING!"

Her expression shifted—only for a moment—from a look of anger to a look of sadness. But I wasn't going to fall for her tricks. Not again. Not when she had already deceived me on more than one occasion.

"You've been claimed now," she whispered, tugging at my hold. "You *need* Director. You *need* the Ministry!"

I slapped her across the face. Hard. "I don't need anyone. Certainly not you."

She laughed as blood filled her mouth. "Is that what you thought about Mother and Father? Is that why you killed them?"

My ears rang as if I'd been struck as well, and my mind went numb. "I did not kill them."

"No?" She laughed again. "It's amusing how far you're willing to go to deny it, even to yourself. You're a monster, Athena. You're a killer. And now that you've performed the ritual, your power will grow beyond your ability to control it. The only way to harness it is to be trained by the Ministry."

Somewhere in the distance, Margaret screamed, dragging my attention from my sister long enough for her to jab me in my ribs and flip me over, this time pinning me.

"You won't make it out alive," she roared. "You need the Ministry!"

I tilted my chin up, peering back at that damn balcony. The scene was mostly obscured by shadows, but I caught a glimpse of Sinner's toned body. He was still shirtless, his muscles rippling under the moonlight as he fought against three guards.

Margaret was fighting, too. She'd just landed an elbow to Director's side when Katherine dug her knee into my chest, pulling my attention back.

"I'll never help them," I gasped, barely able to take a breath. "They're monsters."

"They are?" She tossed her head back and laughed,

then glared pointedly at the balcony. "Look around you! Who's the monster here?"

The man slinging shadows may have looked like a monster to some, but not to me. He was a quiet force, a saving grace—

"Katherine." A man stepped out of the woods to my right.

She immediately sat up straighter and loosened her grip on me.

He edged closer, his focus fixed on her. "Let her go."

"What are you doing out here?" she asked.

As he came into focus, I recognized him. Benedict, her claimed.

Another scream echoed from the balcony, this time from Director.

"She won't understand!" Katherine pleaded.

Benedict stepped closer, eyeing me for one second before returning his gaze to Katherine. "We're leaving. Now."

"Don't." She crawled off me completely, as if she'd forgotten that she saw me as a threat. What the hell was happening? "You know what will happen if you do."

I pushed myself into a seated position, turning back to the mansion in time to see Sinner running out the front door, one hand clasped with Margaret's.

My heart leapt. *They made it. He had her.*

An instant later, dread swamped me again. We were surrounded. Dozens of guards closed in on us. We didn't have much time, not if we—

"We're leaving," Benedict said again.

Katherine looked at me with wide eyes full of fear rather than anger.

I stood and took off toward Sinner and Margaret, leaving the lovebirds to deal with whatever mess they were working through.

"Margaret!" I screamed, throat raw. "Sinner!"

Somewhere in the shit show that was this life, I had started thinking of them as my family. And that was absolutely terrifying.

As I was pulling Margaret into my arms, Katherine and Benedict caught up. I spun, keeping my friend behind me, ready to fight, ready to kill them both if they got in our way.

But before I could throw a punch, Benedict raised his arms, and the five of us disappeared.

sinner

I gripped Mags's hand like my entire fucking life depended on it as we fell through the air.

With a heavy thump, then another, we landed on solid ground like we were dropped from the sky.

With a groan, I snapped my eyes open to find Mags, Athena, Katherine, and the motherfucker who just...who just *teleported us.*

Between one breath and the next, I was on my feet and barreling toward him. "What the fuck do you think you're doing?" I wrapped a hand around his throat and squeezed, shoving him backward. "Where are we?"

He held his hands up. "I'm on your side," he choked out. "Those guards would never let you leave alive. Any of you. I got us out of there."

"Benedict is a tier two. He can jump through space. That's his gift." Katherine stumbled a few feet away, then bent at the waist and vomited. As she stood, wiping the back of her wrist over her mouth, she grimaced. "I can't say I approve."

I loosened my grip a fraction but didn't release him.

"Why?" Athena asked from behind me as she, too, found her footing. "Why would you help us? Katherine hates me. She was all for letting the Ministry use us as weapons."

Benedict gave Katherine a sideways glance. "Just because she is my claimed doesn't mean we share the same beliefs. She wasn't trapped in those dungeons. Not like I was."

I dropped my hand and stepped away, my heart thumping wildly.

"That was a stupid decision," Katherine said, her face scrunched up in disgust as she backed away from the vomit on the ground. "They'll come for us. You know they will."

Benedict shrugged. "They'll have to find us first."

"I have to say," Mags said, stepping up to my side. "I'd considered a whole bunch of outcomes, but this was not one of them."

The five of us stood in a circle, eyeing one another. The air was thick with tension, as if we were all considering which of our new counterparts we could trust. Then Mags started laughing. Actually laughing.

It was quiet at first. Somewhat restrained. But it quickly turned into a full-on fit. She clutched her stomach and bent over as laughter erupted from her.

God, my sister was crazy.

Athena giggled, bringing a hand to her mouth like she

could stop the sound. Within seconds, though, she gave up and laughed out loud. Benedict caved next. It was almost... refreshing? When was the last time I had heard a sound so light, so full of promise? It sure as hell wasn't during the months I'd spent in those dungeons.

Katherine didn't give in. Why would she? She was against all of this. She'd likely try to betray us again. Though what did it mean that she was tied to Benedict?

They were so different. He'd stepped in and teleported us out of there without hesitation.

Why? Why would he risk his own life to save us?

"We need to find shelter for the night," I said, turning away from the group of ridiculous children. "It isn't safe. Like Katherine said, they'll come looking for us."

The laughter slowly died, leaving me feeling only a little guilty for being the cause.

"I know where we are," Benedict said. "We're in the northern lands."

Oh, fuck. "You teleported us *halfway across Ashora?*"

He lifted one shoulder in a half-hearted shrug. "The power of the blood moon strengthens my gift. All I wanted to do was get us somewhere safe."

"Does the Ministry have other jumpers? Other people who can follow you?"

"Not that I know of," he said. "Maybe deployed, but none stationed with Director."

I scanned our surroundings, taking in the less dense forest. The leaves here were lighter, the trunks taller. They didn't suffocate us in thick greenery like the forest before.

The shelter was sparse, the grasses nearly reaching my knees.

"Where is the nearest town?"

Benedict took a look around. It all looked the fucking same. Months ago, I might have had a better sense of direction. But now? I'd spent the last several months trapped in a dungeon. I had no clue what was up and what was down.

Benedict pointed ahead of us. "That way. It won't be far."

"Great." I still wore no shoes. Athena, either. I was very aware of my lack of shirt, her lack of, well, clothes. Everyone else was dressed more appropriately than we were, but we all needed shelter.

Fast.

The others fell in line behind me as we headed in the direction Benedict claimed would lead us toward civilization. In reality, I didn't fucking know what we were headed toward. But we couldn't stay out here forever.

The Ministry would come for us. Nowhere was safe.

SILENCE. I never minded silence. I preferred it. Why make so much noise talking when simply *not* talking was far more enjoyable? Half the shit people talked about was a waste of time, anyway. A waste of breath, too.

For hours, we trudged through the tall grass in the darkness. The bottoms of my feet were screaming, cut and torn by the landscape. Katherine hadn't said a word since we'd taken off. Even Mags and Athena had been mostly quiet, only whispering every now and then at the back of the group.

For the first time in my life, this silence drove me crazy.

I actually sighed in relief when somebody finally spoke up.

"Wait!" Mags yelled. "Slow down!"

I spun around to find Athena stopped with one hand pressed to the trunk of a tree while Mags stood beside her, holding her up. "She needs a break. She's bleeding!"

I scanned Athena quickly, assessing her injuries. She had gone through a lot tonight. We both had. But where my feet were sore and raw from walking, hers were literally covered in blood.

"What the hell happened?" I asked, closing the distance between us. "Why didn't you say something sooner?"

"I'm fine," she breathed. "I just need a minute."

Her long dark hair hung loose around her face, stringy and damp with perspiration, her throat now bruising in the obvious shape of handprints that I could only assume belonged to Katherine.

Her, I would deal with later.

"We can't keep walking like this," I said. "Benedict, can you jump us the rest of the way?"

He sighed. "Unfortunately, I used every ounce of my power to get us out of the mansion. I've never jumped with five people before. It'll take hours to regain even a fraction of it."

My gut twisted painfully. Dammit. "Okay, we need a

new plan. You can't keep going when your feet are practically falling off."

"I said I'm fine," she argued, her eyes meeting mine with that same stubborn fire she'd shown me the day we met.

"I can heal her," Katherine stepped forward.

Athena was already holding up her hand. "Absolutely not."

"Don't be so stubborn." Katherine took another step toward her sister. "You clearly need it—"

"I said *no!*"

The group fell silent as Athena's words echoed off the trees. Katherine could heal her. I'd seen her do it multiple times in the dungeons, and we had seen her power at work during Director's dinner.

But Athena wanted nothing to do with her traitor of a sister. She sure as hell didn't want her kindness. That was a feeling I knew very well.

"Fine." I stepped forward and eased Mags out of the way. "Then I'll carry you. We can't be all that far anyway."

"Are you serious—" Athena's words were cut off when I scooped her up, but she clung to my neck and held tight. "This is ridiculous! I can walk!"

"No, you can't. And the more injured your feet are tonight, the harder it will be to travel tomorrow. Don't be stubborn."

With a giggle, Mags started back down the path. Katherine rolled her eyes and followed, Benedict stepping into stride with her.

"You're unbelievable," Athena whispered, even as she sank into my hold.

I basked in the feel of her small body as I held her to my chest.

"You can't carry me the whole way. You're not wearing shoes, either, you know."

"My feet are tougher than yours," I reminded her. "And you haven't seen *unbelievable* yet."

athena

Sinner and Benedict were aghast by how tiny the town we stumbled upon was. Katherine and I, though, had grown up in a small home in the middle of nowhere. To us, this place was huge. Yeah, I had gone with my siblings to the nearby market once or twice back home, but it wasn't exactly a town. Just a few nearby farms getting together to trade.

This? This was...this was incredible. Dozens—no— *hundreds* of people littered the streets, even now, when it was well after midnight. They laughed. Chatted. Drank. Shops were lit up, merchants selling fruit and meat. Strings of lights crisscrossed above the cobblestone streets, shrouding everything in a magical glow. Everything but me. The illumination only emphasized how scantily I was dressed as I was being carried through town by this man with no shirt.

So, yeah, that was great.

"This way," Benedict said. "There's an inn right up here."

I clung to Sinner's neck, trying my best to be as unassuming as possible. He'd had carried me for well over an hour without a single complaint. Yes, he was huge and muscular, but he wasn't a damn superhuman.

"Will you stop doing that?" he hissed in my ear.

"Doing what?"

"Stop trying to hold yourself up. You insult me by assuming I can't hold the weight of you."

"I'm only trying to help!"

"Well, don't." He held me tighter. "I don't need your help, I can manage just fine."

Fine. I relaxed in his arms as we approached the inn. Benedict held the door open as Sinner ducked into the cozy building. Margaret and Katherine were already inside, speaking to a young woman behind a wooden counter.

"We need rooms for tonight, please. At least—at least three."

The woman eyed us. To say we were out of sorts was an understatement. Sinner and I were barefoot, practically naked, and bleeding. Katherine and Margaret were dressed in white clothing smeared with blood. The only person who looked even remotely close to civilized was Benedict, whose white suit was covered in dirt but lacked the bloodstains the rest of us couldn't hide.

He stepped forward and pulled money out of his pocket.

At least someone here could pay. Maybe he'd be useful for more than teleporting.

"We only have two rooms." She sniffed. "It's a busy night. Take it or leave it."

Benedict rolled his eyes. "Fine. We'll take them."

After taking the cash, she handed over two keys. "The kitchen will be open all night if you're hungry." She eyed me and Sinner. "And try not to get blood everywhere, please?"

Sinner ripped a key out of Benedict's hand, readjusted his hold on me, and stormed toward the hall flanked by several closed doors. "Mags, let's go!"

"Where are you going?" Katherine yelled behind us. "I want to stay with my sister!"

"No!" we yelled in unison—Mags and me and even Sinner. Okay, that warmed a part of my heart that it shouldn't have. My new friends were protective of me. Call it the power of the blood moon or whatever, but it was actually kind of nice.

"We'll find you when we're ready to talk," Sinner hollered over his shoulder as he handed the key to Margaret.

Once she'd closed the door behind us, Sinner finally set me on my feet.

We let out matching sighs in unison. For the first time all evening, I let my shoulders relax. Let my guard down— just a little—as we were finally shut away from the noise of the town.

Even in our quiet journey over here, I'd been on edge. It was impossible to relax in Katherine's presence.

"We shouldn't trust them," I said.

Margaret had already peeled her shoes off and was

launching herself onto the large bed in the center of the room. "Your sister really hates you, huh?"

With a scoff, Sinner walked over to the far window. He looked out of it for a moment, assessing the view, before double-checking the lock and yanking the curtain closed.

"It's safe to say we can't trust anyone," he said. "Anyone outside this room."

I smiled. "Aw. You trust me?"

He arched a brow, giving me a strange look, one that unsettled my stomach. "Benedict turned on the Ministry tonight. Just like that. Why would he do that? Why now?"

"Did you have much opportunity to talk to him at the mansion?" I asked Margaret. "Or Katherine? Did they tell you anything?"

She propped herself up on her elbows. "They didn't talk to me much, but I did catch them fighting a few times. Doesn't seem like Katherine likes much of anybody."

"You'd be right. I still can't believe she tried to stop me from leaving. Is she really that delusional?"

Sinner shrugged. "There's got to be something in it for her. Maybe Director promised her something in return for your compliance."

"Maybe." My chest tightened. She was my freaking *sister*. My *family*. Sinner and Margaret protected each other. They'd die for each other. Sinner had practically torn himself apart when Margaret was in danger.

Then there was Katherine. She was indifferent to my suffering. She wanted to force me into staying. The anger in her face when she was fighting me... I didn't understand it.

But I'd figure it out. There was no way in hell I would let her trick me into working with the Ministry. Never once in the time they had us held captive did I consider it.

Burning them to the ground? Killing Director with my bare hands? Now *those* thoughts had crossed my mind.

The Ministry claimed to be helping mystics, when in reality they kept us chained and crippled so we'd be forced to rely on them to survive. And why hunt us all? Why scour the edges of the continent looking for us?

Power. Control.

They couldn't win the war without us. They'd discovered that a long, long time ago. An entire army of earthly soldiers was nothing compared to a small group of tier threes.

But did the mystics even want war? I didn't know enough to understand the consensus, but it was clear the Ministry brought violence to the gifted who were only wanting to live in peace the way we had been.

No, I would never help them. Not in a million years.

My stomach growled deeply, causing both of my companions to look my way. I put a hand over my stomach, not that it did anything to mute the sound.

"We need food," Sinner announced. "And clothes."

Ha. That was an understatement. I looked like a lady of the night coming in here dressed like this.

Hell, after what happened earlier tonight, I felt like one, too.

"Stay here," he said as he strode to the door.

I glanced at Margaret, expecting her to protest, but she was sprawled out on the bed, arms and legs spread wide, with her eyes shut. Damn her for her ability to fall asleep so easily.

"Are you kidding?" I hissed. "I'm coming with you!"

He spun, glowering. "No, you're not."

"I am. What if you see Katherine and Benedict out there? Margaret will be fine here as long as the door is locked. I'm coming."

Did I really need to go with him to find clothes and food? Probably not. But adrenaline still buzzed in my veins. I needed to get out of here. Needed out of this room, out of this damn inn.

"Fine," Sinner said. "But the second we find what we need, we're coming back."

I scoffed. "I wasn't planning on touring the entire town, if that's what you thought."

Pocketing the key, he rolled his eyes and stomped away. As he pulled the door open, his back muscles rippled. Dammit, the move was sexy. I was used to seeing Sinner without a shirt, but things felt...different now.

Even looking at him felt like a violation, like he could read my every thought.

The hallway was eerily quiet. No sign of Katherine or Benedict. My feet screamed with every step, but I bit my tongue and pushed through the pain.

"You shouldn't be walking." Sinner's voice was barely above a whisper. "I'm perfectly capable of getting food and clothes on my own."

"You haven't been in the real world in months," I reminded him. "I'm not letting you loose out there by yourself."

He turned in the dark hallway, his body casting a shadow over me. Electricity arced between us, even though we weren't touching. God, he was close. So close that if I reached out, I would brush against his—

"Don't trust me, New Girl?" The smile he gave me was the cocky, annoying one he'd graced me with a thousand times in the dungeon. The one I hated.

My chest tightened with a sensation I refused to believe was disappointment. "Back to the nicknames, are we?"

"If you're going back to being stubborn, then yes."

I crossed my arms over my chest and pulled myself up to my full height. "You don't intimidate me. Everyone else might be quaking under your stare, but not me."

He moved even closer. "No?"

My body ignited as he drank me in, lingering on my lips, then my neck. His gaze dropped lower and lower, and memories of just hours ago flushed my entire body.

Not only was my reaction a chemical one, but a piece of me I had buried deep, deep down, a piece of me I tried very, very hard to ignore, came to life as well.

"When were you going to tell me about that little power of yours?"

All my bluster evaporated, and I squirmed. "I don't want to talk about this right now." I took a step back and slipped around him, only to be stopped when he shifted his massive body and extended one muscular arm.

"You're going to tell me everything," he said, caging me against the wall. "Every last piece of it."

My heart took off. His words were more than a threat.

More than some masculine intimidation tactic he used to get what he wanted.

He'd seen something during the claiming. Pieces of me. My past. My magic.

My magic. Was I really accepting the fact that I did, in fact, have magic?

I gritted my teeth. Some secrets couldn't stay buried.

"Fine," I said. "Food first. And a fucking drink."

"YOU'VE EATEN," Sinner growled, breaking the silence that settled over us for the last thirty minutes. "Now start talking."

"Wow," I said, picking up a cold bottle of ale.

Sinner had found a spot at the back corner of the tavern next to the inn. For a crowded town, the place was surprisingly empty. Only a handful of other patrons mingled in the dining area, all of whom were on the other side of the space. Only a few people stared at our absurd appearances, but we were almost hidden in the back, and they moved on quickly.

These people had their own lives to worry about.

Taking advantage of the privacy we'd been given, Sinner pushed me to talk.

Fine. He wanted to talk? I would talk. He wanted to know how sick and twisted my life had been?

I might as well grant his wish.

I swallowed the liquid in a few gulps. "You should

really get a drink," I said. "After what we went through, you deserve it."

Sinner scoffed. "I don't drink."

"Really?" I arched a brow. "That's surprising."

"Why do you say that?"

I shrugged. "Big, tough guy who wants everyone to be afraid of him. I don't know. You seem like the type."

He lowered a forearm to the small table and angled closer, the intensity of his attention searing into me. "You don't know shit about me. You have no idea what my life was like before you met me. I'm not the guy you think I am."

I nearly choked on my drink. "Trust me, I know more than you think."

He stilled. "And what is that supposed to mean?"

Tension thickened in the air. He knew exactly what I was talking about. He had seen pieces of my life just as I had seen pieces of his.

"You know what I mean. I saw things."

"What. Things."

I'd never known Sinner to be a laid-back guy, but this version of him was slightly unnerving. He nearly buzzed with anticipation, but something else, too. Fear, maybe?

Hell. After what I'd seen, I didn't blame him.

"Tell me. Now."

I inhaled, then forced all my nerves away with a long exhale. *He has no reason to be mad at you, Athena. It wasn't your fault you were forced to swap life-altering memories with him during the claiming.*

"I saw you and Margaret. She was younger. Cute." I smiled, unable to fight the way my heart tugged at the memory of my friend. "She's still cute, don't get me wrong, but she looked softer." I shrugged. "I saw you. You were younger, too. Not nearly as strong yet. You were tied to a chair with your arms tethered behind your back."

Darkness flashed in his eyes. He knew exactly what memory I was talking about.

"And your father was there."

I breathed deeply again, waited for him to speak. To confirm that he knew what I meant. Anything. Instead, he stared at me, his face an emotionless mask.

"He—" I snapped my mouth shut. Sharing this information didn't feel right, even if it was a real memory for Sinner.

The details were too personal. To speak of them felt too violating.

The Sinner who'd been tortured and bullied by his own father was not the Sinner sitting in front of me now, yet somehow, he was.

Those were the experiences that molded us into these cold, heartless creatures, weren't they? The hell we endured shaped us into the people we'd become.

Life had turned us into warriors. And how cruel that was, to leave so many others untouched.

Not like I was a warrior myself. I was nothing. Nobody. I hadn't endured the things that Sinner had. What I had seen...

"He what?" Sinner pushed.

I dropped my focus to the table between us, unable to hold his angry gaze. "He tortured you. Whips. Knives. Weapons I've never even seen. Your shadows were everywhere, but he wanted more. He wanted you to be more."

A wicked smile grew on his face. "He wanted me to be a killer."

"I know." I clasped my hands in my lap. "I saw that too."

"Don't make me do this." Young Sinner was nothing like the emotionless man I'd come to know. Young Sinner was softer. Kinder, even. It broke my heart. I knew what happened to soft hearts like his.

His shadows surrounded him, lacing up his body, twirling around his limbs as if they could protect him. As if they could stop him from what was about to happen.

"This is for your own good, Elijah!" Sinner's father was tall, with messy hair like his son's. But there was no kindness there. Only sinister intention lurking behind his gaze. And the way he looked at his son? The way he tightened the ropes around Sinner's body until the boy screamed? That man deserved hell. Worse than hell, even.

Then there was Margaret, who was in the corner, crying.

"See what you do to your sister?" the older man yelled. "All of this is to protect her, understand? Show me your power and I won't have to push her like this. You would rather it be you than her, wouldn't you?"

Sinner's eyes widened, his expression absolutely heartbroken. Because his father was not asking for a simple show of his shadow magic.

His father wanted death.

Across from Sinner sat another boy about the same age. His eyes pleaded with Sinner's, but there was something else under his gaze, too.

Forgiveness.

Forgiveness for what? I wasn't sure. Not until a few moments later.

"Kill your friend. I know you're capable of it."

"I don't want to," Sinner cried. "I don't want to do it!"

"It's okay," his friend stammered. "It's okay, Elijah. I won't blame you for what you have to do."

I could practically feel the turmoil in Sinner's blood. His friend or his sister, both innocent. Both too kind for this world.

Sinner had once been too kind for this world, too. But what happened next was the first step in turning him into the monster he was now.

His father marched over to young Margaret and gripped her arm until she screamed. He pulled a silver blade from his belt and ran it down her cheek, causing a thin trail of blood to appear. "Do it," he ordered. "There is no way out of this. Do it or she dies, too."

"I'm so sorry," Sinner sobbed. "I'm so sorry, I'm so sorry, I'm so sorry." The apology was a chant. A prayer. A mantra that I would hear in my dreams for the rest of my life.

I'm so sorry I'm so sorry I'm so sorry I'm so sorry I'm so sorry.

Shadows erupted from Sinner's chest, wrapping around his friend's body and squeezing until they both screamed.

And then, abruptly, the sound ceased.

And an emptiness opened up in Sinner's gaze as he took in what he'd done.

"See?" His father said, kneeling in front of him with a disgusting smile on his face. "That wasn't so hard, was it, my boy?"

The man across from me cleared his throat, his focus still fixed on my face. "Then you know what I'm really capable of." His tone was dry, vacant. "And you also know I'll do anything to protect my sister."

I finally found the courage to stare back at him. "He was your friend," I said softly. "That was cruel of your father. He had no right."

With a dark chuckle, Sinner leaned back in his chair. "He had no right to do a lot of things. You saw only a glimpse of what he was capable of. But that doesn't change what I am. If he hadn't forced me to become a killer, someone else would have."

A pit opened up in my stomach. "I don't believe that."

He surveyed me, brow furrowed, then huffed a breath and flipped the conversation entirely, putting me on the defensive.

"And what about you? When did you realize you were a killer?"

I froze. "I don't—"

"Your entire family. I almost can't believe it. Katherine was right about you."

I slapped my palm on the table, making the plates rattle. "Katherine knows nothing about me."

"She knew you were powerful. Director, too."

"They guessed. They never actually knew."

Sinner stared at me silently. To be honest, the silence was worse than the barrage of questions and rude comments. It unnerved me, to be caught in his silent scrutiny. I wanted to know what he was thinking. What he thought about me now that he'd seen so much.

Did he think of me as a monster, too? Would he ever look at me the way he did when we were locked inside those barriers tonight?

"You saved Margaret's life back there. When you used your magic to strangle Director." His tone was a touch softer now. "I didn't think you could really do it."

I said nothing. He could feel my magic now, just as I could feel his, but the fight back at the mansion had been so chaotic, so fast, I didn't realize what I was doing until Director was being strangled.

"I can't control it," I said. "It just happens."

Another silence fell over us.

"Is that why you're so afraid of accepting it?"

Heat pricked at the backs of my eyes, unwanted emotions welling inside me. "I didn't mean to hurt anyone."

Another beat passed. "I know."

I choked back a sob. "I never wanted to hurt my family."

Another.

"I know."

When I finally looked up, Sinner was watching me, though rather than the cold glare I'd become so familiar with, his expression was soft, his eyes swimming with pity.

We sat like that until the food had grown cold and the

rest of the patrons had filtered out. I didn't say another word. Neither did he.

But I could feel it; a change in the connection between us. A fundamental alteration to what tethered us.

Rather than bitter hatred, there was an understanding now.

And as much as I hated to admit it, it was comforting.

sinner

"How are we supposed to buy clothes?" Athena asked as we slipped out onto the street. "We don't have any money and we look horrific."

I chuckled. "Money isn't always necessary. I thought you had more skills in society and whatnot?"

Though I kept my focus fixed ahead, I felt her eyes shooting daggers at me.

"What?" she asked, her tone full of defiance. "You plan on selling your body on the streets? Looking like that, you might earn enough to buy one shoe."

As we navigated down a narrow path, I put a hand on her waist and lowered my head. "Why? Would that bother you?"

She rolled her eyes and stepped out of my reach. "Don't flatter yourself."

It was a relief, really, that Athena could joke and sass after everything she'd endured tonight. After everything she'd endured for some time, really. I didn't want to push her for more information about the deaths of her family members or the power living in her veins. The power she hated so much.

Because I knew exactly what that felt like. I knew what it was like to hate a piece of what fundamentally made a person who they were. Instead of accepting the darkness like I did, she had pushed it away. Locked it in a cage. She had killed her entire family—Katherine aside—though none had happened because she'd actively wanted to do so. She couldn't control herself. She hadn't been trained or forced to use her magic every day like I had.

What my father did was nothing short of evil. He made me do things I couldn't even bear to remember. But being forced to use my powers meant learning to wield them in the way I wanted.

Gifted, they called us. More like cursed.

Of all the men in that damn dungeon, I seemed to be the only one who hated who I was. The others were almost proud of their gifts. Some could move small objects. Read thoughts at will. Teleport, apparently.

But nobody could kill with the shadows that bowed to them.

Death.

That was my gift.

I supposed Athena had been cursed with a version of that gift as well. Though based on the well of power I'd encountered, hers ran far deeper. I'd yet to see what she was truly capable of. Even now that I could taste it, I could sense it more than I ever had before, I could wield it even, if

I wanted to, but there was an instinct inside of me to tread lightly.

Athena thought I'd finally discovered her secret. But there was more to it. Facets of it she didn't even know she was hiding.

"Here," she said, tugging my arm as we approached a clothing store. She was right about one thing. We looked absolutely insane.

We needed clothes, and damn, Athena needed some shoes. We both did.

She released her hold on me, but before she could step away, I caught her hand and tugged her body to mine. "Follow my lead," I ordered as we crossed the threshold.

The shop was small, just a few racks of clothes with enough room for us and the shopkeeper who greeted us.

"Welcome," the woman said. "You two look like you're in the market for some warmer attire!" She was pretty. Not *Athena* pretty, but pretty.

"That, we are," I answered with a smirk.

She blushed and averted her eyes. She was around my age, maybe younger. "W-well," she stammered, "we have a few things over here that could work out for you and your..." She peered at Athena and paused.

"My sister," I replied.

Athena hit me with a glare so full of hatred I'm surprised I didn't drop dead, but I kept the arrogant smile on my face.

We picked out clothing quickly, Athena glowering at me the entire time. I chatted with the shopkeeper, worming my way into her good graces, and by the time we had what we needed, she was happy to let us return later with our *payment.*

Out on the busy street again, Athena smacked me in the arm. "Are you kidding me! Your sister?"

I fought a smile. "The plan worked, and you know it."

"Oh, please." Though she hid behind her sarcasm, anger emanated from her. Maybe I was sick, but I kind of liked that.

I guided her across the cobblestone. "Let's get back to the inn before Mags wakes up and decides to go make peace with Katherine and Benedict."

The walk back to the inn was quiet. Peaceful. Even though Athena's limp was back—and the urge to do the same was hard for me to fight—the night was enjoyable. More than enjoyable. The lights strung across the narrow street created a beautiful glow, illuminating the people we passed. The longer we walked the more obvious it became that the citizens here were actually happy.

It was hard to come to terms with such contentment. Such normalcy. How could life be continuing on like this when I had endured so much? How could so many people be living their lives, smiling, when I could barely breathe?

It felt fucking crushing at times.

Back at the inn, we found Margaret still out cold. Of course. She had always slept soundly. Unbothered. Peaceful.

That, I was thankful for. I would have kept watch over her every night if it meant she could rest without being disturbed by nightmares.

Athena tiptoed farther into the room, clearly not wanting to wake her.

"This way," I whispered, motioning to the small bathroom on the other side of the room.

She stiffened, looking from me to the closed door and back again.

My mind swarmed with a million questions about her reaction. Damn, I wished I'd manifested the power to read minds.

Before I could ask what the problem was, she tiptoed over to the bathroom door.

I followed her inside and shut the door behind us without a sound.

I dropped our armfuls of clothes on the small white counter next to the sink. The room was small but clean, with a toilet, and a small shower in the corner. It was luxurious compared to the facilities in the dungeons.

Knowing I didn't have to worry about the dozens of other men walking in on Athena was the greatest part of all of it.

Freedom had some benefits, I supposed.

At least for now.

With her back to me, she turned the nozzle and the water beat down against the tile.

Steam quickly followed, fogging up the small, cracked mirror that hung over the sink.

"You shower first," she said. "I'll wait."

"No, you go. You need it more than I do."

She cocked her head to the side. "Are you telling me I stink?"

With a harsh inhale, I gave her a once-over. "Athena, you're covered in mud and blood."

"And you're not?"

Annoyance flared in my chest. "Are you always this stubborn?"

"Only when you're being this annoying." Eyes narrowed, she assessed me.

Damn, she was an absolute mess. And she was fucking beautiful. With every hour, my power became more responsive to her, more protective. It urged me to reach out, to run a finger down her dirty cheek.

Instead, I balled my fists at my sides and turned toward the door. "Hurry up," I ordered. "It'll be light out soon."

For a few seconds, she didn't move. For a few seconds, I pictured the way she might step forward, put a hand on my shoulder, force me to face her.

I hadn't always wanted to be this person. I hadn't longed to be the cold asshole who brushed her off at every turn. I played games with her. I knew I did. She was confused and vulnerable and she had been through so fucking much, and I'd done nothing but make it worse.

After everything she had been through...

"Fine," she said. "Don't turn around."

I stayed put while she stripped the tatters of her white dress from her body. I fucking hated that dress. It reminded me too much of the Ministry. They'd taken so much from her. From us.

But in the end, they hadn't broken us. They never would. Athena would have submitted completely during the claiming if it meant freedom.

But at what cost? What was she willing to give up in return for control over her life?

Some freedoms were an illusion. I knew enough to know that.

The sound of the water hitting her body distracted me from my thoughts, allowing the muscles in my shoulders to relax. I slumped against the sink and stared at myself in the steamy bathroom mirror.

I didn't recognize the person looking back at me.

I'd hated myself for a long, long time. Since long before I met Athena. But somehow the way she smiled at me, the way she looked for me in a crowd and lit up when I was near, made me hate myself even more.

Because she only saw a glimpse of who I really was. Yes, she'd seen the moment I killed my very first childhood friend, but that was only the beginning. Would she ever look at me the same if she knew the truth?

My heart clenched tight enough to make me suck in a breath. Not likely.

People like Athena didn't belong with people like me. I would only ruin her.

The sound of water falling in the shower kept me steady, kept me here, in this moment. The steam soaked into my skin, the smell of lavender soap inspiring emotions I wouldn't name.

But fuck if my power didn't like it all. A lot.

"Sinner?" Athena asked from behind the shower curtain.

"What?"

"Do you feel different now? After the claiming, I mean?"

She shut the water off and snagged a towel off the counter without pulling the curtain back. When she did appear, she'd secured the plush white fabric tightly around her body.

I watched her through the mirror, eyes meeting hers, as she stepped out.

"Different how?"

She shrugged as if she was asking a perfectly casual question. "Anything, really. How do we know it really worked? What if it didn't? And what if they know that?"

"It worked."

"How do you know that?"

I couldn't explain the primal sensation that had developed deep in my bones. My power had been satisfied. Unlocked, really. Unchained. And along with it, she was there. The essence of her. The knowledge that I could wield her power again if I wanted to, the same way she could wield mine.

"Have you tried to use my shadows?" I asked, spinning to face her.

She adjusted the towel around her body. "Try them how?"

"They're a part of you now." I dipped my chin. "They'll protect you. They'll obey you."

She lowered her focus to the bath mat, shifting her weight. "I don't know how to control magic."

"It doesn't matter. Will it, and they will obey."

Her eyes met mine, a turbulent sea of doubt. "I'm not strong enough. I don't think I—"

"You're afraid to use your power. I understand why. But my phantoms? They won't hurt you. They won't hurt me, either. You can trust them. You can trust me."

I reached out and ghosted my fingers down her bare arm.

She shivered, and goose bumps erupted across her chest. "What if I lose control?"

The pit inside me widened, ached to be closer to her. "You won't."

She still didn't believe me. I would have to prove to her that she could trust me.

I let my magic loose, let my shadows pour from my chest and darken the room around us. Athena sucked in a sharp breath.

"See?" I murmured. "They won't hurt you. I honestly don't think they would hurt you now even if I wanted them to."

"Because we're claimed?"

"Because we're claimed."

"You're saying you can use my power too?" Her wide eyes met mine.

I nodded.

She stepped forward, gripping my biceps, her lips turned down in a pained frown. "Please, Sinner. Don't. My magic is different. It's dark, I can feel it. It's... It feels evil. Don't use it."

What I told her was true. I understood her reticence.

But she'd never become strong by avoiding it. She would never learn how to control it.

But now was not the time to push her.

"Fine," I said. "If you don't want me to use your power, I won't. Not until you ask me to."

Her face softened, and her shoulders lowered. "Okay. Thank you."

Silence fell between us, but she didn't pull away. Didn't step back.

"What if they find us and take us back there?" she asked, her grip on my arms tightening.

"Then we'll fight them. And we'll win."

Her lips parted as she studied me. Water dripped from her hair and rolled down her shoulders and chest, disappearing beneath the white towel. "And what if she makes us claim with someone else? What if she tries to use our magic by mixing our power with—"

"Don't." I crooked a finger beneath her chin and lifted it. "Nobody will ever touch you, Athena. You are my claimed. Mine. No, we didn't have sex, but we won't need to. It makes no difference. Every ounce of me can feel you now. Nobody else will claim with you. Ever. Do you understand?" My voice came out rougher than I anticipated, but it made no difference. The words were true.

She blinked a few times. "Yes, I understand."

"Good. Now get dressed."

She was silent then, though I could sense the thoughts engulfing her. This happened often, even back in the dungeons. It was like her thoughts didn't have an off switch.

And I could only imagine what she was thinking now.

I stripped off my pants and stepped into the shower, damn near moaning when the water hit my back. My power rumbled in my veins as I used the lavender soap she'd just lathered all over her body. I scrubbed my skin raw, though I eased up when I cleaned my feet. The soles were bloody, but the skin would heal soon. They weren't half as bad as Athena's wounds.

I finished my shower quickly, then wrapped a towel around my waist before opening the shower curtain. Athena sat on the counter with her back against the wall, her legs stretched out. Her eyes were closed. Damn. Could she really sleep in that position?

Her new clothes were two sizes too big, but at least her body was covered.

Her bare feet swayed slightly back and forth in the air, snagging my attention.

I acted on instinct. I knelt before her and lightly picked up one foot.

She flinched but didn't pull her foot away. "What are you doing?"

"Checking your wounds."

An expression that looked an awful lot like confusion crossed her face, making my chest tighten. I mean, fuck, was she not used to being taken care of?

I silently cursed myself for the thought. Of course nobody had taken care of her. Her family had seen her as a monster.

They'd avoided her—Katherine and her parents at least. Of course they didn't take care of her.

The thought made me want to wring Katherine's neck. I didn't blame Athena for rejecting her sister's offer to heal her wounds. I would carry her anywhere she wanted to go for as long as she needed before I'd let Katherine touch her.

Why would her sister want her to stay with the Ministry? It still made no sense. Unless she hated her sister that much…

The idea that anyone could hate Athena sent a burning rage into my heart.

"Why?" she asked.

I kept my focus on the bottom of her foot, making sure she had truly gotten all the dirt out of the cuts. "Why what?"

"Why do you care?" she asked, her voice more timid than I would have expected from her. "Why are you helping me? We're supposed to hate each other, remember?"

I scoffed. "That was before we got out of that godforsaken dungeon. And that was before the claiming."

"So you're helping me now because we're claimed."

I held her ankle but I sat back on my heels so I could look up at her. "The claiming honestly has nothing to do with it."

Her eyes went wide, like she was as shocked as I was by my words. It had been my cover for the last few weeks. That I only cared about her because of the claiming. I'd only helped her because performing the claiming was my ticket out of those damn dungeons.

But somewhere along the way, sometime during the dark nights, under the spray of the shower, maybe while she whispered with Mags, things changed. And my emotions were only amplified when I was given access to her memories.

I realized I would have protected her regardless of the claiming.

Why? Probably because I was the biggest idiot I knew.

Don't get attached. Don't get close to anyone. That was my number one rule. I didn't allow myself to worry about anyone but Mags. Not if they were destined for the same fate as my first childhood friend. The one I killed while he stared at me in horror.

But we were long, long past that now.

She didn't say anything else as I stood and adjusted my towel. Though she did turn before I let it fall to the ground.

"Come on," I said once I'd pulled a pair of pants on. "You need to sleep."

"We both need to sleep."

I scoffed and held out a hand. "I'll be okay. Don't worry about me."

With her palm against mine, she slid off the counter. "I do worry about you."

My heart fucking cracked. Yeah. I was so, so screwed.

She held my gaze for a handful of seconds. Enough to light up the shadows running through my veins. They wanted her. They wanted to protect her. To keep her safe. To heal her.

They wanted to consume her, too.

But I had already taken too much from her. I wouldn't touch her again unless she asked for it. And even then, only if it was completely of her own free will.

Fuck, I would never let that happen. I would be the only person to ever see her in her pleasure like that again.

Before I could do anything stupid like run a thumb across her pink lips, she turned and stepped into the bedroom.

Mags was still sprawled across the bed, so I settled on the floor near the window and stretched my legs out in front of me. I'd been sleeping on a cot for months. This wasn't any worse. In fact, I was more comfortable than I ever remembered. Here, I knew that door was locked. I knew Director wouldn't be barging in to take Mags from me.

And for the first time in a long time, I actually started to feel hope for the future.

athena

Benedict ran his fingers through his dark hair and exhaled loudly. "I can't simply teleport us all back there. That would be suicide."

"Why not?" I asked. "It worked before!"

"Because they weren't expecting me to help you. Hell, *I* wasn't even expecting me to help you."

The five of us stood in our room at the inn. It was cramped, but when Katherine and Benedict brought us breakfast, my stomach growled loudly again, and I begrudgingly allowed them to enter.

"We can't go back," Katherine said. "Not unless we're turning ourselves in."

Margaret cocked her head, licking the butter off her bread dramatically. "I wonder sometimes, Katherine. Truly. What is wrong with you?"

I choked back a howl of laughter.

Katherine gasped and pressed a hand to her chest. "Excuse me?"

Margaret shrugged, her expression light. "Clearly there is something deeply and disturbingly wrong with you. I'm just trying to figure out what exactly it is."

Sinner coughed beside me as Katherine's face turned red.

"We have to go back." Benedict stepped forward. The more time I spent around him, the more I liked him. Though I couldn't help but pity him, too. He must have really pissed someone off to be paired with my terrible sister for the claiming. "There are mystics in those dungeons just like us. It's wrong. We can't leave them there."

"And where would we go afterward?" Katherine cocked a hip, her chin lifted in derision. "There isn't a place on the planet that's safe from the Ministry."

The room fell into silence. That had been the question, the one thing stopping us. We could storm the Ministry, sure. We could pretend like the five of us had any chance against the hundreds of guards surrounding that dungeon and we could attempt to get the others out of there.

But then what? Where would we hide dozens of rebel mystics in a world where mystics are being hunted?

"Actually, I've heard of a place." Sinner, who had been quiet all morning, leaned casually against the wall with his arms crossed over his chest. "I've heard of places where mystics live together. Small communities safe from the Ministry's reach."

Katherine laughed out loud, shrill as ever. "You seriously think communities of mystics the Ministry doesn't know about exist?"

Margaret put down the rest of her bread. "My brother's right. Where we're from, people talk about them. And I wouldn't say that the Ministry doesn't know about them. It's more that they're too afraid to confront them. If they did, they'd be outnumbered. Outpowered."

A chill ran down my spine. If what they said was true... there could be an entire rebellion awaiting us.

Yet that still didn't solve the issue of getting into the Ministry's camp without dying.

"All right." Sinner pushed himself off the wall. "Benedict, you stay here with Mags. Come up with a plan to infiltrate the Ministry. You two—and Katherine—know the grounds better than we do."

"Where are you going?" Katherine asked, her eyes narrowed to slits, her whole being radiating suspicion.

Sinner straightened, grasped my wrist, and pulled me toward the door. "I've got one day to teach Athena how to use her power. We're getting started now."

Before I could argue, I was pulled out of the inn and into the bustling streets. Like last night, the energy of this town lit my body aflame. Excitement and nervousness both flitted through me. I relished it. This was like nothing I had ever felt before.

Sinner pulled me between two buildings, leading me away from the crowded main streets of the bustling city. He ignored my protests and questions, just like I figured he would, and didn't stop walking until we reached a grassy field on the outskirts of the town. I could still see the inn in the distance, but we were at least a half mile away from any living being.

"You can't be serious," I said as I finally extricated myself from his hold. "I can't learn my gift in one day."

In the soft morning light, his face glowed. His skin was slightly pink from the sun exposure—exposure he hadn't seen in months—and his muscles rippled with each movement.

And those dark eyes...

"You can and you will," he replied. "You don't have a choice. We can't make it through this without you."

I put a hand on my chest. "Aw, I'm flattered."

"Don't get cocky." He fisted his hands at his hips. "It took me years to learn how to control my shadows. Now we're going to teach you."

"You're forgetting an important detail in all of this."

"Oh, really?" He stepped forward, brow arched, head bowed over me. "What is that detail?"

I didn't back away as I craned my neck to look up at him. "I don't have phantoms to wield. And every time I've used my magic in the past, bad things have happened. One day of training won't help." I tried to keep my voice strong, but the crack in my words betrayed my fear.

My power wasn't the kind that could be reined in. How was I supposed to learn to control death itself? Evil personified?

No, I wouldn't do it. Not when there was so much at stake.

"You can't be afraid of yourself forever."

Unease coiled tight in my belly. "I don't see any other way."

Sinner tipped his head back and huffed at the sky like he was looking for answers.

Good luck with that.

"Okay, new plan," he said. "If you're afraid to use your own magic, fine. You'll learn to use mine."

I swallowed past the lump that had suddenly formed in my throat. Shit.

"We share power now. You can feel it, I know you can."

As if on cue, that tether tugged at my chest like it had each time Sinner had used his magic since our unfinished claiming ceremony.

I hadn't had time to really assess the sensation. It all happened so fast, and then we were running.

But holy hell. He was right. I could wield Sinner's shadows.

"Fine," I sighed. "Teach me how."

A wicked smile spread across his face. Shadows pulsed out of his chest, right above his heart. They did not flood the area like I had seen them do before. These were slower shadows. Subtle. And completely under Sinner's control.

At the sight of those black wisps, my own chest tightened. He was standing close enough that if I reached out, I could touch them—

"Will them to come to you," he ordered.

Uncertainty fluttered through me. *Yeah. Like it would be that easy.*

I took a deep breath and closed my eyes, silently urging the shadows to move closer. It felt ridiculous. This was all... it was all magic, for god's sake.

Still, I willed them forward. With my hands at my

sides, I turned my palms up, and I pulled, as if there was a physical string tethering me to each of the black clouds that snaked around Sinner's body.

I pulled and pulled and pulled.

And got nothing.

"You don't want it bad enough," Sinner said matter-of-factly.

A humph escaped me as I let my shoulders sag. Was this guy on drugs? "Um, yes, I think I do. Our lives are at stake here."

Sinner laughed under his breath while he shook his head. "And when have you ever cared about your own life?"

"Excuse me, but I do possess a little self-preservation, thank you."

"Really? This is the first I'm hearing of it."

I glowered at him. *Real good, Athena. Great scary work. I'm sure he's trembling right now.* "I understand what's at stake here. Those people in the dungeons will continue to suffer. That's not a life I'd wish upon anyone."

A darkness flickered in his eyes, but it was gone as quickly as it had come. "Then act like it. Control these shadows. Their lives depend on it. We have no chance of standing up to the Ministry if you're not using a gift."

My heart rate spiked. I hadn't wanted to believe that I'd need to, but the earnestness and concern in his tone struck deep. We were their hope.

Possibly their only hope.

Instead of pushing the shadows from his chest again, Sinner held one hand out between us. A single shadow appeared, twirling like a tiny tornado in his palm. "Show me how badly you want it, then."

My entire body tensed at the sight of it. Each time I saw his magic, I had a stronger reaction to it, a stronger attraction to it.

As if that string between me and this shadow had tightened, I was drawn closer.

Somewhere in the pull of his power, I moved my own hand and laid it on top of his palm.

It was quiet out here, no sounds but the chirping of birds in the distance and the rapid beating of my heart.

Want it bad enough.

I did want it. I wanted this more than anything. Sinner was right. We had no chance if I wasn't using a gift. Sinner could wield death, yes, but I could too. We could do it together.

I wanted it.

He kept his hand steady beneath mine. Like a rock, unmoving.

Where we touched, a fire ignited and erupted up my arm. I fought the urge to step closer. To grip his forearm. To pull his body flush against mine.

Focus, Athena. You want him, but you want his power more.

I slowly lifted my hand from his.

And the shadows followed.

Between his palm and mine, the dark clouds spread, swirling and whispering, rattling wildly like an animal caged between us.

"It's working," I breathed.

"It's working," he repeated. "Now, more."

Without his touch to guide me, my body buzzed. This close to him, power flooded me. Only now did I realize that my body's reaction to him was so much more than lust. It was as if my power literally craved his.

I could wield his power. *I could.* I was meant to, that's what the whole claiming was about. I had done it at the mansion, too. I had actually controlled his phantoms.

So instead of backing away, instead of closing myself off to that feeling of want, I leaned into it.

And the damn shadows followed.

I took a step back, and although it felt like fighting against a magnetic pull, the shadows followed. They wrapped around my arm, coiling up my shoulder and caressing my neck. "Oh my god," I whispered.

He grunted, his lips ticked up on one side. "God has nothing to do with this."

The shadows pulsed at the sound of his voice, but they remained coiled around me, wrapping me further in their darkness.

When I met Sinner's gaze, he was smiling.

A rare smile. A real smile.

It was kind of freaky.

"Good," he said. "Now pretend I'm your enemy and unleash them on me."

HOURS LATER, I had gotten the hang of basic shadow wielding.

I was also dripping in sweat, completely exhausted, and slowly losing my inhibitions. That last part was due to my prolonged proximity to Sinner.

My head tilted up to the sky as my knees dropped to the ground, and I caught my breath. Simple shadow movements had turned into intense combat training, which turned into fighting like my life was on the line.

In Sinner's world, it *was* on the line.

I understood that, but damn, I was tired.

"You're getting better." He dropped to the ground beside me, legs bent, arms resting on his knees. The annoying asshole hadn't even broken a sweat.

"I still can't kill people with the power like you can."

"You don't know that until you try it."

A laugh bubbled out of me. "Oh, are you offering to be my test subject?"

He shook his head, but I saw the smile that crept onto his lips before he covered it up. "You'll have plenty of test scenarios when we make it back to the Ministry."

"If I don't die first."

It was a joke, but the truth in the words hit hard. Sinner was right. Until now, I'd rarely cared about my own life. Lately, though I felt as if, for the first time in my life, I had something worth fighting for.

The Ministry had to be stopped.

God, who was I? Had I become a rebel meant to shake up the government?

I didn't hate it. Someone had to do it, right? End the corruption of the Ministry or die trying.

It was quite the motto.

"You're not going to die. I won't let you."

I closed my eyes and relished the way the sun warmed my face. "Careful. It's starting to sound like you actually care."

When he didn't quip back, I turned to look at him. The sun cast shadows across his face, but there was no hiding the emotion that rolled through his dark eyes.

"You're my claimed, Athena. What we feel for each other on a personal level isn't important. But my power is now connected to yours. Forever. I'm not going to let you die. My shadows won't allow it. *I* won't allow it."

My face heated. I never could have predicted the scary, sullen tier three from the dungeons would care even the smallest amount about me. Nobody had ever cared about me. Why would they? I was a monster. A killer. A waste of oxygen, as my sister once said.

They were right, of course. Mystics were supposed to be valuable. Talented. They were supposed to possess what the world needed.

Sinner didn't even know the half of what my power was capable of.

Once he learned, he would think differently of me.

"Let's go." He stood, brushing off his pants. "The others should have a plan by now. If they haven't killed each other yet."

I groaned. "Can't we just lock Katherine up and take Mags and Benedict with us? It would help morale."

Sinner pulled me to my feet effortlessly, and I caught myself on his bicep before I stumbled directly into his chest. "Keep your enemies close. Don't forget that."

Sinner the wise. I'll add that to the list of his surprising qualities. "Fine," I said. "But I want it on record that I tried to be the bigger person."

We headed back toward town, wandering side by side. "Really? When did that happen, because I distinctly remember you rolling around in the mud and fighting while you tried to kill each other."

I flipped my hair over my shoulder and brushed past him. "Well, I mentally tried. And that's really all that matters."

By the time we got back to the inn, the sun was setting and the energy had shifted. Even from the hallway outside the door I could sense how tense the rest of our group had become. The weight of the situation was coming down on all of us.

Good. I didn't mind that it felt heavy. It *was* heavy. If we failed, those men would stay locked in those dungeons. The Ministry would get their way. Again.

Sure, some of those men likely deserved to stay locked away. Some of them would need some serious therapy. But most were redeemable, and if we didn't get them out, the Ministry would use them for their own twisted games.

We hadn't even seen war. Hadn't even touched that part of the problem, yet.

When I didn't reach forward and open the door, Sinner stepped up behind me. He stood so close that when he took a breath, his chest brushed against the backs of my shoulders. To my surprise, he grasped my upper arms. His breath caressed the side of my neck as he whispered,

"Don't be afraid of your sister. I'm just waiting for the right time to let you practice your shadows."

He reached in front of me and pushed the door open.

"There you are!" Margaret jumped up from the edge of the bed. "I was starting to think you two left us here."

"It was tempting," Sinner replied. "But we have work to do. Please tell me you came up with a plan."

The bed was covered in sheets of paper, all full of notes, drawings, maps, and what looked like schematics.

Wow. They really had spent all day brainstorming.

"What is this?" I asked.

Katherine stood near the window, looking out, as if she hadn't noticed our arrival.

"This is everything I know about where they're keeping the rest of the mystics," Benedict said. "I've only been underground a few times and it's very complex, but it's nothing we can't figure out."

My chest expanded a fraction. "You sound confident."

"Look at this." He handed me a piece of paper.

It was a diagram of the underground tunnels layered with one of the camps above ground. "When you were at the mansion for the claiming ceremony, you were here." He pointed to an area on another paper. "Which is only about a mile from here." He pointed to the map with the dungeons.

"That can't be right. We were in a car for nearly an hour when we were transported for dinner and the claiming," Sinner said. His voice had hardened. Grown more serious.

"We're instructed to drive around to confuse mystics who don't have the proper security clearance."

I studied the maps. We were really that close to the rest of the mystics the night of the blood moon?

"And how many men are protecting these places? What types of gifts will we be fighting against?"

Margaret picked up another piece of paper. "Here. We compiled a list of the gifts of every guard we've encountered. Of course, it would be nice if we had Katherine's help, but someone is being stubborn."

Every eye turned to my sister.

"Really?" I asked, my heart sinking. "Still?"

She finally turned her gaze away from the window. "I don't want anything to do with the massacre you're walking into. That's what will happen, you know that, right? They'll kill you all."

"Not this again," I groaned.

"It's true." She stepped toward us. "You can draw your maps. You can make your plans. But do you really think your scary little boyfriend is strong enough to fight everyone?"

I ignored the little boyfriend comment, but beside me, Sinner stiffened. "Why are you so adamant that we're going to die?" I asked. "What do you know?"

She rolled her eyes. "Nothing."

"I've known you my whole life, Katherine. You're stubborn, but you're not an idiot. You know Sinner's abilities are far stronger than most of the generals in Director's army. What is it you know?"

"I don't know anything, Thena! And neither do any of

you! Do you think the Ministry gained all the power they have by allowing gifted to infiltrate them so easily? You're smarter than that. There are other mystics out there with powers you've never even considered. Trust me."

"Do you know other threes?" Sinner's voice echoed off the walls. "Or powerful twos?"

She crossed her arms and leaned against the windowsill. "The Ministry has been operating for decades. Use your imagination, Sinner."

God, she was annoying. Of course there would be mystics with powers we hadn't seen before, but we were bringing the literal power of death with us.

"We can be in and out of there before they even realize what's happened," Benedict interrupted, saving us all from drowning in the growing tension. "That's our best shot. We don't have to fight everyone alone, either. The second we open the gates to the dungeons, we'll have dozens of other mystics with us."

"You can't take down every guard." With a shake of her head, she turned back to the window.

"So this is what you've been in here doing all day? Arguing with each other?" I asked.

"No," Margaret said. "After about an hour, we banished Katherine to the corner. Benedict and I are optimists. Glass half full, etcetera."

"So we're running on optimism here?"

She lifted one shoulder. "Optimism and a plan. Here. Look at this."

For the next hour, Benedict went over every detail. He walked us through every note. Every diagram. They had even drawn scenarios where the plan could go wrong, where we would have to jump ship if shit hit the fan.

I couldn't lie. It seemed like it could work.

Hope blossomed in my chest and a hint of excitement coursed through my veins.

Katherine kept her mouth shut, thank god, and Sinner made a few adjustments to the plan, insisting that he and I stay together at all times.

And I tried not to blush like an idiot at that. It was for the purposes of magic, nothing else.

"The guards open the doors of the dungeon to refill the supplies at dawn. I'd suggest we get a good night's sleep, then set out first thing tomorrow. We can camp out one more day if we need to, but the sooner we get in, the better."

Dawn. We had until dawn.

"Can you teleport us all there? Are you strong enough?"

"Yes, but I'll need time to recharge. We'll stop near the Ministry, and I'll rest there." He pointed to the map. "We'll stay here for the day and move in before the sun rises."

Benedict locked eyes with each of us one by one, his expression full of confidence. Thank god. I would rather him be ignorant and confident than pessimistic. Either way, we were going through with this. Either way, this was happening.

"Katherine," Benedict called out. "Let's go. We need our sleep, too."

She scoffed. "Like it'll matter." Without bothering to glance at any of us, she sauntered out of the room. A moment later, a door down the hall slammed shut.

Benedict followed with a sigh.

"That was *pleasant*," Margaret cheered. "I hope you two had a better day than I did."

I cringed. "I'm not exactly a killing machine yet."

"When the time comes, you'll be ready," she replied. "I can feel it. You're a natural."

God, I hoped she was right.

sinner

I closed my eyes and steadied my breathing in hopes that I could actually get some rest. I'd been lying here for hours when Athena shifted in the bed. She silently rose and crept toward the door, closing it behind her with a quiet snick.

If I were a normal, non-obsessed man, I would have minded my own business. But I wasn't. I had completely lost my mind, had thrown all common sense out the window.

So I silently stood, made sure Mags was still fast asleep, then crept toward the door just as Athena had.

Rather than open it, I pressed my ear to it, listening.

"What do you want?" she whispered.

For a moment, I thought she'd heard me. But before I could respond, another whispered voice cut through the night air.

"I'm giving you one last warning, Thena. We can sneak

out of here. We can be gone before the morning. They'll have no way to find us."

Katherine.

"Are you joking?"

A beat passed.

"I'm not leaving." Athena said again, her tone full of fury. "These people need me."

Katherine let out a derisive laugh. "You're seriously choosing these people over your own family?"

"These people *are* my family now. Not that you could understand that kind of loyalty. And aren't you the one who left your family in the first place?" The hushed whispers grew more intense.

"Oh, please. You wouldn't know family if it was staring you in the face! It's why you have none left! You killed Mother. You killed Kylar, then Father. That's when I knew I had to get out of there. You even killed sweet Jasmine. I never could have imagined you'd be capable of that. And in less than thirty-six hours, you'll have killed me, too."

"Stop."

I had to fight the urge to rip the door open and strangle the last breath out of Katherine's pesky throat. She had no idea what the weight of a gift like Athena's cost.

Athena had paid the price many, many times. In fact, she paid the price every time she closed her eyes, every time those tortured memories crossed her mind.

I would know.

"Have you told him all of it?"

"Stop it, Katherine."

"Does he think the two of you are alike?" Katherine

laughed, her tone pure malice. "Does he think you're both death wielders, gifted with a curse and ready to slay the whole Ministry?"

"I said that's *enough*!"

Neither sister spoke again, but there was a rustling of fabric and the sound of footsteps moving closer. "You're a monster, Thena. You are worse than a death wielder. Worse than *any* tier three. You know that, don't you? People like you have no redemption. Not after what you did."

"Then why do you care? If I'm such a lost cause and you really think we'll fail, then why not let me do it? Why not let me get caught? Why are you even here?"

"I'm trying to convince you to work for the greater good. Help the Ministry. At least then you'll be killing for the right reasons."

"What would you have done?" Athena asked, her voice wavering in a way that made my chest ache. "If you were me, what would you have done?"

I pictured the way Katherine scowled at her sister. No respect. No love. "If I were you, I would have killed myself a long time ago. The world would be a better place without you. And once the Ministry has you again, they'll see it."

I could barely hear the sound of her retreating foot-steps over my own pounding heart. The door was opening before I knew what I was doing. Athena stood in the hallway, shoulders slumped, feet bare, her eyes glazed over.

When the door clicked shut behind me, I gently grasped her arm. "Hey," I whispered. "What are you doing out here?" I wouldn't stir up more pain by telling her I'd heard that entire, gut-wrenching conversation.

Athena opened her mouth, then snapped it shut without replying, her focus fixed on the floor in front of her. She was lost somewhere I couldn't follow her, some-where deep in the caves of her mind.

It killed me to see the pain, to know that I couldn't follow her. I hated that Katherine had pushed her there with nothing but lies and hatred.

"Athena." I ran a finger down the side of her face, trying to make her snap out of the trance. "Athena, come back to me."

"I don't want to be a monster." Her voice had never sounded so weak. "I never wanted to be this person."

"You're not a monster. You know you're not."

She finally looked up, her eyes brimming with tears. "I killed my family." The words were barely audible. "I wanted them dead. That's why they are dead."

A single tear crested her lashes and tracked down her face.

Without hesitation, I scooped her up and hugged her tight.

She was so tiny, yet she looped her arms around my torso and held me equally as tight.

Fuck, I could have died at the relief.

Like that, she cried. Her entire body shook. The tears came and came until they soaked my shirt. She buried her face in my chest, muffling her cries. Still, I held her. I would have held her forever.

"I hate who I am," she whispered. "Katherine hates me,

but it doesn't even matter. Nobody hates me more than I hate myself."

I didn't think I had a heart, but I felt it breaking in that moment. Shattering. Icing over.

"Don't worry." I kissed the top of her head as if it would help. As if I could break through the numbness that had enveloped her. "I hate me, too."

Her sister was wrong. We were alike. There was nothing Athena could do that would make me turn on her. She was part of me now. Her soul was part of my soul.

People like Katherine would never understand us. She would never know the feeling of standing in the darkness alone at night, wishing for pain, wishing for an ending.

Because even pain was better than living in this void. The apathy that spread like a disease, that called me home. That summoned me forward.

I couldn't slip back into that trap. Not now. For years, I'd lived in the darkness, in the abyss. But then I met Athena.

And when she clung to me, when she sobbed against me, her body shaking, I realized I had escaped it. That was strange, wasn't it? That we never knew we were out of that hole until we threatened to slip right back into it?

Part of that realization was terrifying. But the other part was comforting.

Like coming home.

I held Athena until her tears dried. Until her sobs were silenced. She didn't try to explain. She didn't have to. I wouldn't ask. This was her battle, and she had been fighting it alone for so, so long.

She would never have to fight alone again.

"What are you doing awake?" she said, finally peeling herself from my grasp.

"I need your help with something."

Before she could ask questions, I slipped quietly back into our room, tugging her along with me. The moonlight trickling in from the window was bright enough to illuminate all the lists and plans Benedict had written out. I took a seat on the floor beside them, and Athena followed my lead.

"What are you doing with these? You're not changing the plan now, are you?"

I inhaled deeply, eyes closed, then blew the breath out and zeroed in on her. "No, I'm not changing the plan."

She eyed me carefully, her eyes puffy and red. "Okay, then what?"

I picked up what I believed was the list Mags and Benedict had compiled of all the other known gifts in the army and handed it to Athena. "Read this to me."

Lip caught between her teeth, she eased the paper from my grasp. "You want me to read you this list?"

"Yes."

A beat passed. "Why?"

"Because I'd like to know what's on it." I nodded at it. "Now, please read."

She looked down at the list, then back at me, then down at the list again. When her gaze returned to mine, her brows were drawn together, her eyes more focused than they had been all night. "You can't read it?"

"If I could read it, I wouldn't be asking you to do it for

me, now would I?" The words were harsher than I had meant for them to be, but Athena didn't flinch away. She didn't laugh at me, either, which was a relief.

Not like I cared, dammit.

"But I've seen you reading. You read that book in the dungeons almost every night."

I forced myself to keep my eyes locked on hers. "Pretending like I knew what the hell those words said was more entertaining than staring off into space. Please." I motioned to the paper. "We don't have all night."

She cleared her throat, the sound loud in the quiet room. "Fine."

And then, without even a snicker, she began to read.

Jumper
Earth manipulator
Water wielder
Mind reader
Advanced strength
Healer
Unknown—?

It was a decent list, but there would surely be more. More we'd yet to come across.

More like me.

"Does Margaret know?" she asked after a while.

"Does she know what?"

"That you can't read? She clearly can." She glanced at

the page, then back up at me. "Considering she wrote this list."

I shifted, stretching my feet out in front of me. "Like most people, she assumes I have the basic skill of literacy. My father taught her how to read. He taught me other things. It's not important."

She studied me a little too intently. It took more strength than I'd like to admit to not squirm under her inspection. I had never told anyone. It had never come up, really. Until now, I hadn't been forced to read for survival purposes.

But now that she knew, would she see me as weak? As less than? I was Sinner, the terrifying tier three with literal death magic who couldn't even read the damn list.

But she did not look amused.

She looked sad.

And somehow, that was worse.

"Okay." I plucked the sheet from her hand and gave her another. "Now this one."

She read every word from every sheet of paper on the floor, even the labels on the diagrams. Every note. She didn't laugh once. Didn't bring up anything about my deficiency.

She simply read.

And then she read them all again.

And again.

It wasn't until the sun was nearly rising that my eyelids grew heavy. The last thing I heard before I drifted asleep was the sound of her voice.

And it replayed in my dreams, chasing away the night-mares, chasing away the horrors.

And I slept.

THANK GOD FOR SHOES. Mine and Athena's.

The others changed, too, no longer wearing those ridiculous white outfits. We packed the few items we had gathered over the two days at the inn, ate as much as we could handle, and hit the road.

I wouldn't miss this little town. Crowded places weren't for me. But I would miss the way Athena and Mags gawked at every tiny thing they passed, laughing and holding on to each other like they'd never seen anything better.

One of the delights they encountered was a dog wearing a sweater. It was fucking ridiculous.

We walked through town and into the woods, the same way we had come from. Benedict said it would be easier to jump from an open space.

Katherine remained silent. Thank fuck, too, because I wasn't sure I wouldn't draw blood if one shitty remark left her lips. Not after how she'd treated Athena last night.

The fact that every person in Athena's family *but Katherine* had died?

It perplexed me. Deeply.

"All right," Benedict said as we reached a small clear-ing. "There's no going back once we're there. We'll be in range of the Ministry. There's nothing we can do but move forward with our plan after this."

Nobody spoke.

"Great. As long as we're all on the same page." He adjusted the strap of his bag across his shoulder. "Everyone hold on."

Mags immediately wrapped an arm around Athena and held a hand out to Benedict.

Athena turned to me and smiled.

I twined my fingers with hers, ignoring the shadows that wanted to break free at her touch.

God, I hoped this worked.

"Three."

I took a long breath.

"Two."

Katherine pulled a silver object out of her pocket. I didn't realize until it was too late that it was a small dagger.

No, no, no—

"One."

She stabbed Benedict in the gut.

Shit.

athena

I had known chaos. I would say my entire life had been one long stream of chaos, actually. But what I felt after we jumped? It took that term to an entire new level.

We landed on solid ground with a thud. There was a crack, but because of the adrenaline coursing through me, I couldn't tell whether I was hurt or whether the sound came from someone else.

At the sound of a scream, I had my answer. It was a deep voice. Benedict, maybe?

Sinner's shadows pulsed against my palm. I opened myself to them like he taught me and let them cloud around my body, then Margaret's. I wasn't concerned that they'd hurt us. I knew now that they had a mind of their own.

And they protected their family.

I blinked, willing my vision to clear, desperate for the world to stop spinning.

Sinner pulled his hand away from mine, and an instant later, a second scream echoed off the trees.

This time it was Katherine.

"What the fuck are you doing?!" Sinner pinned her to the ground with a hand to her throat and screamed into her face.

Beside them, Benedict dropped to his knees.

"Oh my god." Margaret and I rushed to help him. "You'll be fine," I said, though I had no clue whether that was anywhere close to the truth. Especially when I caught sight of the dagger protruding from his stomach, right above his belly button. "It's nothing."

His face had drained of all color. "I'm so sorry," he breathed.

"Don't be." Margaret was already tearing away a piece of her shirt and applying pressure to the wound. "We're going to pull this out and you'll be fine, okay? It's going to be fine."

Her words sounded oddly confident. Sinner was still shouting in my sister's face. She, in turn, was blabbering self-righteously.

"We can't do this!" she screamed. "We can't!"

"Well, it's too fucking late for that, isn't it!" Sinner's voice echoed off the trees around us.

Margaret gripped the handle of the dagger and pulled, and instantly, more blood gushed from the wound.

"Get over here and heal him!" I yelled.

Katherine barked a laugh. "He can't help you! Nobody can!"

My stomach lurched. "He's your claimed!! Why the hell would you do that?"

Her own claimed. She actually stabbed the man she was bonded to in order to stop us from jumping.

"You can take her power, right?" I asked Benedict.

His eyes had gone hazy, his head wobbling.

"Benedict, listen. You can use her healing power since the two of you are bonded."

Katherine laughed, though the sound was cut off when Sinner put pressure on her throat.

"Not unless she lets me." Benedict coughed, and blood seeped down his chin. "She's had her power shut off from me since we performed the ceremony. I can't access it if she doesn't want me to."

What? I turned my attention to Katherine and Sinner. He was waiting for the signal to kill her. I knew that look.

It was a look far past anger. Far past fury.

"Heal him." I marched over to where she was splayed out on the dirt.

Sinner backed away enough so I could tower over her.

"Heal him," I gritted out. "He is your claimed."

She sputtered another laugh, and I kicked her in the ribs to shut her up.

"It's too late." She rolled to her side, grimacing. "Good luck freeing anyone without him. You're stuck. You're all stuck."

Benedict slumped against Margaret, who pressed the cloth harder against the wound. Not that it did much good. He was losing blood far too quickly.

"Athena," she cried out. "He needs help."

Benedict coughed again, blood spattering the ground in front of him. "It's okay," he breathed. "You don't need me. I was just going to speed up the process, remember?"

"We *do* need you." Margaret shook him. "Who else is going to keep me company when these two are off saving the world?"

My chest tightened. No, no, no. I hadn't felt like this in a very, very long time. This desperate.

And feeling desperate was a very dangerous thing.

Eyes locked with Sinner's, I silently pleaded for him to understand.

I pleaded for everyone to understand.

"Katherine." I knelt so my face was only inches from hers.

Immediately, her manic smile evaporated.

"Heal him."

The words were more than a command.

My power came to life, thick and palpable in the air.

Head shaking, she dug her heels into the dirt, trying to scramble away. There was nowhere she could go, though. Nothing she could do. "No, Athena, don't—"

"Heal him."

My body buzzed as I let that magic flow out of me, as I let that animal out of its cage. *Heal him. Heal him. Heal him.* I looked at her as I played the vision out in my mind. I pictured her kneeling before her claimed, using her power to heal him.

Katherine was in the middle of another protest when she went rigid and the words died on her tongue.

She couldn't fight me. Not when I had already seen it in my mind.

She pushed herself onto her knees and crawled to Benedict.

Without another moment of hesitation, she held her hands over his wound and began to heal him.

Margaret cursed beneath her breath, but I ignored the reaction. I kept my focus fixed on Katherine. I let my emotion pour into the magic. It was unlike anything I had ever felt. Far different from when I had used my power in the past.

Previously, it had been like drawing from a shallow well. Its limits well-defined. My fear at the forefront of my mind.

But now? Now, I was unstoppable.

Sinner slipped his hand into mine. He didn't pull me away, though.

No, he let his magic pour into me, too, giving me his strength as I commanded Katherine to heal against her will.

I didn't stop until Benedict slumped in relief and his breathing came easier.

"Athena," Sinner whispered. "She's done."

His voice echoed off the corners of my mind.

"Now back away from him."

Face blank, Katherine obeyed my orders, a mindless slave under my control.

"Stay there."

When she came to a stop several feet away from Benedict, I finally released my hold on her and the world came crashing back to me, the silo that was my power now merging with my surroundings.

Benedict tucked his chin, breathing heavily as he examined his now healed wound.

Margaret stared at me, eyes wide. "Holy. Shit."

When I turned to look at Sinner, his irises were almost black, his expression unreadable.

"Athena," he breathed.

I shook free of his hold and backed up. I didn't want to hear it. He didn't have to tell me how dangerous my gift was.

He didn't need to say it out loud. I already knew. Fuck. I controlled minds.

And that was much worse than the ability to kill.

No longer under the hold of my magic, Katherine laughed.

And laughed.

And laughed.

"You really thought you were getting better, didn't you? You thought you were no longer a monster?"

"Monster?" Margaret stood and stepped forward. "You're the one who stabbed him, Katherine! What the actual hell!"

She looked from Margaret to Sinner, the manic smile returning. "Did you see that? She took away my free will!"

Margaret scoffed. *"She saved his life!"*

Sinner pressed a hand to my lower back. "You're lucky she didn't do much worse. You deserve nothing less than death."

"Are you all insane?!" My sister flung her arms out.

"You have no idea what she can really do! You have no idea what it's like to have your free will stripped from you!"

I couldn't speak. Couldn't allow myself to think about what I'd done.

Sinner's shadows spread along the ground, between our legs and around us, lapping up at Katherine's feet like hungry dogs ready for a feed.

Sinner's shadows.

But Sinner wasn't controlling them.

No, they were coming from me.

He was letting me wield his shadows.

"You hurt any of us again and you'll meet the fate you deserve."

"DO you think what Benedict said was true?"

Sinner and I sat alone near a shallow stream as the moon rose above us.

He turned and assessed me, his lips pressed together. "Which part?"

"The part about only being able to use Katherine's magic if she lets him."

He shrugged, but kept his focus set on the water. "It's possible, but it seems unnatural. It would be very hard for me to shut my magic off from you."

"Can you feel mine?" I asked. "I can feel your phantoms." I held my hand up and watched them coil around my fingers. "It's almost like they want me to wield them."

Sinner smiled without looking up. "Yeah, they're manic

little things. They don't like to sit still. Ever since I announced that I would claim you, they've been pushing their limits trying to get to you."

I swallowed. "Can you feel my magic like that? I mean, what does it feel like to you?"

For a long time he was quiet, the only sound the trickling of the stream.

I resigned myself to not getting an answer. That was okay. It was an absurd question, anyway. I couldn't control my magic. I had only been able to use it to heal Benedict because there was nothing in that moment I wanted more than for him to be well.

It was nothing like Sinner's shadows. There was no presence to be summoned. It was like...it was like a nightmare coming to life. Could he feel it too? Could he feel how terrible it was to wield, how treacherous it could be?

"It feels like a storm." His voice blended with the smooth song of the river. "Like something I know is coming but should prepare for."

My heart thumped painfully against my breastbone, and all words escaped me.

"But it doesn't feel dark. It isn't...it isn't scary. Not to me. I know I could wield it freely if I needed to. If you allowed me to."

I nodded. "You could probably control it much better than I could, even if I had time to learn how."

He scoffed. "I doubt that."

"I'm serious. It may have looked like I had control back there, but I didn't. If an intrusive thought had wormed its way into my mind while I was using my power, the magic could have made it happen, just like what I did to Katherine. I could have hurt you. I could have hurt Margaret." Tears prickled at the backs of my eyes, but I sniffed them away. I was tired of crying.

Sinner finally lifted his head from the water and faced me. "Did you not see how incredible you were back there?"

My heart stumbled. "What? I—"

"Benedict would be dead if it weren't for you. You do know that, right?"

I shook my head. "He got lucky. Things could have gone very, very wrong. I could've—"

"But you didn't." He leaned in until I could smell the light scent of lavender soap wafting from him. "Every time I let my phantoms out, I risk hurting someone. They can kill. You've seen it. You feel it. The difference between this?" He held his hands between us until a small tendril tickled my face. "And instant death? It has nothing to do with control. It's all about intent."

My breath hitched. "You learned to control your powers years ago. I've had one day of practice."

"It doesn't matter. It's your power. *Yours*. It will bend to you. You are its god. Not the other way around."

I picked at my fingernails, at a loss for how to make him understand.

"If I were you," he whispered, "I would have killed her a long time ago."

A laugh slipped out of me before I could stop it. Damn, it felt good.

"Trust me, I've come close. She was lucky she wasn't around when I—"

I snapped my mouth shut before I went any further. *The other times I killed.*

"You're not as terrible as I thought you were when I met you," he said.

I glanced up at the truth in his words, frowning. "You didn't know anything about me then."

"I'm great at reading people. But you surprised me."

I tried and failed to hold back a laugh.

"What?" he asked.

"Nothing. It's just." I choked on another fit of laughter. "Great at *reading* people."

For a second, he stiffened, and my heart sank. I was sure I'd pissed him off. Hurt him by joking about his insecurity.

But before I could formulate an apology, he reached down and splashed water in my face.

With a squeal, I scrambled away.

He followed, his hands cupped and full of water. He tossed it at me as I pushed myself to my feet, still giggling.

I turned, ready to run, but before I'd made it a step, he caught me, spinning me around and hoisting me off my feet in one strong movement.

"Stop!" I laughed. "Stop it right now! Put me down!"

"Oh, you think this is funny?" he whispered, his breath against my neck sending a shudder down my spine.

He flexed his fingers, tickling my sides.

"No! No, it's not funny at all!" I only laughed harder.

The clearing of a throat stopped us dead. Heart pounding, I turned. Sinner came with me, still holding me tight, though the grip had turned protective.

"Sorry to interrupt," Margaret said. "Benedict is looking for you, Elijah."

The breath left my lungs in one relieved whoosh.

With a nod, Sinner sidestepped me. Though he peered over his shoulder, giving me one last look that promised he would finish what he started later.

I bit the inside of my cheek to keep from smiling like an idiot. I couldn't possibly have feelings for him. It would never work between us. I was too complicated. Too unlovable.

And he was...well, he was Sinner. A tier three. A soldier who would do anything for his sister.

"You call him Elijah?" I asked when he was out of earshot.

Margaret glanced back to where her brother disappeared into the woods. "That's a long story. He's *Sinner* to everyone else, but he'll always only be Elijah to me. Even if it pisses him off. It's nice to see you two getting along, though. He doesn't get along with anyone, actually. Anyone but me."

I fought a smile. "I noticed that. How did you end up so friendly when he's so..."

"Antisocial?"

Another laugh escaped me. "I was going to say selective. But yes."

She kicked at a stick, smiling. "He wasn't always this way. He used to be as crazy as me."

"Sinner? Crazy? I hardly believe that."

"It's true." She crossed her arms and stopped, her lips

tugging down in a frown. "He's protective of me now, but only because he blames himself."

Trepidation threaded through me at the sadness in her tone. "Blames himself for what?"

She took a breath and kicked at the dirt. "When we were kids—well, I guess he was a teenager then—our father was on one of his rampages. He usually took his anger out on Elijah, but this time, he wasn't there. Not at first."

My stomach dropped. Mags was usually so light-hearted and soft. Hearing the hardness in her voice felt so wrong.

"He wanted me to be strong like him. He yelled, telling me to prove myself, to show him what I could do. He looked down on me because I wasn't a tier three." She huffed a dark laugh. "I'm not even close. Anyway, he didn't like what he saw. He thought if I went through the claiming, I would get stronger."

No. No, no, *no.*

"He tied me up. I tried to block it all out. I was so young then, I had no idea what the claiming even was. And I was so confused." Her hands were balled into tight fists at her sides, her knuckles white. "But Elijah showed up, thank god, and he stopped it. It was the first time he had ever killed anyone of his own free will."

My stomach lurched. "Sinner killed your father?"

Tears welled in her eyes. "I wish he would have done it long before then. Not for me, I would have been fine. But he wasn't." Her voice wavered. "He hasn't been fine for a long, long time. You call him Sinner, because that's the name he chose for himself after what he did. But I'll never, ever call him that. He knows it, too. He'll always be Elijah to me, even if he pretends Elijah is dead."

I closed the distance between us and pulled her into a tight hug. *Oh, Margaret.*

"It's nice to see him with you. I wasn't sure he'd be able to live with himself after the claiming. Not if you...well... he'd never force himself on anyone. Not after what he saw. Not after what he'd been through."

My throat stung. "He'd do anything to protect you. And now, so would I. Even if you are a little crazy at times."

She smiled up at me, the look as refreshing and sweet as ever. Only now that I'd had this glimpse into her past, I could see what she hid beneath that smile. Happiness wasn't so easy to come by, not even for her. We all had demons. We were all running from something.

"I'd protect you, too," she said. "And I know he would. He already has."

He already has.

What he didn't know was that he'd never have to protect her on his own again. He would never have to be that monster again, not if he didn't want to.

I saw through that mask. I saw the real him, the softer him, the damaged him.

And I was not afraid.

sinner

The sky was purple, the sun just cresting the horizon as the three of us stalked through the forest. Mags put up a good fight, but eventually I convinced her to stay behind to watch Katherine. Though I didn't tell her, I couldn't focus if my baby sister was near. I didn't need her mixed up in the chaos that was about to break loose.

We were half a mile from the dungeons, assuming Benedict's map was correct. Katherine had healed him, but his power wasn't fully recharged. He could teleport a short distance if he really needed to, but we all agreed it would be best for him to save it for the fight.

I had a feeling he would need it.

We spent all morning going over the plan again, but it didn't make this any easier. It was truly three of us going up against an entire squadron of guards.

Mystic guards.

The sound of an engine sliced through the silence, and

we darted into the trees and dropped to the ground without a word.

Breathe in. Breathe out. The truck came so close I was sure I would have to kill anyone inside it.

But rather than stopping, it idled past. Neither of the men in the cab even looked our way.

"That was close," Benedict whispered as the engine noise faded.

Too close. But that meant the camp was nearby.

"Let's go," I ordered as I hauled myself up.

We jogged for another handful of minutes before voices and movement ahead had us checking the hand-drawn map.

"That's it," Benedict breathed. "Everyone ready?"

Athena nodded, jaw set. She was different today. More determined. More energetic. More alive.

Why did that terrify me?

"Ready." I clenched and unclenched my fists. "We get in as fast as we can and bring as many of them as we can. Simple and easy."

And then we were moving.

We crept forward slowly and soundlessly until familiar tents came into view.

That was the place they had kept me all those months. Locked underground like I didn't exist. Up here, the two dozen or so soldiers walked around like what was happening was entirely normal, like this was simply another day of work for them.

Disgusting.

Athena stayed close behind me, thank fuck. My power

was rattling the bars of its cage, desperate to escape me and protect her. I could feel the danger nearby like a prick on my neck. Yes, these soldiers were dangerous. They had weapons and far, far greater numbers.

But we were dangerous, too.

Benedict peered around a tree and held up a hand, signaling us to stop.

The two of us stepped behind another tree, making sure to keep him in sight, and waited.

Guard change. Right on time.

Lighthearted voices and laughter drifted on the wind, only angering my phantoms more. Like they deserved to laugh.

They didn't deserve to even live.

Benedict was right. When the first wave of guards stepped away from the small door that led to the dungeon, that was our cue. The three of us moved seamlessly forward, barely a shadow. The guards were distracted chatting with one another, allowing us to slip by. Benedict propped the door open and ducked in, followed quickly by Athena.

I went last, reminding myself the whole way down the stairs that I was not a prisoner this time. This time, I was getting out.

We all were.

The door shut behind us, trapping us inside. There was truly no going back now.

"Quickly," Benedict whispered. "We don't have long before the guard—"

Out of nowhere, an armed soldier appeared, and Benedict ran face-first into him.

My magic slipped from me in an instant, my shadows coiling around the guard's neck and squeezing.

I didn't apply enough pressure to kill him. Yet. Just enough to knock him out.

Benedict froze, his focus fixed on the body as it fell to the floor.

Athena pushed his back softly. "Go," she whispered.

With a shake of his head, he strode forward once more. We ran into two more guards as we coiled through the underground hallways. I memorized every turn, burning the route into my memory. I knew Athena was doing the same.

"There." Benedict stepped aside. At the end of the hallway was the massive, solid door that led to the dungeon.

My body buzzed at the sight. Beyond it was what we'd come for. The men we would set free before we got the fuck out of this place.

"We need the key." Athena knelt next to the most recent incapacitated guard and fumbled with the ring at his belt.

There were at least a dozen.

She cursed beneath her breath as she ran to the door.

The pounding of my heartbeat sounded like footsteps stomping toward us. I kept my focus trained down the hall, sure I wouldn't hear anyone who approached over the sound. Adrenaline pumped through my body. We only had seconds before more guards came down here for their shift.

We only had seconds to let the others free.

The first key didn't fit. Neither did the second or the third.

But the fourth one clicked.

"Thank god," she breathed in relief. It took a few minutes to undo each lock, and my nerves pulsed with each second.

"Let me." I sidestepped her and pushed the massive steel door forward. It creaked and groaned, as if fighting against the pressure, but I didn't stop until it was wide open.

And just like that, we were back in the dungeon we had spent so much time wishing we could escape.

I squinted in the darkness of the underground and stepped across the threshold. Behind me, Athena did the same.

From the back of the room, a laugh pierced the air. *Carter.* "Back so soon, lovebirds?"

athena

After the quickest rundown of what the hell Sinner and I had been through in the last couple days, Benedict got to work jumping anyone who wanted to leave.

Some of the men were still skeptical, and question after question was lobbed our way.

"If we do this, there's no going back," Sinner explained. "But this is our best chance at surviving."

Carter stood in front of a few of the guys with his arms crossed over his chest and his jaw set. He wasn't buying this. "More like our best chance at getting killed."

"If you stay here," I chimed in, "you'll be the Ministry's pawn forever. You want to play that game? Fine. But the more of us who act now, the better the chance we all make it."

"How the hell are you even here right now?" Leon asked. "You just walked in without being stopped?"

Sinner and I exchanged a glance. "The coast is clear for now. But it won't stay that way much longer."

Leon frowned. "This is dangerous. There's a reason the Ministry is so powerful, and it isn't because they let the unclaimed escape easily."

"Most of the guards are looking for us elsewhere. They would never expect us to come back to the dungeons."

"Then why did you?" he asked, stepping forward. He seemed almost angry that we had come back at all. "Why'd you come back?"

Benedict jumped back, grabbed another, and was gone again.

Sinner cleared his throat. "We weren't going to leave you all to the same fate. It's bad enough that the Ministry has so many mystics in their clutches. If we get out now and band together, we stand a chance at fighting back."

Fighting back. A chill racked through me. We really were starting to sound like rebels.

Benedict appeared in front of us, breathing hard. "We have to move faster."

There were too many mystics for him to move out this way. Each time he jumped someone out of the dungeons, he grew weaker. We had already spent too much time here, exposed, and there were more than a dozen guys left.

"Okay," Carter said. "I'm sick of this place, anyway. Could use a change of scenery. What do we need to do?"

"Athena." Sinner leaned in close. "It's time for plan B."

"What's plan B?" Leon asked. "We charge out of here and pummel anyone who gets in our way?"

Sinner shrugged. "That's pretty much the plan, yeah."

"I don't know if I can jump anymore," Benedict breathed. "Not for a while, at least."

"You've done a great job," I said. "The guard coverage was pretty sparse, and we're all mystics, right? We can escape the old-fashioned way. We knew this was a possibility."

These men—thank god—practically buzzed with a violent energy. I understood it. They had been trapped for months—some of them even years.

Not only were they eager to escape.

They wanted vengeance.

"We stay together," Sinner announced. "Leave no one behind. Understand?"

The men, to my surprise, agreed. Nobody had a snarky comment to share. Not this time.

"Great. Out this door and up the stairs. There are armed guards waiting, but as far as we know, they have no idea what's happening down here. Take them by surprise. Then turn right and sprint into the woods. Follow the tree line. Margaret will be waiting for you. And if you're comfortable using your power, don't hesitate." Sinner clenched his fists at his sides. He did that frequently when he was nervous, I realized.

"You're coming with us, right?" Carter asked.

"We'll be right behind you," I answered. "Now, go."

Without hesitation, the men began funneling out of the dungeon.

It was Sinner's idea to wait until everyone else had escaped. They were fighters. They would be okay leading the pack.

We were here to finish the job.

We stood guard as the guys moved one by one, stepping over the bodies without hesitation.

"Something doesn't feel right," I whispered as the guys filed up the stairs. "This seems too easy, doesn't it?"

Sinner's jaw tightened as he watched the men ahead of us. Some pride lingered there, but something else, too.

I turned and checked the other hallways again—all empty.

"Benedict, you go next," Sinner ordered.

With a nod, he jogged up behind the last prisoner.

I saw the grenade rolling down the hall a second too late. Before I could even scream, Sinner's body slammed against mine, and the world went dark.

"OH, good. You're alive. You can finally join the party."

I cracked my eyes open at the sound of the one voice that had the power to make my skin crawl. Director stared back at me, an absurd smirk tipping her lips, her face and neck mottled with bruises.

I was strapped to a familiar metal chair, my hands secured behind me. Breath held, I searched my surroundings, and I only exhaled when I found Sinner sitting opposite me in a similar position.

His eyes were full of fury. Full of rebellion. Full of fight. *Good.* He hadn't given up yet.

This was just a bump in the road, right?

I would do whatever it took to get us out of here. There

was no way I'd let Sinner get so close to freedom only to have it ripped away again.

"You miss this place so much you really had to come crawling back?" Director asked. "I'm shocked."

When I didn't answer, she slapped me across the face hard enough that I tasted blood.

When a guard behind me gripped my shoulders and pulled my slumped torso back, Sinner growled.

"What can I say?" I gritted out. "It must be the welcoming hospitality."

I focused on my breathing, searching for Sinner's magic. Why hadn't he used his power to kill these people yet? Margaret was far from the reach of the Ministry. There was nothing holding him back now.

My eyes met Sinner's, and his magic tugged like it always did. Like it *wanted* me to wield it.

Just as I readied myself to pull, just before I forced his shadows out, his gaze shifted. "Athena, don't."

Confusion swamped me. "What? What's going on?"

Director crossed her arms, her expression smug. "Did you really think you could escape? Did you think it would be that easy to get past an entire army, to get out of this place with all of your friends in one piece?" Her derisive laugh echoed off the stone walls. "You two are a hell of a lot more stupid than I thought you'd be, which is saying quite a lot. But don't worry. Time with the Ministry's army will fix that."

She lifted her chin and focused on something behind me. I couldn't see what was happening, but Sinner's eyes filled with pain, with grief.

My chest constricted painfully. "What's going on?"

"I'm sorry, but I can't let her get hurt. Not again."

When they dragged Margaret into the room and dropped her bloodied body on the ground between us, I cried out.

"The two of you will follow every direction I give," Director said. "Or precious, precious Margaret will pay the price for your disobedience."

Shit. Shit, shit, shit. How the hell had they found her? They must have had another jumper, someone who knew where we'd been.

"I'm so sorry," Margaret whispered.

"Don't," Sinner interrupted. "Don't apologize."

She sobbed, her body shaking. "I'm sorry, Sinner."

Director skirted around Margaret, sauntering right up to Sinner, and, without warning, stabbed him in the thigh.

It was like she had stabbed me instead. His cry of pain was enough to crack my chest wide open.

Margaret screamed, too. Tied up and on the floor, all she could do was watch as her brother writhed in pain.

sinner

Despite the agony coursing through me, I pulled at Athena's power. She wouldn't use it. Not when she thought that imposter on the floor was my sister.

It took a moment for me to understand. I'd run through it time and again, wondering how they could have found Mags and gotten her here so quickly.

But then she called me Sinner, and it clicked.

My sister never, ever called me Sinner. She despised the name.

This wasn't Mags. It was all a trick.

A moment after I'd begun to pull on the source of power from Athena, though, I was cut off.

Heart thundering, I blinked at Athena, silently begging her to look at me.

Director was rambling on about victory and justice.

The pain in my thigh was excruciating. It only worsened as the knife was yanked out, then plunged right back in.

Fuck. They really held a grudge, didn't they?

I yelled out again, unable to keep the pain locked inside.

Director raised her hand again.

Then froze.

Athena froze, too. Her magic surrounded us, filled the room. It was invisible, imperceptible. To everyone but me. Now she was unleashed. Uncontrolled. She was really doing it. She was wielding her magic.

My phantoms purred inside my chest.

Not only had she stopped Director from stabbing me a third time, but she'd gained control over the four guards standing behind her. Each was frozen mid-move, their eyes wide.

"Drop the knife," Athena ordered.

Director obeyed instantly, and the blade hit the floor with a clatter.

"Now untie us." One second passed. Two. Then the guards moved in, one working on my hands, the other on my feet. Two untying Athena as well.

The moment I was free, I was on my feet. Athena was, too.

"Wait!" the person pretending to be Mags said. "They'll hurt me if you use your power!"

Athena narrowed her eyes at me, and in that moment, I knew she also saw the truth. *This wasn't our Mags.*

She still had control of every other person in the room.

"We're leaving," she said. "Lock yourselves in this room once we're gone and don't come out."

I limped forward, pressing a hand to my wound to stanch the blood. Fuck, this might actually work. I let my shadows flood out of me, a warning to anyone who might stand against us.

"Good." Athena fought back a smile. Her expression fell, though, when she caught sight of the gun holstered in one of the guard's belts. "New plan," she said, her tone scarily even. "Shoot them all. And then shoot yourself."

The guard unsheathed his weapon.

Pointed it at Director.

Slid the safety off.

I held my breath. This was the moment that would change everything. The moment that would go down in history as the beginning of the mystics' victory.

The bang that followed came from the other side of the room, startling us.

The door had flown open and slammed into the wall.

Director stepped forward. "Shield, drop their visions."

A man to her right raised his hand, and the room shifted. The walls changed color, and the woman we believed to be Director vanished. So did the Margaret impersonator. Director, the real Director, was flanked by six regular guards.

It was a fucking trap.

"Athena." I pushed my shadows out, willed them to protect her, but they went silent, dissipated. My powers were being blocked.

"Good luck using your power while Leon here is with us."

The hair on the back of my neck rose. Leon? What the hell was he doing with them? He was using his power to *help* the Ministry?

My chest stung with betrayal. Fuck. I could only imagine how hard this truth was hitting Athena.

"What the hell is going on?" she asked, her eyes wide.

No, no, no. This wasn't happening.

We had played directly into Director's plans.

"I knew you were strong, Athena. But mind control?" Director laughed.

I tried again and again to push out my shadows, but nothing happened. I tried to pull at Athena's power, too, but got nothing.

Director clicked her tongue. "You are not just a tier three, are you?"

"I don't know what you're talking about." Athena lifted her chin, though her hands trembled at her sides. "Whatever you think you saw, you're wrong."

Director crossed her arms, wearing a look of mock pity.

"Even after the claiming, I wasn't quite sure what your power was. It's why we set up this diversion. So you would finally show us."

No. A growl escaped my throat.

Director hit me with a smile that made my stomach roll. "Claiming with a four? Once you've come to your senses and realized we're on the right side of this war, once we give you full access to your magic, you'll be unstoppable. Your father would be proud of you." Bile rose in my throat. *I was going to rip her fucking head off.* "You two will be very, very useful to my army. Especially now that you are claimed."

"No." Athena's voice cracked. "It's not possible. Fours don't exist."

"I'm so sorry," Leon said, his face a ghostly white. "I never wanted to do this."

It was not only my power that was suppressed, but my entire being. I fought against it with everything I had, I fought against the pressure, fought against the fading consciousness. I reached out to Athena, my hand brushing hers, but before I could find purchase, my vision went dark.

"Don't worry," Director said. "You two will fit in nicely in the barracks. Shields everywhere. Nobody uses their power without permission. You'll spend the next four months training, then you'll help us win this damn war."

<hr>

CONTINUE WITH BOOK 2: CURSE THE HEART

thank you!

Thank you so much for reading Beg The Night. Each book of mine is special, but this one holds a very dear place in my heart.

Athena and Sinner have both gone through so much, and this is just the beginning! I cannot wait to continue this world and give you more romantasy fun with this series.

If you loved this book, please consider leaving a review on Amazon and Goodreads! This helps indie authors like me find our readers!

And if you're looking for more information on my books, special editions, signed copies, or anything else, you can find it at www.authoremilyblackwood.com

You can also join my reader Facebook group, Emily Blackwood's Faeries, for giveaways, publishing news, and fun faerie things!

Happy reading, besties!

acknowledgments

This book was a beast. Starting a new series is always terrifying, but this specific story has lived in my head for so long, I wanted to do the characters justice.

Thank you to Lauren, who listens to my ramblings and helps me turn my jumbled ideas into actual stories. You're my biggest cheerleader in this industry and I truly couldn't do it without you.

Thank you to all my beta readers, Lexi, Morgan, Sarah, and Lauren. You're my favorite hype women and you have no idea how much I value your feedback on my new baby. I appreciate you so, so much.

Thank you to everyone who has continued to follow me in this career. I'm just a fantasy-obsessed woman with too much free time and coffee, and the fact that you all continue to read these stories I write means the world to me.

You can keep up with me on social media, primarily Instagram and TikTok, at @authoremilyblackwood.

You can also find signed copies and special editions of my books at authoremilyblackwood.com

also by emily blackwood

<u>The Fae of Rewyth Series</u>

1. House of Lies and Sorrow

2. Prince of Sins and Shadows

3. War of Wrath and Ruin

4. Trials of Saints and Glory

5. Queen of Fae and Fortune

<u>The Golden City Series</u>

1. Wings So Wicked

2. Blood So Brutal

3. Crown So Cruel

<u>The Demons Duet</u>

1. Demons and Darlings

2. Deals and Daggers